RULE NUMBER FIVE
A HOCKEY ROMANCE NOVEL

J. WILDER

Copyright © 2023 by J. Wilder
All rights reserved.
J. Wilder
Rule Number Five
No part of this book may be reproduced in any form or by any electronic or mechanical means, including information storage and retrieval systems, without written permission from the author, except for the use of brief quotations in a book review.

Editing: One Love Editing

AUTHOR'S NOTE

So you may have noticed that I have two names now. Jessa Wilder and J. Wilder.

I set it up this way so people who only like contemporary romance don't accidentally stumble into my trigger-happy series. But both names are still me!

What to expect from a J. Wilder book:

J. Wilder writes fluffy contemporary romance steeped in delicious smut. If you want squishy, warm, happy feelings, and quality spice, her books are for you.

Rule Number Five has a unique story behind it. Way back in 2019 I fell in love with Sidney and Jax and published their book: The Study Date.

After publishing 6 additional books I realized

even though I'd laid out the bones of their story I hadn't done them justice.

So, in June of 2022 I had the wild idea that I would unpublish The Study Date and edit the hell out of that book to republish.

At the time, I thought it would be a simple process that would take no time at all. Boy, was I wrong.

This turned out to be one of the most intense editing processes I've ever done. I switched chapters around, deleted some, and re-wrote others. Until it was everything I ever wanted it to be.

For those of you who've read and loved The Study Date, don't worry. Sid and Jax's love for each other is still there, just with some added excitement and fun.

I hope you love Sidney and Jax as much as I do.

Happy Reading!

Join Jessa's readers' FB group. **ARC SIGN UP EXCLUSIVE**. You'll get updates on Lucas and Piper's book creation and all kinds of fun extras. I'm dying to hear what you think!

TRIGGER/CONTENT WARNING:

Parental neglect, past death of close loved ones, mature sexual content.

Rule Number Five is a complete **STANDALONE.**

For more books by Jessa Wilder, visit Jessawilder.com

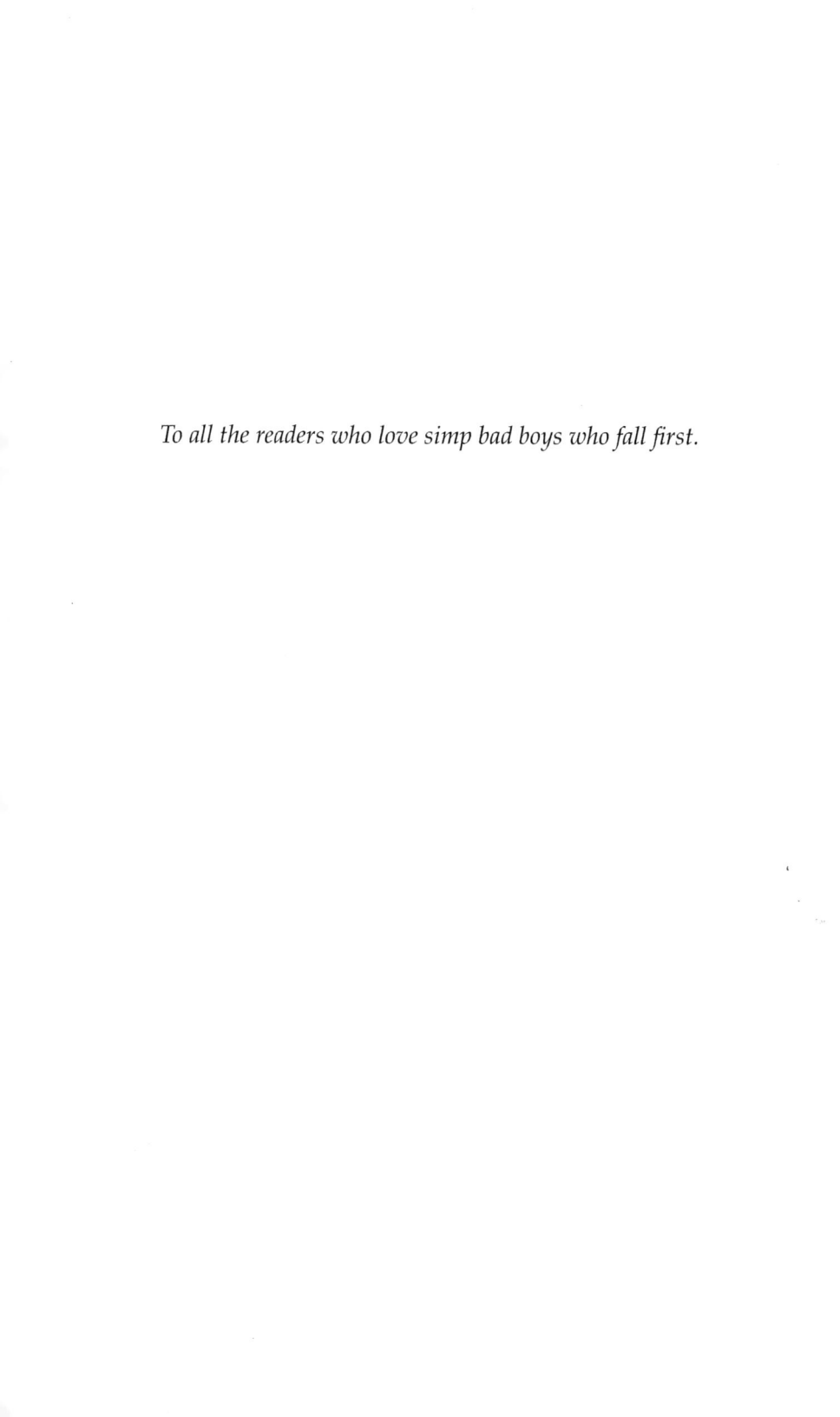

To all the readers who love simp bad boys who fall first.

ONE
JAX

"YOU'VE GOT to be fucking kidding me, man."

Alex met my gaze across the table and grinned, showing off the lipstick smeared on his cheek. He'd been practically fucking a redhead in our booth for the last fifteen minutes, and her moans had officially reached soap-opera-acting level of ridiculous. Not that I minded if a girl wanted to get laid, but that wasn't a puck bunny's MO. They were out to catch a free ride and didn't give a single shit if they liked you or not. A shiver crawled down my spine. It made me feel used and dirty. I had to get the hell out of there before he convinced her to get on her knees beneath us.

Not that I expected anything less. Alex had always been a bit of a puck slut.

He gave me an unapologetic shrug but disentangled himself, dropping her feet to the floor, then smacked her ass. "How about you get us a beer, sweetheart?"

"How about you come with me?" Even though we all knew she would do it anyway, she still pouted when he just stared at her. With one last look, her shoulders dropped, and she walked off in a huff toward the bar.

The club was in a warehouse with giant concrete pillars that divided the space and multicolored strobe lights pulsing over a dance floor. On the furthest side, there was a long glass bar serving every type of drink you could think of.

"She's going to spit in your beer," I said with a grin wide enough that I knew my dimple was showing and raked my hand through my messy brown hair.

Alex laughed. "Eh, never know. I might like it."

"Alright, fucker." Standing, I grabbed my coat from the booth. "I'm out before she comes back with friends."

"Hey, you're supposed to be my wingman," he argued.

"If I wanted to catch bunnies, I'd have stayed at the rink." Sure, I was down when he asked, still high off our win, but I wasn't interested in these girls.

"Fucking picky bastard. Hold up," Alex grumbled under his breath and searched the crowd before a slow smile formed on his lips. Then he gestured toward the other side of the club with his chin. "How about them?"

I followed his gaze to a girl at a bar-height table.

She was tall, blonde, and had a deep tan that gave her a sun-kissed look. By the way Alex looked at her, she must've been his type, but I was too blindsided by the hot-as-fuck brunette standing beside her to notice.

"Fuck me," I said low under my breath as I took in the brunette. She looked like some kind of sexy librarian, wearing a short pleated skirt, thigh-high socks, and chunky black boots. She smiled at her blonde friend, then dipped her head, getting ready to take a shot.

My mouth watered when she licked the web between her thumb and pointer finger, getting it ready for her friend to pour salt on. She had a devious-looking smirk on her face, and I counted with her. One. Two. Three.

Next, she sucked the salt off, tossed back the shot, and bit into a lemon. I swallowed hard when a sexy little shiver ran through her. I wanted to be the reason she trembled like that.

"I'll see you back at the house, buddy."

Alex was talking, but I didn't register his words. The brunette dragged her fingers through her hair, pulling it into a high ponytail, revealing a sexy silver layer underneath. This girl was just full of surprises. She fucking owned the hot nerd thing she had going on, and I groaned, tracing the line of her neck. There was a spot below her ear that looked biteable—

A hand landed on my shoulder, snapping me out of my daze, and Alex smirked at me.

"What?" I asked, ignoring the rasp in my throat.

"I said I'd see you at our place." His voice practically screamed, *I told you so*.

The brunette propped her elbows on the table, her back straight and her ass angled out behind her. My pulse kicked up, sending my blood rushing down. Jesus fucking Christ.

"The brunette is mine." I growled the words, and Alex just laughed, smacking my shoulder.

"Yeah, buddy. Tonight's going to be a good fucking time."

As soon as she bent over, all my attention focused on where her fingers glided over the thin band of visible skin between the top of her sock and the bottom of her skirt. I was already walking before she stood. I didn't know who this girl was, but tonight, she was fucking mine.

Alex walked right up to the blonde and gave her a cocky smile. "Besides being sexy, what do you do for a living?"

He should've been arrested for that line, but it hadn't let him down yet. By the way the blonde smiled, it wouldn't fail him now.

The librarian choked on her drink and shook her head. She looked like she was about to say something, but her friend cut in.

"Does that ever work for you?"

Alex moved closer, his voice dropping low. "Don't know. Does it?"

I didn't hear the blonde's reply because now the brunette's attention was on me. Her teeth ran along her bottom lip as her gaze slowly worked its way up my chest. *That's it, baby. Look at me.*

As if she heard my thoughts, her eyes flashed to mine, startling when she found me already watching her. I ran my thumb over my lip, exactly where she gnawed on hers. As a result, her cheeks flushed a deeper pink. So fucking adorable.

"I'm Alex, and this dickhead's Jax. He's been dying to talk to you, so I took pity on him and brought him over."

Fucking asshole. I cut him a glare, but I was distracted when the librarian introduced herself. "Sidney."

Her name felt good rolling over in my head, but before I could say anything, a guy cut between us, wrapping his arm around her waist and handing her a drink. "Drink up. Curtis wants to dance."

He was tall, but not as tall as me, with a lean frame and perfectly styled hair. When she smiled up at him, a jolt ran through me, and a muscle ticked in my jaw. Disappointment mixed with something much more dangerous coursed through me. I tipped back on my heels, needing to get a grip on myself. This girl was fucking trouble.

The guy leaned in closer, his mouth just above her ear, but he spoke loud enough for me to hear. "Oh, he's hot and jealous."

The fuck? He gave her another squeeze, then let go, burying his nose into the neck of the man behind him. In the seconds it took for me to catch up to what was happening, the shorter guy had wrapped his arms around him. Sidney gave them a warm smile, and relief flooded me, knowing the guy was already taken.

He held his hand out. "Hey, man. I'm Anthony, and this is Curtis." He pointed to his boyfriend, who grinned at me.

"Jax." I took a long sip of my beer, and everyone looked at me with identical smiles, but not Sidney. Her gaze was fucking molten. Oh, she liked me jealous. If she stuck around, I had a feeling she'd get what she wanted.

Her friend—I thought she said her name was Mia—grabbed Alex's hand and began tugging him to the dance floor. "Let's dance."

He didn't need any encouragement, already heading in that direction, and Anthony and Curtis followed them.

"We'll catch up in a minute." I stalked toward Sidney, happy she didn't contradict me. No, her gaze was warm on my skin, and there was a slight smile ghosting over her lips. I practically towered over her, her slight frame completely blocked out by my larger one.

The group gave us knowing looks, then dispersed into the crowd.

A giant balloon floating above the table caught my attention. I swear my heart stopped dead as I stared at the blue congratulations balloon with a baby on it. All the blood drained from my head, and my attention went back to Sidney.

I swallowed hard. "Is that for you?"

Her mouth twitched and pulled to the side before she let out a laugh. "You should see your face right now."

Her voice lowered with a subtle rasp, only made sexier by her amusement at the same time her grin grew, until it was practically blinding with pride. "My internship at Parliament was accepted today. Apparently, this was the only congratulations balloon available." She laughed. "Anthony thought it was hilarious."

Not pregnant. My muscles relaxed, and the circulation returned to my body as I slowly registered her words. "No shit, seriously?"

"Don't be too impressed. I need another letter of recommendation. Those two got a little prematurely excited." She nodded, watching me a bit too guarded. I fucking hated that she lost some of her confidence.

I leaned in closer. "Hey, you've got this."

"How can you know that?"

I'm overwhelmed by the need to wipe the unsure look from her face. "I bet you're at the top of your class, right?"

She bit the side of her cheek before answering, "Yeah."

"You've already got other recommendations?"

"Yeah." She stood straighter now. Good.

I pushed harder. "Do you think you can kick your internship's ass?"

She smiled at me, eyes brighter than they were a second ago. "Yeah, I do."

"Then don't worry. You've got this."

She let out a deep breath, and her entire body relaxed. I clipped her chin with my curled forefinger. "I'll leave a good impression on you so you remember me when you make it big."

Heat flushed across her chest, and I followed it up her neck, running my tongue along my top teeth. She was so fucking responsive. I wanted to find out if she blushed like that everywhere. She shifted forward but stopped herself with a hand on the table.

Come on, Sidney. Come get me.

She broke eye contact, looking at her hands. "Do you come here a lot?"

It was a random change of subject, but it was a start. "Enough to know you don't."

She huffed out a laugh and shrugged. "I don't go out much. Busy preparing to be that 'important politician' you were talking about. I've got to keep my image clean."

The things I wanted to do to her were anything but clean. I tipped my voice low until it was a gravelly rumble, forcing her to step into me to hear. "Do you go to school here, Sidney?"

She sucked in a breath when I said her name and bit her lower lip. Fuck. She needed to stop doing that. I was already too fucking turned on.

Her mouth pulled to the side. "Yeah, one semester left. I go to the University of Windsor."

A spark of interest flashed in my chest. "Yeah?"

She gave me a quick nod, and that interest turned to anticipation of seeing more of her.

"Me too. Kinesiology major." I moved in closer

until the toes of our shoes brushed against each other, and she was forced to tip her chin up to meet my gaze. She took a deep breath in, and energy kicked up around us, drawing me closer. I lowered my head above her, keeping my voice steady. "I bet you're a poli-sci, right?"

"You've got it." Her throat lifted with her swallow.

Come on, Trouble. Ask me something.

She didn't disappoint. "So, kinesiology, that's impressive. Planning to work for some pro sports team when you graduate?"

"Something like that." I rolled back on my heels, and she raised a brow. She studied me, clearly not happy with my vague answer, but I didn't want to ruin this moment by bringing that into it.

Sidney stepped back, creating distance between us just as a server walked by. They connected with each other faster than I could warn them, sending Sidney tipping forward. I caught her in my arms, and her touch was like a live wire shooting straight through my veins. The scent of citrus—orange and grapefruit—surrounded me, and I had to fight back a groan. Heat practically poured off her where we connected, soaking into my skin. She stared at my mouth, with heated eyes. She didn't move, and I didn't interrupt her as she took me in fully. Fuck, the way she was staring at me turned me the fuck on. I swallowed hard, then lowered my lips above her ear and murmured, "Caught you."

"I... I didn't mean—" she said, flustered.

Deciding to put her out of her misery, I gestured toward our friends. "At this point, if Alex gets any closer to Mia, they're going to become one."

She lifted onto her toes, placing a hand on my shoulder for balance, and craned her neck to see them. I knew she felt my low rumble under her soft touch.

Her fingers curled into my shirt, but she didn't face me when she said, "Is he always like this?"

I lowered my chin to her ear, focused on the millions of goosebumps that rose over her skin. "A shameless flirt? Pretty much."

Sidney leaned back, her gaze traveling from my mouth to my eyes, and I spread my fingers over her back, tugging her closer. She made a soft sound that had my breath catching in my throat and my dick growing hard. I searched her face, wanting—no, *needing*—to know that she felt this too. That I wasn't the only one driven fucking crazy just being near her.

A sensual grin formed on her mouth. "Are you hitting on me?"

"Maybe. Is it working?"

Her smile grew. "Maybe."

My grip tightened, her words sounding distinctly like a yes. She was throwing off *fuck me* signals, and god, I hoped I was right. I paused, not sure where to go from here. At first, I found her hot, but fuck if I wasn't more interested now. There was something about her. She was clearly smart, and there was a level of sass coming off of her that had me itching to—

"Want to dance?" Sidney asked, cutting off my thoughts.

"Fuck yes." I practically growled the words, and I was rewarded by her shiver. Sidney entwined our fingers, and I followed her like a lost puppy, but who could fucking blame me? She looked delicious in her short plaid skirt with a white slim-fitting T-shirt that had come loose.

Sidney picked a spot on the dance floor out of sight of our friends, turned to face away from me, and swayed to the beat. She moved in slow, languid motions that made my dick harder with each second I watched her. My hands curled with restraint, and Sidney's breath caught in her throat when they landed on her hips, tugging her back into my chest. *Fuck.* She rolled against me until her ass pushed into my groin, driving me insane. My mind chanted the same thing over and over, like some kind of fucking caveman. *Mine.*

I needed to take her home tonight, or it would fucking kill me.

Blood rushed to my already rock-hard cock when I ran my fingers just below her skirt and squeezed her exposed thighs. A low growl escaped the back of my throat when her entire body trembled in my grasp. Fuck, she didn't know how close she had me to the edge. She leaned her head on my shoulder, tilting it to the side, making room for my mouth, and hummed when I licked up the narrow column of her neck.

"You smell so fucking good," I groaned, burying my face in her shoulder.

She whimpered, and I flipped her to face me, needing to capture it with my mouth. We were so close her breath fanned over my lips, but she tucked her chin to stop the kiss.

The fuck? I dropped my forehead to hers, breathing in each of her breaths. Sidney's hands ran up my abdomen, and I groaned deeply when she dug her nails into my chest. Her lips were pink where she bit into them, and I fucking craved to run my tongue along the marks. Her mouth formed a perfect pout, and I shifted close enough that it nearly brushed mine with each inhale.

Sidney made a low, pained sound before jerking her head back. She sucked in several breaths, and her eyes widened on me.

Ice filled my veins, replacing the heat that had been building. Did I read her wrong? Did I push her too far? "I'm sorry. Whatever I did, I'm fucking sorry."

She let out a long sigh, then shook her head, a smirk forming on her full lips. "That's rule number one: no kissing."

She shifted back a few inches, and my hands tightened on her hips, not letting her go. My gaze flicked from her mouth to her eyes and back, trying to process anything but the desire to taste her. I dragged my teeth over my bottom lip, and she tracked the movement while her tongue wet hers. Sidney's words finally broke through the haze of lust, and they hit harder than they should. "What?"

"Rule number one." She leaned away, but her fingers still dug into me like she didn't want to let me go. Good. I didn't fucking want her to.

My gaze searched hers as if I would find the answer there. Sidney was already turning away, but I caught the disappointed look in her eyes. She gestured to her table with her thumb. "I need a drink."

Me fucking too, Sidney.

She pulled from my grasp, and I immediately missed the feel of her. What the hell was happening? One minute, we were all over each other, and the next, I stood here stunned. She was already at the table before I snapped out of it.

"What do you mean rule?" I asked as soon as I reached her.

She finished her tall glass in a few sips. "Just what I said. I have rules for this type of thing."

"What sort of thing?"

"One-night stands."

"What if I want it to be longer?" Where the fuck did that come from?

"That's rule number two: one night only."

My brows pinched together, not sure what to make of it. I should've been happy she was down for one night. Hell, I should've been ecstatic. What guy didn't want that? Apparently me, because her taking more off the table didn't sit right.

Curious, I played along. "Okay, I can respect your game."

Her glare was ruined when she hiccupped. "Rules, not a game."

My hands rose in surrender. "Sorry. Rules."

"That's better. Look, we're getting way off course here. You're hot. I'm pretty sure you think I'm hot. Come home with me." She hiccupped between her words and swayed on her feet.

I caught her, holding her closer than necessary, and tried not to preen when she wrapped her hands around my back. Her pupils were blown wide, and I swallowed hard when her tongue snuck out, wetting her bottom lip.

So fucking pissed at what was about to come out of my mouth, but I'd never been and would never be the type of guy who brought a drunk girl home. No matter how tempting she was. "It fucking kills me to say this. And it *really* fucking does, but you've had too much to drink tonight for this conversation."

She frowned.

I slid my phone toward her. "How about you give me your number and we can do this again? Sober."

She chuckled, shaking her head. "Nope, can't do that."

I raked my fingers through my hair. "Tell me this isn't another rule."

Sidney propped her chin on my chest and smirked, looking sexy as fuck. I tipped my head back to the ceiling and took in a deep breath. Please, fucking god. This couldn't be happening. I had never chased a girl in my fucking life, and this girl had me hooked. "What if I gave you mine?"

She scrunched her nose. Fucking adorable. "Rule number three: no exchanging phone numbers."

"How the fuck does that work?" I had to stop myself from tightening my grip. I was getting dangerously close to being an asshole, but come the fuck on. These rules were killing me. "What happens if you're into a guy?" If only my boys could see me now. I'd never live it down.

She gave me an apologetic smile, and I already knew what was coming. "Breaks rule number five."

"Tell me," I deadpanned.

"Being into a guy leads to dating, dating leads to relationships, and relationships lead to feelings. Rule number five: no falling in love."

A muscle ticked in my jaw. "How many rules do you have?"

"Five."

"What's the fourth rule?" Someone grabbed my shoulder, twisting me to face him and effectively cutting me off.

"Congrats, buddy. That goal was insane," he screamed over the music, and his breath reeked of beer.

"Goal?" Sidney's head tilted to the side, looking me up and down as if seeing me for the first time.

The big guy beside me wore my team's teal hockey jersey. He turned around, showing her the back, where the last name Ryder was written across it in large white letters. He faced her and smiled.

"Yeah, sweetheart. You going to pretend you don't know you're hooking up with the Huskies' star forward?"

"Jax Ryder?" she asked with a little shake of her head like she was telling me to say no.

"Yeah." I swallowed hard. For the first time, I got the impression my name was going to backfire on me.

Her shoulders slumped, and she looked so fucking disappointed before lifting onto her toes and leaning closer to me. Her eyes were wide as she searched my face, and I wished I could make out their color in the dim club light. I reveled in the heat of her body pressed tightly against my chest as she brought her mouth closer to mine, so close I could feel her breath fan across mine. My mouth watered, and it took everything in me not to close the distance. *Come on, Trouble. Kiss me.*

"That's really too bad, Jax." She closed the distance, kissing me just to the side of my lips, then broke away from my arms, brows pulled together. She took a step toward her friends, nearly tripping as she did. I so wanted to help her, but her words caught me up. "Rule number four: no hockey players."

"You've got to be kidding me."

"Nope." She gave me a downcast smirk and wiggled her fingers goodbye before turning around.

My gaze tracked her ass the entire time, and a slow smile curved across my lips. I never could resist breaking the rules.

TWO
SIDNEY

"WELL, Mom. I got the email last week. One more recommendation, and it's a done deal." A gust of wind raised goose bumps over my neck, and I flipped the collar of my blue wool jacket to protect my ears.

"Don't worry, though. I've never failed to win a professor over before. I don't plan on fucking it up this time." My hand flew up to cover my mouth as soon as the words came out.

"Sorry, I guess I'm too old to wash my mouth out with soap, anyway." I joked and brushed the dirt from around her gravestone, arranging the faux flowers in their plastic vase. The ground was frozen solid, so it was more habit than necessity, but I couldn't stop myself from fussing each time I visited.

"I wish you were here."

My fingers trembled as I traced the words engraved in the stone.

A loving mother
Gone too soon.

"I could really use one of your cheesy motivational speeches right now." I sniffed, pausing a second to control my breath. "Sometimes, I try to guess what you'd say: *You can do anything you set your mind to.* Or your personal favorite: *Your dreams are worth the sacrifices you make.*"

A chill climbed up my legs, and I shifted in place. "You were right, Mom. I've been sacrificing, and I'm so close I can taste it."

An icy tear rolled down my cheek, and I wiped it away, not wanting it to leave streaks down my cold cheeks. You would've thought the eight years since the accident would make this easier.

"I miss you. I miss your hugs, the way you always knew what to say, and breakfast in bed when it's raining." The words caught in my throat, and I had to take several breaths to get myself under control. She'd left me five years ago, and there was nothing I could do about it. "You'd be proud of me. I'm following in your footsteps. I'm going to make it. Promise."

Not able to stay any longer, I kissed my fingers and placed them on her headstone. "I love you, Mom. Happy birthday."

I headed back through the maze of sidewalks winding through the graveyard and plopped into Mia's nineties car. It was in rough shape, but it still worked. She already had the heat blasting, and I rubbed my numb fingers together in front of the vent. Mia gave me a warm smile and placed her hand on my arm. "How're you doing?"

I shrugged. "Better than last year, not as good as next. At least I had good news this time."

"You know she'd be proud of you no matter what, right? She'd want you to be happy."

Rationally, I knew that. Of course I did. But Mia didn't understand what it was like to know you're the reason your mom didn't get to live her dream. Well, at least one reason.

"Being in politics is in my blood, just like it was hers." I shook off the heavy feeling that always weighed on me when I visited my mom. "Thanks for getting up at dawn to come with me. I don't know what I'd do without you."

Mia searched my face, and her normally sunny expression softened with concern before she joked, "Anthony's going to be pissed when he wakes up and finds out you came here without him. You know he's trying to beat me for best friend status."

I smiled. "You're both my best friends."

"Yeah, but I'm *the* best friend."

My shoulders shook with suppressed laughter. "You know I love you both, right? There doesn't have to be a winner."

"Uh-huh. And you don't need to be first in class. Just think, we could've slept in today. Not that you've ever skipped a class a day in your life."

I scoffed. "Day one is syllabus day. It's literally the most important day."

"Are you seriously trying to pretend you haven't contacted your teachers?"

I rolled my eyes. "Yeah, but not all of them answered."

"'Cause it was Christmas break." She shook her head and nudged her shoulder against mine before putting the car into drive. "You're buying breakfast, though."

Anthony met us at the diner. His light brown hair was in a tidy swept-to-the-left style, and his black-framed glasses slid down his nose as he checked out my short black skirt and the vibrant blue jacket. He lifted a strand of my chestnut hair, revealing the pure white highlights peeking from underneath.

"Looking good, cupcake." He didn't bring up my mom. This wasn't the first time I'd visited her grave, and they both sensed I needed to talk about something else. Anything else.

I gave him a small smile in acknowledgment, and I sat at the 1950s-style table. It was covered in a red cloth that played on the white-and-black tiled floor. It was so on theme I half expected the waitstaff to wear Rollerblades. My mom would have loved it here. I sniffed and blinked back the burning in my eyes. I was in desperate need of a distraction.

"So, are we going to talk about that insanely hot guy from the club?" Mia raised a perfectly defined brow.

That'll do it. Images of clear gray eyes and full, lush lips had me feeling light-headed. Jax had been on my mind more often than I'd like to admit, and every time I tried to convince myself he was just some random potential hookup, a voice at the back of my head called bullshit. That night was so intense that if it wasn't for him putting a stop to things because I was a little too tipsy, I would've broken my rule and gone home with him. Hell, I may have even begged a bit.

Anthony spoke around a mouth full of pancakes. "From the way you two were grinding all over each other, I thought you were going to combust. Hell, I thought I might combust. Girl, I cannot believe you didn't take him home."

I couldn't believe it either. Honestly, men shouldn't be able to be built like that. To move like that.

"He's a hockey player." I shrugged.

"Yeah, and?" Mia looked at me expectantly.

And I didn't get involved with self-indulgent, arrogant, cocky assholes who only cared about themselves. Not that he showed any signs of that, but I, of all people, knew exactly how hockey players thought. They had surrounded me my entire life, after all. "And you know that's rule number four."

She sighed loudly, and the server looked over at us. I gave her a wave and glared at Mia. She shook her head in disappointment. "You know those rules are stupid, right? The guy was fine as hell."

All the more reason to keep the rules in place. A guy like that was hard to walk away from. I knew the type of girl I was. Before I knew it, I would wrap my entire life around him like some kinda clingy octopus. Hey, it was important to know your weaknesses, and being a needy bitch was one of mine. No doubt stemming from my bottomless pit of daddy issues.

Anthony messed up my hair. "From the way you two were moving, I bet he'd be good in bed too."

I could already feel the blush rising in my cheeks. "The rules are nonnegotiable."

Mia sighed, her dislike of my rules clear on her face. "Okay, but it was only one rule. The hockey player part doesn't *really* matter if it's only one night, does it?"

"How'd that go for my mom?"

Her eyes widened. "I'm sorry."

I covered Mia's hand and gave it a little squeeze. "It's fine. Hockey players are arrogant pricks that are selfish in bed. I'm better off with my vibrator."

Anthony leaned in and whispered so only we could hear. "Please tell me you at least used him as material for your 'self-care.'"

A flush crawled up my neck, and my face felt like it was catching fire. I'd imagined Jax's full soft lips pressed against mine, my fingers digging into his messy sandy-brown hair, and the weight of him pressed between my thighs more times than I could count.

Mia squealed. "Oh, you totally did. Dirty. I bet it was good."

Heat pooled between my legs. Yeah, too good.

THREE
JAX

SIDNEY CROSSED the street in front of my truck, and I had to stop myself from beeping the horn. Her deep brown hair was down around her shoulders, hiding the silver streaks I knew were underneath. She wore plaid tights under a black skirt that hit mid-thigh that switched as she walked and an oversized bright blue coat. She had a cute punk-rock librarian thing going for her today that was doing a number on my ego.

It had been over a week since the night we danced, and I didn't think she understood what kind of challenge she'd laid down with those rules of hers. I swear my dick was hard for days. The only relief was from my own fist, picturing her pressed against me, head tilted all the way back, pupils blown wide, and the perfect way her tongue wet her bottom lip before she pulled it between her teeth. Even in my memories, the need to soothe the red dents with my tongue was overwhelming. Fuck, my mouth watered just thinking about it.

But nothing, and I do mean nothing, topped the crashing disappointment that sank low in my gut when she'd shrugged and walked off. Because I was a hockey player, of all things. That was supposed to get me laid, not cock-block me.

Her rules landed like a challenge, and I'd been looking for her ever since. Here she was, dropped in my path like it was meant to be.

I parked in a teacher's spot, not giving a single shit if I got a ticket. If I didn't hurry the fuck up, she'd disappear again. I practically jumped out of the truck, feet pounding on the cobblestone path, and tried to catch up to her. When I turned the corner, her blue coat had vanished in the sea of students heading to class.

Where the fuck is she?

I huffed out a breath, pushing down the disappointment of losing her, and headed toward the coffee shop. Was it stalker behavior to show up earlier next Monday and wait, hoping to see her? Probably.

What the actual fuck was wrong with me? It had been one night. Not even. Nothing but a fucking moment between us, but her rules had dug their claws into me ever since. I hated it as much as I enjoyed the thrill of finally being interested in someone.

"Hey! Aren't you Jaxton Ryder?"

Small hands clamped around my arm, halting my

steps, and a blonde stared up at me, her doe eyes wide. I gritted my teeth, stopping a sudden sneer from crossing mouth when she leaned against me. It took every ounce of self-control not to shake her off.

"I know you're him. You took us all the way to finals last year." Her voice was sickly sweet. She was trying to be cute, but that shit was not attractive.

Alex nearly fell off his chair this morning, laughing, when I put on a beanie and grabbed my sunglasses. His smug ass thought it was hilarious that I believed I could pull off a "Clark Kent"—his words, not mine—and walk around unrecognized.

Fucking great.

"I heard you're playing next weekend. Maybe I can come by after the game?" she said, her voice soft, attempting to be seductive, but she couldn't hide the underlying hint of desperation.

I didn't miss the fact that she said "after" the game. Her baby blue eyes, bleach-blonde hair, and decent rack should've tempted me, but she had that needy gleam to her. She thought if she could catch me, she could keep me.

She was wrong.

I stepped back and removed her hand from my chest. "I'm sure the guys will be happy to see you."

"You won't be there?"

I deadpanned, making sure she got the point, "Oh, I'll be there."

Her face crumpled into a pout, but I turned before she could say anything.

"Have fun at the game," I said dismissively over

my shoulder and walked away. Maybe I sounded like a dick, but that girl had *stalker* written all over her. She'd no doubt gotten here early just to corner me on my way to class. The irony that I'd been considering doing the same to Sidney was not lost on me.

Today was the first day of my last semester of college. In a couple of months, I would have a degree in kinesiology, and then I would be off to play for the Boston Bruins. They'd drafted me three years ago when I was still playing Juniors. I was all set to go right to the pros, but my meddling mom had sent me a list of players who *sucked it up* and went to college. So here I was.

Unlike football and baseball, the NHL drafted most of their players before they got to college. They used a loophole where you didn't physically sign the contract, but you were committed to the team. It was to the point that if you played college hockey and weren't drafted, you were likely a second-tier player.

My long strides ate up the distance as I walked along the cobblestone path to the coffee shop. A buzz of noise greeted me when I entered. The place was so packed students with early classes, the line stretched around the wood bistro tables to the front entrance. It was set up exactly like every other cookie-cutter cafe chain, cash at the front and pickup line down the side.

I removed my beanie, tucking it into my pocket, and my gaze landed on the girl directly in front of me. A grin lifted the corner of my mouth, and my heart beat in my ears.

Found you.

Sidney's foot tapped incessantly, and she'd checked her watch at least three times in the past thirty seconds. She hadn't seen me yet, but I couldn't look away from her. Sidney stepped fully in front of me and glared at the cute barista, who was trying to skip her to take my order.

"I'll have a large dark roast. Please." Her voice was sharp. The type you would expect from a coach, not a mini-skirt-wearing co-ed.

Entertained, I waited my turn quietly and watched her walk to the other end of the counter without spotting me. I quickly placed my order, ignoring the way the barista was leering at me, and circled around the cafe so I could approach Sidney from behind. I stepped into her space, not touching but close enough to drop my mouth to just above her ear and whisper, "There you are, Trouble. I've been looking for you."

She shivered, and my gaze followed the goose bumps that trailed down her arms. We were frozen for one blissful second before she spun around and laughed. "Oh, shit!"

A low chuckle rumbled in my chest, and my grin turned up in the corner. "Surprised to see me?"

She turned back to face the counter, and my mouth quirked at the tinge of pink that crawled up her neck. "I didn't expect to see you again."

I put a hand to my chest. "I'm hurt you don't remember I go here."

She huffed out a half laugh. "Oh, I remember. Plus, I wasn't exactly in my right mind by the end."

"No, you weren't. What do you say we try that again?"

"Oh, so you're looking to get your ego hurt?"

Fuck, I loved the sass on her.

Before I could answer, the overeager barista turned a carnal smile my way and leaned all the way over the counter, giving me a perfect view of her full tits. "Made yours special."

I grabbed my coffee, ignoring the phone number written across it in red marker and the lipstick print of her kiss. She gave me a little smirk.

"Thanks," I said, voice flat.

Sidney's gaze pierced mine before she rolled her eyes.

There wasn't enough light in the club to make out their color before, and I was momentarily sucked into their depths. They were brown around the edges, lightening to a crisp apple-green center. She was gorgeous, and her annoyed expression at the barista was fucking adorably hot.

"That happen a lot?" Sidney gestured to the barista.

"Sometimes." I shrugged and took a sip of my burning hot coffee and tried not to wince when the hot liquid touched my tongue.

Sidney chewed the side of her cheek, and her eyes zeroed in on the scrawled number on my cup. She looked annoyed, but there was an underlying emotion there I couldn't make out. The same electric current from the bar pulsed between us and held me frozen in place.

I knew it was fucking real.

Her chest rose rapidly, clearly as affected as I was. I lowered my head to her ear so only she could hear me. "Seriously, I want to see you again."

"Sidney… Sidney… going once, going twice." The barista called her name in a snarky, acidic tone. Jerking her gaze from mine, Sidney blushed the sweetest shade of pink. I wanted to reach out and direct her attention back to me, but the barista huffed, refusing to be ignored. Sidney and I turned to see the employee's jealous expression as she looked between us.

"How about Friday?" I asked, but Sidney had already stepped away to grab her coffee.

I moved to follow, but a giant of a guy stood in front of me. "Hey, man! Great game Saturday. You better be taking us to finals this year."

"That's the plan, buddy." I normally kept to myself, but people coming up to me was inevitable since we'd won finals last year. I tried to spot Sidney before she disappeared again, but I only got a glimpse of her walking toward the door. *Fuck.*

I disentangled myself, refusing to lose her again, and shouted over my shoulder. "I'm out. See you at the next game."

I pulled my beanie low over my eyes, avoiding people's stares, and followed through the door. I pushed it wide in my hurry and jerked back when it hit something solid.

"Oomph." Sidney made a loud squeak sound and tripped forward. She lifted her cup out of the way, narrowly avoiding spilling it everywhere.

"Shit, sorry." I caught her arm, stabilizing her before she could tip forward. Nothing like being hit with a door to ruin her morning.

"Uh-huh." Sharp green eyes narrowed on me. "Didn't save enough time by skipping the line?"

"Hey, I didn't skip the line. She just got mine ready faster." Even I didn't believe my bullshit.

Her brow quirked. "You mean when she leaned over the counter and gave you her number?"

"What? Jealous?" I tipped my head to the side and gave her a playful smirk. "Did you want her number? You could always go back and ask her."

"She's not really my type."

"Oh yeah? What's your type?" I knew I wouldn't like the answer before she said it.

"Skinny emo musicians."

My hand covered my heart. "Damn, that stings. Why do you have to do me like that?"

There was a gleam in her eyes as she worked to secure her lid and looked at her coffee like she'd saved her child's life and murmured something under her breath about stupid guys and coffee gods.

Sidney faced me with one hand on her hip. I was a big guy, standing at six foot three and two hundred pounds of muscle, refined from years of playing hockey, but I was inclined to think she could take me from that look alone.

My apology halted, my tongue twisted, and my brain full-on stuttered. "It's a nice morning out."

Commenting on the weather? That was the best you could come up with?

She was equally unimpressed, and a crease appeared between her brows, making me want to slide my thumb across it until it relaxed.

"Is it, though?" She tilted her head to the side, and smirked. "I'm running late and barely made it to my favorite coffee shop, only to have some hot, self-entitled hockey player cut in front of me."

"First, as I said, that was all the barista. Second, you think I'm hot, huh?"

"Are you really fishing for compliments? Isn't it a little early for that?" She sounded flirty, and a hint of hope rose in my chest.

"How else am I going to get you to notice me?"

"Oh, I've noticed you. I'm just not interested."

"Ouch." But she was interested. It was written in the way her chest was rising with rapid breaths, the slight pink hue of her cheeks, and the heat in her gaze. "Your rules, right?"

She patted my shoulder, delivering her next blow. It just enticed me further. "Yuppers. You should really give up now."

"I like a challenge, Sidney."

Her darted between mine as she scanned my face, no doubt wondering if I was serious.

So fucking serious.

I itched to know what would've happened the other night if she didn't have her stupid rules in place and what it would take to get her to break them.

"Well, you're not going to win this one." She huffed out a laugh and took a few steps toward the second exit door, bringing me back to reality.

How long had we stood in the coffeehouse entry? She made a show of opening the door. "After you."

I eyed her apprehensively as I walked through; she looked too pleased with herself to trust. "Thanks."

"It's the polite thing to do." Sidney's mouth quirked at the side, and her words were beyond sarcastic.

The tension built between my shoulders. This girl was under my skin, and I was finally in a position to catch her.

Nothing about her made me want to be polite. I walked through the door, and my mouth twitched at the high-pitched squeak she made. She let out a little groan of exasperation when she saw me smiling but struggled to contain her smirk. I love that I was getting to her.

There was a long path that connected the cafe to the building my class was in. I didn't like the idea of splitting from Sidney, having already lost her twice, but before I could say anything, she stopped to shove her BCPT textbook into her overfull bag. A thrill went through me as I realized we were in the same class.

Man, she looked good, bent over. The little minx

scratched her face with her middle finger as I walked by. Guess she didn't like me checking out her ass.

"Behavioral Change, yeah? Looks like we'll be spending the semester together."

She sucked in a breath and, her brows pinched together.

Good. I needed to get under her skin the way she burrowed under mine since she'd been pressed against me at the club. My body hummed with a rash idea, and I picked up my pace, putting a decent amount of distance between us. Then I pulled one of the weirdest asshole moves there was. I held the door open way too fucking early and waited. It always looked super polite, but it put the other person in an awkward position. Do you pick up your pace? Do you smile? Do you keep smiling all the way there, or do you smile twice?

Two girls walked through. "Thanks, Jax," they both said in a singsong voice, as if I was holding the door for them. I took a step back, nodding in their direction, but my gaze stayed on Sidney.

Her brows pulled together, and she bit the side of her cheek, trying to figure me out. She must have noticed my mischievous grin because she slowed down, ignoring me altogether. Her movements were exaggerated as she casually checked her phone, taking her time. I could see a slight grin as she turned her head away from my stare, looking sexy as hell. That earned her points in my book. She wasn't backing down—she was enjoying the game.

"Could you go any slower?" I called out.

"Some of us like things to last more than a few seconds." By the way her eyes sparked to life and dared me to say something back, she knew exactly what her words implied.

I couldn't hide the laugh from my voice. "Fast or slow. All that matters is everyone gets to their destination. Right?" I held the door at the top, forcing her to walk beneath.

"Sure, keep telling yourself that, big guy." She was so close, the top of her head skimmed the bottom of my arm, and her shiny, dark hair bounced as she walked. I couldn't help but breathe her in. She smelled delicious, her citrus-vanilla scent immediately drawing me back to the night at the club. I shook my head and did my best to snap out of the memories.

I tried to reach the next door first, but she beat me by a second. She spun and hauled it open for me. Her eyes narrowed in challenge. "Don't worry. I've got it."

She stood there, hot as fuck, and I had to take a beat to shake out my head. She looked fucking devious. Somehow she turned opening doors into a fucking dare, like she knew exactly how to get to me.

Game on, Trouble.

"Thanks, but I wasn't worried. I knew I could count on you." I ran my tongue over the edge of my teeth and walked toward her, giving her a side-eye. As soon as I got past her, I hauled ass up the stairs, taking two at a time. The stairwell was crowded, but people moved out of my way when I wore my game face.

Sidney was forced to slow down, trying to avoid bumping into people, and I could hear her apologies as she struggled to follow me. Her laugh was breathy as she panted, finally breaking through the students. We shared a conspiratorial glance, and I grinned. I couldn't fucking help it.

My heart pounded in my chest as I beat her to the next door. I pulled it open and did a little bow, smiling so hard my cheeks hurt. "After you."

Already at a half run, she had the advantage and raced past me, yanking the classroom door wide with so much force she nearly hit herself. Her coffee sloshed as she dodged the impact, and she looked at the now near-empty cup with disappointment. She was going to miss that.

I stalked toward her, blood rushing through my ears as adrenaline pumped through my veins. God, I loved chasing her. I moved slowly, no longer in a hurry to get inside. She was cornered between the door and wall, exactly where I wanted her.

"I win." She smiled triumphantly.

I hummed in appreciation. There was something about this girl I couldn't resist. "That's a case of perspective."

I placed one hand on the door and the other on the wall, effectively trapping her between my arms. A thrill went through me when her wide eyes darkened when they met mine. The world quieted around us, all my attention on her shallow breaths that came out in pants as her gaze dropped to my mouth, and her tongue snuck out, wetting her bottom lip before biting it. Fuck, I wanted to free her it from her teeth and replace them with mine. My heart pounded in my chest, and it took everything for me not to close the distance between us. She visibly shivered, watching me with dark eyes, and it took an obnoxious amount of willpower to back away. "I wouldn't want to break your rules."

Her brows pinched together, and I inwardly smiled at her look of disappointment. When this was over, she would be chasing after me. I clenched my jaw, leaving her before I did something desperate, and walked into the room. We were still five minutes early, but the class was practically filled to the brim. It was tiny, with only a few rows of desks, not surprising for such a specialized course.

Looking up, I couldn't help but grin. There were only two seats left.

FOUR
SIDNEY

MY HEART POUNDED in my chest, and I had to take several deep breaths to get it under control. What the hell just happened? One second, we'd been bickering, and the next, I was chasing after him through the halls. He walked into class without a hint of defeat and more than a bit of humor in his eyes. Like he hadn't just pinned me to the wall, making me burn for him. For a brief moment, there was a possessiveness about him, like he was going to kiss me then and there, and then a wall went up between us, and he reminded me of my rules.

I would be a liar if I said I hadn't thought of him since that night at the club. Oh, no. He'd played a starring role in more than one of my fantasies. It kept replaying in my dreams like I was mourning the night that could've been if I hadn't shut it down.

Why did he have to be a hockey player, of all things?

In hindsight, he had all the typical markers: messy hair, giant build, cocky smile. I normally had a radar that spotted them a mile away. Apparently, I had let a much lower region control my actions that night, or I would've clued in sooner.

I would love to say I was behaving like a prickly porcupine because the barista tried to skip me in line, but the reality was all my defense mechanisms snapped into place the second I saw him. It was that or nuzzle into him like some desperate puck bunny. I hadn't been obsessed with him or anything. I just hadn't *not* not thought about him.

I walked into class and gulped down the last sip of coffee before tossing the empty cup into the garbage with a frown. Dammit, I was looking forward to drinking that. I skimmed through the classroom, looking for a spot, and scrunched up my nose when I spotted the remaining empty seat.

Of course it was beside him. Of course it was. I laughed, putting my hands up in the universal—I surrender—gesture as Jax held the chair for me. He looked chivalrous, but the gleam of victory in his eyes told me otherwise.

As I got closer to him, I could practically feel his gaze track over my body, like he couldn't quite figure me out. I did the same, taking in his appearance. I'd been too caught off guard in the cafe to check him out. He looked strong and sturdy, like he'd find it easy to pick me up and toss me around, and his wide chest stretched his dark shirt, making the barest definition of his muscles visible. He wore fitted gray sweats that hung low on his hips. It was a typical jock outfit, but he made it look sexy as hell. I dragged my eyes up over his sharp jaw, landing firmly on his full lips, which turned into a cocky grin at my gaze. I snapped my eyes away, acting extremely interested in the floor tiles, and tamped down all my indecent thoughts. This guy was completely, one hundred percent off-limits.

"I still won." I pretended my face wasn't bright red and slid behind the two-person wooden desk into the chair he held out for me.

"Not a fucking chance." He gave me a victorious smile as he took the seat beside me.

I couldn't help my grin. "Nothing in the rules says anything about chairs. Doors only."

"Do you have rules for everything?" His laugh rang out through the class, but it was cut short when everyone in the room turned toward us. They fixated on him. *But honestly, who could blame them?*

He stiffened and slid a blank mask over his face. He looked like someone good at keeping others locked out. It was a huge contrast from his grin a few seconds before. While I sat here, heart pumping with the exhilaration of the last ten minutes, he looked unaffected, almost bored.

What the hell?

My phone vibrated, and I did my best to covertly check it, rolling my eyes at the message.

Dad: Sorry I missed dinner. You know how it is. I promise I'll catch up with you next week.

I shoved my phone back into my bag, determined not to let my dad standing me up *again* distract me from class.

Most people had turned forward, but there were a few holdouts still looking this way. I twirled my finger, gesturing for them to turn around, and they spun to the front in a dramatic fashion.

Really mature, Sidney.

My arm pressed against Jax's when I pulled my laptop out from my bag, and I could feel it vibrating with his suppressed laughter. A smile cracked my face, realizing he wasn't as collected as he looked. I knocked my elbow into his, which earned me a sideways smirk. *That's better.*

His voice was so low when he leaned in close and whispered, "Have a hard time making new friends? Maybe challenge them to a chivalry race."

This totally isn't flirting. Nope. "I've got plenty of friends."

"Really? How many?"

Well, I had three friends. But they counted for at least a dozen. "So many."

He raised a brow, not believing me. "We should go out sometime. I'd like to meet them."

Little did he know he already had. "I don't know. Our club's pretty exclusive." Exclusive to hanging out at home, eating pizza, and watching old reruns of reality TV.

"Okay. Then just you and I."

Did he just ask me out? My heart was about to

pound out of my chest. The guy was hot. Like, roll off a magazine cover hot, and his confidence just made him all the more enticing. I twisted in my chair, already feeling warmth grow in my lower stomach as memories of dancing with him at the club flooded my brain, stealing all rational thought, and barely managed to respond.

"I see you forgot rule number two."

He raised a brow, but he was cut off before he could reply.

The professor cleared his throat, looking right at us.

Shit.

He pushed his glasses up the bridge of his nose. "As I was saying... Welcome to Behavior Change Persuasion Technology. I'm Dr. Carter, and I want you to take a good look at who's sitting beside you because these are your assigned seats for the rest of this class."

Dread settled in my stomach. How was I supposed to survive the entire semester sitting next to *him*? I was going to lose my damn mind.

Jax looked over, one eyebrow raised. Could he tell how much his attention was getting to me? He was like sitting next to a vortex, impossible not to be sucked in. He directed his entire body toward me and searched my eyes, trying to read my expression.

My already warm face grew hotter. It was potent to have someone like him direct all of—*that*—toward me. He stared a bit too long, and I could feel my skin pebbling at his attention. This man was... dangerous.

Jax had that natural air about him all sports stars had. He'd taken off his beanie, and his light brown hair was in a naturally mussed state, and his eyes stood out with their light gray hue, surrounded by thick lashes. He scratched his neck over a tattoo peeking out above his collar, then pushed his sleeves to his elbows, revealing muscular forearms. Discreetly, I drew in a deep breath. He smelled fantastic and oddly comforting, a subtle woodsy scent mixed with masculine aftershave I hadn't noticed at the club.

"You might need this," Jax said and slid his coffee toward me. His voice was a low rasp, drawing me in until all my attention was on him—

Oh no. He was not allowed to be sweet.

Jax's mouth curled up on the side, his amusement doing nothing to abate my flustered state.

Quietly as possible, I took the rest of my stuff from my bag, having left it for the last minute. I needed to figure out how to ignore him, or I wouldn't survive this class.

A note was passed across our desk to Jax, and my patience disintegrated as I saw the name Lindsay in bright pink letters, followed by a phone number. I growled up at him, "Rein in your little fan club. Some of us need to take this class seriously."

His eyes darkened, and he opened his mouth to say something, but not before Dr. Carter called out to me, "Is there a problem?"

Shit, shit, *shit*.

"No, sir." I wrung my hands together in my lap, body stiffening.

"This is a serious class, and I expect your complete attention. If you can't show your classmates the respect they deserve, you need to leave."

"It won't happen again, sir, I promise."

Anger rose in my cheeks, and I slowly turned to shoot daggers at Jax. His grin only widened, making me want to explode. My hands clenched, and I closed my eyes, taking deep breaths. This was exactly why I stayed away from hockey players. They were nothing but freaking trouble, and Jaxton Ryder was no different. Sure, he might have been charming, funny, and apparently thoughtful, but that was the chase. I turned him down. I might as well have waved a giant red flag in front of his too-competitive ass.

Dr. Carter continued. "As I was saying. To get here, you had to be the best of the best, but you've never experienced this class." I glanced over at Jax, but he focused on the professor, who was giving a once-in-a-lifetime speech. "The next four months will be some of the most grueling you've experienced. I'm here to make sure you succeed in the real world, which means I won't go easy on you. You got yourselves this far, and how well you do is in your hands." He proceeded to list off facts with his fingers.

Ten percent will fail.

Thirty percent will be below average.

Thirty percent will be satisfactory.

And only five percent will be top of the class.

"As an extra incentive, the top three students will get a personal recommendation letter from me."

Blood rushed through my ears and drowned out Dr. Carter's next words as I was overwhelmed with both excitement and fear. The exact thing I needed to secure my internship was being dangled in front of me like a freaking carrot. A carrot that might as well be twenty feet in the air for how hard the professor described this class.

Dr. Carter was halfway through the syllabus when I dropped back into reality. We were going to be quizzed weekly, which was more than the typical midterm and finals.

"Most of you have good reasons for joining this class, but let me be clear, if you do not have one, it's best you leave. This course will be grueling, and your advisor should have informed you of that before you signed up. You either give one hundred percent, or you're doomed to failure."

A sense of dread boiled in my stomach. *Breathe, Sidney. You've got this.*

This was my last shot at getting a recommendation. All the more reason to keep my shit together.

"The weekly quizzes do not count toward your final grade. They're there to help you determine if you should drop out before the cutoff. If you aren't passing them, you won't pass the midterm, where you'll present all your work in front of the class."

I swallowed hard. I needed that recommendation letter.

For the next hour, I listened to what had to be the

most intense first lesson ever given. Begrudgingly, I was thankful for Jax's coffee. Not that I'd ever tell him that.

Dr. Carter closed his laptop and put it in his bag. "Decide what you're going to do, and you're free to go." He paused at the door. "And good luck."

I was practically shoved out of the way as classmates surrounded Jax. One cute brunette started in. "You could come by my place. I have it all to myself, so we won't be interrupted." She winked in his direction as if what she was implying wasn't perfectly clear.

I snuck out around them, ignoring Jax calling after me as I escaped class.

FIVE
JAX

AS SOON AS I got home, Lucas, our starting defenseman, met me at the door. He was a big man and he wore a bright pink shirt that he swore contrasted nicely with his dark brown skin. "Want to tell me why you're tagged in a million tweets about running after some girl?" He used his massive form to block me in the doorway and waved his phone in my face with Twitter open. Sid's and my little competition was on full display as he scrolled.

Tweet: Who's the mystery girl?
Tweet: Hold on to your panties, girls, because this you've got to see.
Tweet: We want some of whatever got into Jax Ryder.

I shrugged. "Nothing to tell."
There was no way I was getting into it with him.

As it was, I would already get shit in the dressing room. Hockey players were huge gossips.

Lucas looked at me with amusement written all over his face. "Bullshit."

"Seriously, man. Drop it." I walked past him into the living room, where both Alex and River chilled on the couch, playing a game on our giant flat-screen. From the way he yelled, Alex was losing badly.

"Come on, man! Mr. Reserved can't go running through the halls and not tell his best friends what the hell happened." Lucas was practically falling over himself, getting a kick out of ripping into me.

Alex, a forward, slammed his controller onto the couch, his dirty-blond hair falling out of its bun, and grabbed his phone. You'd think he would've learned no one beat River when he was committed to the win.

"Oh fuck, there's a video." Alex watched for a second, and a sly smile took over his face. "It's not some girl. *It's the girl.*" He grinned as he jumped from the couch and pointed his phone toward me. "She lay her rules on you again, bro?"

Lucas cackled. "This I've got to hear."

Oh, hell no. This needed to stop right the fuck now. There was a sofa separating Alex and me, creating an obstacle I didn't need. Alex was big and fast. *Fuck it.*

I scrambled to jump over the couch, knocking him on his ass, but as soon as I grabbed the phone, he tossed it to Lucas, laughing at my failed attempt to take it.

I shouted to our right winger, "River, you gonna help me out here, man?"

"Not getting involved. I heard she's cute, though." He gave me a wink and raked a hand through his pitch-black hair before starting a new game.

I walked slowly toward Lucas, cornering him like a scared buck ready to bolt, and lunged to grab the phone. Sidney's laugh rang out through the room as the video played. The sound was free, open, no holding back. None of the fake giggling that I was used to.

It was really too fucking bad she shut me the fuck down. *Again.*

"Christ, man, you were laughing." Lucas looked at me with genuine shock. I wasn't a big laugher; I tried not to think too hard about why. I mean, I put on a good show, but that was what it was. A show. Lucas's head was still bobbing from the screen to me, a grin curving his mouth.

I'm never going to live this down.

River's dark head snapped up. "You like this girl, Jax?" His eyes searched mine, head tilting with the question.

Did I like her? Fuck, I wasn't going there. "Nah, man. Just another girl."

Alex laughed. "Just another girl who turned you down."

River looked over at me with disbelief in his voice. "Wait a fucking minute. This is the girl from the club?"

I tried to blow it off with a shrug. "She's not into hockey players."

Alex laughed from the other side of the room. "Sure, buddy, *that's* why she left you high and dry." He shared a look with Lucas and River, and the three of them smirked, calling me out on my bullshit.

I had to pull my shit together before these guys found out how twisted this girl had me. I gave her my coffee, for fuck's sake. Some uncontrollable urge to do something nice for her and wipe the dejected look off her face. So, like a sixteen-year-old with no game, I slid my coffee over. Worse, I caught myself watching her drink—her soft mouth indenting on the lid—more times than I cared to admit.

Alex threw a pillow at me. "You've got it bad, man."

Luckily, I caught it right before it smashed into my face. Bastard caught me daydreaming.

I grabbed my bag from the counter, intent on making an escape. Our house was set up with two bedrooms on the main floor and two upstairs. The best part was each of our rooms had an adjoining bathroom. It was out of most college students' price range, but with each of our bonuses, we were more than fine here.

Plus, it was fucking perfect.

We'd been living together for the last three years and had a pretty good system going. Not to say we didn't get on each other's nerves because we fucking did.

I bunched the pillow in a tight ball and whipped

it back at Alex, who stared at the TV, hitting him square in the back of his head. I rushed toward the stairs when he threw it back. It slammed into the wall, barely missing me. As soon as I was in my room, I pressed my back against the closed door and rubbed my hands over my face. I cracked my neck before resting my head against the solid wood and closing my eyes, picturing Sidney's victorious smile. *What the hell was I thinking?*

I was supposed to be keeping a low profile to avoid school becoming a circus. Instead, today's stunt would be blasted all over social media. *This fucking girl.*

I'd been pissed about her no-kissing rule, but *One Night Only* should've worked perfectly for me. I would make a shit boyfriend. I spent all of my time practicing, playing, studying, or sleeping. My whole life was about making it to the NHL. So tell me why I tried to convince her to break it?

It was bad enough I had to worry about my two oldest friends. Lucas was drafted to the Bruins right after me, Alex and River after that. Something I would never let them live down, and we were heading to Boston together when we graduated.

The thing was, Lucas was head over heels for Piper, and pro sports were brutal on relationships. Between road games, mandatory events, and training camps, a player spent most of their time out of town. Then, when they were home, players still needed to maintain their workout and training schedule. I didn't want to watch Lucas's and Piper's hearts get stomped on if it all fell apart. And let's face it, the odds weren't in their favor. Lucas said she was worth the risk, and seeing how they acted together, maybe she was. But if it fell apart, they would end up wishing they'd never met at all.

I collapsed on my bed, resting against the headboard. I couldn't stop picturing Sidney's wide-open smile, bouncing hair, and delinquent gleam in her eyes as she booked it up the stairs.

A small smile forced its way onto my lips, and I let out a frustrated groan. I wasn't that guy; I was the don't talk to me with a side of fuck off type. Now, with the growing attention around my start with the Bruins, I doubled down on being private. Running through the halls was the opposite of that.

Lucas barged into my room, flopping down on the bed beside me like dead weight. He was still scrolling Twitter on his phone. "So, you're into her, huh?"

"You know damn well I don't date, so screw off, man." Lucas was my closest friend. Meaning, he thought he was entitled to know my shit.

"Whatever you say, buddy. From the way you look in those posts, I haven't seen you have fun like that with... anyone." He looked at me like I was some kind of lab rat, and his voice turned serious as he studied me. "At least not since Marcus died."

Marcus.

My stomach dropped. He would've loved this drama.

"What do you want, Lucas?"

He lifted himself off the bed. "We're headed to the Brewhouse."

My stomach growled. I'd planned on staying in, but I guess it had other ideas.

Lucas finally tucked his phone in his pocket. "Honestly, though. How was it?"

I tried to shrug it off, but I could feel the smile build on my lips. "It was fun."

"Just fun, huh?"

"I'm not justifying that with an answer."

"Whatever helps you to sleep at night, kid." His teasing tone was back in full force. Ever since he and Piper finally got together, he'd been on our cases about settling down and how wonderful it was. So, we basically avoided him like the plague.

"You think right before we move to Boston's a good fucking time to date?" Frustration coated my voice. No, it fucking wasn't. Something I forgot when I got within a three-foot radius of one feisty brunette.

"Hey, hurry up." Alex banged on my door. "Quit your man hugging in there, and let's eat." More banging. "Get your ass out here, Jax, or I'm going to comment on each of these posts."

He wouldn't dare, but it was enough to get me up and moving. Even if it was just to knock him out. Sometimes these guys acted like we were brothers, and right now, he was the annoying younger one.

I opened the door, and Alex moved to the side to let me out. He wrapped his arm around my shoulder and dragged me with him out of the house.

"Our agent called, and he wants to *talk* about

today." He air quoted the word *talk*. "Looks like you're in shit."

Rocky had signed Alex first, then took the rest of us on. His primary job was keeping us in line, and he was our go-between us and our future teams. Rocky was a dick but made good deals and knew the business, which was what we needed. I knew how to play, not suck up and PR.

I lifted a brow. "Rocky can fuck right off with that bullshit."

Alex laughed. "Whatever, man, it's your funeral." A sly smile took over his face. "Okay, I want all the details about this girl."

I looked at the ceiling. It was going to be a long night.

SIX
JAX

I CLICKED Submit on my online quiz and watched the "calculate" symbol flash on the screen. First test down, only one million to go. At least that was what it felt like. Several students had already scrambled out of the class with matching looks of terror.

Couldn't say I blamed them. Shit was hard.

I might be a jock, but I didn't fuck around with school, and the quiz had tested my confidence. I cracked my knuckles as the results page loaded and smirked.

A.

Hell, yeah.

A distressed feminine sound drew my attention just in time to witness Sidney drop her head on the desk with a dull thump, making it vibrate below my arms.

She banged her head a few more times before laying it over her crossed arms. She flattened on the table like a giant weight pressed on her, so heavy she couldn't lift her head.

I snuck a peek at her laptop and the B- marked on it.

From the looks of our classmates, it could've been worse.

I mimicked her posture, head laid on my arms, and faced her. "Hi."

Her gaze met mine, and her eyes widened at how close I was. My elbow was only a hairsbreadth from hers.

"Hi." Her voice was quiet. All her usual spark had faded away. Yeah, that had to change.

"Quizzes don't count, remember?" I gestured with my chin toward her laptop.

She huffed and rolled her eyes. "Maybe not for you. You're already drafted to the freakin' NHL."

"Passing this class matters to me. Could you fucking imagine if I made it to the end and didn't graduate?" I scoffed, and a shudder ran down my spine. The newspapers would eat that shit up.

"Sorry... It's just..." She took a deep breath, pausing for several beats before letting it out. "I *need* that referral to finalize my internship."

My head snapped back. "Wait, really? The one you were celebrating at the club?"

"Really. Really." She rubbed her temples, and her fingers slid through her hair, pushing it off her face. Goddammit, she looked like someone had kicked her puppy. I shouldn't care. I barely knew this girl, but I fucking did.

"Hey, we can figure this out."

A soft laugh escaped her, loosening the tension in my chest. "Oh, can *we*?"

I bumped my arm into hers. "Yeah, the fuck we can."

A pale pink brightened her skin as the spark returned to her eyes. "And how do you expect us to do that? I didn't just fail this quiz. I *studied* and failed."

"First, a B- isn't a fail. Second, somehow I'm not surprised that you're as thorough at studying as you were at turning me down."

Her eyes crinkled as she bit back a smile.

That was fucking better.

Her smile turned sheepish. "It's not like I wanted to turn you down. It was the rule—"

"Rules, I know." This girl had no idea how badly I wanted to break all of her carefully crafted rules. I turned my laptop so she could see my grade. "What if I told you I could guarantee you an A on your next quiz? All you have to do is study with me."

"You can't promise that. No one can."

She was right, but that didn't stop me from leaning forward on my forearms, cutting the distance between us. "Try me."

"Just to make sure I understand. You're saying all I have to do is study with you for one night and I'll get an A?"

I pushed my tongue into my cheek. There was that one-night rule again, although I doubted it extended to studying. "That's right."

She laughed, shaking her head. "There's no way."

I waited until her eyes were on mine. "Bet."

"What?" She practically squeaked the question but didn't look away. The green had swallowed the brown of her irises, and her breaths came out in shallow pants as she waited for my response.

I gave her my cockiest smile. The one I'd honed after a lifetime on the ice antagonizing my opponents. "I *bet* you'll earn an A on your next quiz if you study with me one time."

Her head tilted to the side as she studied me.

"And what's in it for you?"

It was a fucking gamble but worth it. "You'll break your rule and give me your number."

"What?" she shot back so fast I had to grab onto the back of her chair to keep her from tipping over.

I didn't answer. I knew better than to open my mouth and accidentally talk her out of it.

"I can't break the rules. Like, I can't." The pupils in her eyes expanded, and she swallowed hard. "Especially not with you."

"Because you think I'm hot."

"Fishing for compliments isn't cute."

"You sure about that?"

Her cheeks flushed, and she rolled her eyes. "What do you want instead of my number?"

"You're telling me you never give out your number? Or just not to hockey players?"

"Of course guys have my number. Obviously, Anthony has it."

I reminded myself Anthony was her roommate,

who had a hot boyfriend, before continuing. "Okay, we're just studying. Think of me as Anthony."

"Like Anthony?" Her brows drew together, and I could practically see her mind working as she stared at the desk. "I get an A and you get my number?"

"You got it."

"Okay."

"That's it? Okay?"

That earned me a smirk. "Yes, oh wonderful Jax. I'd be absolutely honored to study with you." She put her hand across her heart dramatically, and her mouth stretched into a smile. There was the sass I expected from her.

"That's better." I dodged away from her smack. "Where can we—"

"We could grab a spot in the east wing library. The study rooms are already booked for the semester, but there are usually free tables."

She was already looking over her scheduler app. It was full of categories and notes highlighted in different colors. The way she agreed to be partners sounded as if it physically pained her to say yes, but I was her best shot, and we both knew it.

"I'm free Saturday or Sunday afternoons." That way, I could still sleep in from our game the night before.

"Nope, I work at the bookshop most weekends. How about Monday night?"

"I practice late every Monday through Wednesday. We get done early on Thursdays. Would 6:30 work?" Scheduling anything into my life was always tricky. It wasn't that I didn't want to make time for people; it was that I didn't have any.

Sidney tucked her hair behind her ear while looking at her screen. "Yeah, that'll work."

She twisted to put her things into her bag, and her shirt shifted, revealing a long, thin silver scar running from her neck down her shoulder. I wanted to know how she got it. I wanted to know everything about this girl.

Her eyes scanned the empty room. "Well, this has been... interesting, but I've got to get to my next class. I'll see you on Thursday," she said, quickly grabbing her stuff and nearly running out the door.

I smirked. There was no way I would lose this bet.

SEVEN
SIDNEY

MIA: Enjoy your date, hot stuff.
I huffed out a laugh and typed a reply.
Me: You know damn well this is not a dat
Anthony: Keep telling yourself that, Cupcake.

It was not a date because I didn't do dates. It was a bet. One that I wanted him to win.

Wait? Did I want him to win? He wins, I got an A, and he got my number? Was that how that went? Well, shit. I guess I did want him to win. Not that I had high hopes, but at this point, I would have tried anything.

My day had been an absolute nightmare. I woke up late for class, my second one ran long, and work called asking if I could do a double shift on Saturday. I wanted to let the entire week drain away. Instead, I dragged myself to the library to study with Jax. For real, though, I needed to study.

I wore my softest leggings, a light gray sweater, and my favorite pair of chunky black leather boots. Comfortable was the name of the game tonight.

I opened the large oak library doors and smiled. This place had felt like home for the last three years. My schoolwork was all online, but there was something special about coming here. The college had renovated the library a few years back, adding an extension to the entire east side. It gave the space a duality of traditional on the left and modern on the right.

I spotted Jax standing a few feet into the building and swallowed hard. God, there was something irresistible about a guy in an oversized sweater, sweats, and a ball cap. He looked good, relaxed in his skin, and I had to fight hard to keep my eyes from drifting downward.

As soon as he spotted me, his face brightened, and the corner of his mouth kicked up. His gaze drifted down my body from head to toe and then ever so slowly back up again. Jax's eyes darkened when they met mine, but they looked a little sheepish. *Busted.*

He shrugged his shoulders, giving me a boyish grin that showed off his dimple. That was when I noticed he was holding coffees. My heart nearly jumped out of my chest.

"That for me?" I clasped my hands together to stop myself from grabbing it.

"Yes, hello to you too." He held out the cup, amusement clear in his voice.

"You don't understand how much I needed this." Seriously, though, if he kept up with the coffees, he might get himself another stalker.

"I thought you might. I grabbed us a table in the back," he said, gesturing with his head as he led us deeper into the older part of the library. Our desk was tucked around a corner, providing as much privacy as possible in a public space. We sat, and I made quick work of mixing my drink with the sugar and creamer packages on the table.

I took a sip and moaned in the back of my throat. Perfect.

"That's the best thank-you I've got in a while." His voice was a low rasp.

I ignored my hot cheeks and took out my laptop, opening the OneNote document I'd created for this class. It was easier to keep firm boundaries in the professional setting of a lecture hall, but tucked away, even if it was in a library, made everything feel… different. I cleared my throat. "Thank you."

"It's my pleasure." Jax cut into my thoughts and gave me a mischievous grin. God, no wonder women flocked to him.

He leaned on the table, a casualness settling over him. "Where are you from?"

"We're going to do small talk now?"

His eyebrows rose. "Looks like it."

I huffed out a laugh. "Here."

That perked him up. "Oh yeah? What school did you go to?"

"St-Clair High."

"Ha! I went to St. Xavier. We kicked your hockey team's ass."

"Try again. We won Provincials all four years I was there."

He smiled, his cheeks indenting with perfect dimples. "Your team cheated."

I barked out a laugh. "Did not—"

Jax held up a hand to stop me from what would have been an epic tirade about why it was not okay to accuse a team of cheating just because you lost. "So you *do* like hockey? Just not college hockey?"

"Oh, I like college hockey."

"But you didn't recognize me at the pub?" The color drained from his face, and he looked like he sucked on something sour. "Wait? Did you recognize me and this whole rules thing is just a way for you to turn me down?" He took his hat off, ran his hand through his already messy hair, and sighed, "Fuck."

I had to bite back a laugh. "I just don't watch your team's hockey games. I still follow my favorite."

Jax's brows drew together, and his face turned serious. "What team, Sidney?"

He leaned in closer, the intensity of his gaze growing hot until I shifted in my chair. I suddenly didn't want to admit who I cheered for. "It doesn't matter."

"Tell me who your favorite team is," he commanded in a low tone.

Dammit. He wasn't going to let it go. "Brick Bandits."

"No way. No fucking way." His voice came out in

shock, and his eyes widened. "They beat us in the playoffs two years ago. They're why we didn't make it to finals."

I sucked in an apologetic breath between my teeth. "Yeah, they beat you pretty bad that time. It was a good night."

Jax's gaze snapped to mine before he laughed loud enough that we were shushed from the table a few rows away. "Sidney King. That's blasphemy. You don't need to worry about passing this class. They might kick you out for that."

"It'll be our little secret."

"Hell the fuck no. I'm telling everyone."

My heart rate spiked, and I had to swallow it down. "No, no. Like it's funny between us, but there's a whole lot of people who wouldn't think it was funny."

"Why do you think *I* think it's funny?"

Oh shit. "Don't you?"

A muscle worked in his jaw. He didn't look upset, but his eyes tracked mine. He was working something out in his head. "When I win this bet, I want your number, *and* you need to come to a game."

Oh, that was a bad idea. Something told me seeing him play was the last thing I should do. "I'm busy that night."

His brows tugged together. "Doing what?"

"Watching the Bandits kick your ass on live TV."

"You're evil." He patted his hands over his chest and abdomen and looked at his palms. "I must be bleeding with how hard you're trying to kill me."

"Stop being dramatic," I said, smiling.

He leaned forward. His gray eyes were overtaken by the black of his pupils. "I'll just have to win you over as a fan."

I swallowed a shallow breath. "Good luck with that."

He shifted closer. "I don't need luck."

"Why's that?"

He was so close I could almost feel his breath. "I'm good at winning."

I clenched my jaw and locked my legs to stop myself from closing the distance. "And if I don't? Become your biggest fan."

He smirked. "I'll tell Alex, and he'll harass you until you do."

"I'll keep that in mind." I looked away and took a sip of my coffee, finally freed from whatever magnet pulled us together.

"You excited about your internship?" he asked, keeping things light after the intensity of the last moment. Thank god.

I chewed on the side of my cheek before answering. "Yeah, I really am. I've been working hard for this, you know?"

He smiled at me. "Nah, I know nothing about working hard."

"Whatever. I'm sure you've had to work hard your whole life." I was rambling now but couldn't seem to stop. "I'd ask what you're doing after graduation, but the entire school knows you're going on to Boston."

"Technically, it's training camp first, then I start with the Bruins for preseason training." He shrugged like it was no big deal.

I asked another question, "What are you most excited about?"

"That's a tough one. Probably the bigger arenas. I can't explain the feeling of hearing the roar of the crowd."

"I thought you were going to say the chicks." Energy buzzed through me at his smirk.

"Oh, well, them too."

"Thought so." I ignored the slight twinge in my chest.

"How about you, Sid? Are you a secret volleyball star?"

I scrunched up my nose. "No. Sports were never my thing. My mom and I were always really into politics."

"Is that what your mom does, then? Politician?"

A dark, painful fog threatened to overcome me, but the softness in Jax's eyes made it almost bearable. "My mom passed away when I was thirteen. She never made it, but yeah, that's what she wanted to be."

"I'm sorry for your loss." His lashes shadowed his eyes, and he stared at the table for several seconds. Nodding to himself, he took a deep breath. "My best friend passed away a few years ago." He met my gaze, and I could see the grief hidden there. There was an understanding between us now. We both belonged to the same horrible club.

He didn't ask, but I found myself saying it anyway. "It was a car accident. A truck lost control and came into our lane. I was in the back seat but don't remember anything after the headlights. I woke up in the hospital, and she was already gone." I tugged at the collar of my sweater and turned my head, exposing the scar that ran from the base of my neck to my shoulder. "It's how I got this scar."

Jax scanned the scar, and his eyes filled with understanding. "My friend died in a car accident too. He was there one day and gone the next. It took a while to wrap my head around it. My mom did her best to make sure I was alright, but there wasn't much she could do."

It was a strange feeling sharing this moment with Jax. It was somehow both sad and comforting that he knew how I felt without me having to explain. We sat for a long moment, neither of us saying anything. Just soaking in mutual acceptance. Finally, I swallowed hard, nodding, and then we both silently agreed to move on with the conversation.

"So do you have any siblings?" Jax kept the question safe and easy, lightening the mood.

"No, my parents didn't stay together long enough to have more, and my mom never dated after." He raised a brow, but I didn't explain further. "How about you?"

"It's just me and my parents. They've been together for almost thirty years now."

It struck me how different our lives had been. He

obviously grew up surrounded by love, whereas my life couldn't be any more different.

Jax huffed. "So, Sidney. What's with the rules?"

I laughed. "I'm surprised it took you so long to ask. Success takes discipline, and discipline requires rules. And mark my words, Jax, I will succeed."

His brows lifted. "I don't doubt you."

"Good."

"So... you don't date? Like...at all?" he asked, settling in his chair.

I shrugged. "I dated a guy for three years in high school, but we broke up when we went our separate ways for college."

"Not into long distance?" He tapped his pen on the table. I noticed he always fidgeted in one way or another.

"It works for some people, but it's not for me. Too easy to get caught up in your own life and forget about the other," I answered. It wasn't exactly the entire reason, but close enough for this conversation.

"But that was high school. You're in your fourth year of college. You're telling me you just wrote off all guys?"

I gave him my best *what the hell* face. "No... I'm a grown-ass woman, Jax. I can prioritize my own life, and right now, guys are not high on the list."

His head tilted at an angle, and his eyes searched over my face. "So, what is on the priority list?"

"That's easy. My internship. I've spent the last three and a half years working toward it." I leaned back, mirroring his position. "Sacrifices were made, but I'm so close it's all worth it."

He stretched his arms over his head, opening his chest, and his gaze landed on my mouth. "What sacrifices?"

I shrugged. "Big ones."

"Like?" His tongue darted out, worrying at his top teeth.

"No parties," I replied, and his mouth popped open.

"No parties?" His voice lifted at the end.

I smiled at his surprise and continued. "No boyfriends."

"Brutal." He shook his head even as he asked, "You hooked up, though?"

"Yeah, obviously, I'm not an idiot." I laughed at the relief on his face, and I asked a question of my own. "You get it, though, right? You have a big dream."

His shoulders lifted and fell, a sly grin pulling at his mouth. "Funny enough, being a future pro athlete comes with more perks than sacrifices."

He held up his fingers to list them.

One finger raised. "Invited to all the best parties."

Two fingers raised. "I almost never pay for beer."

He looked up and to the right, searching for another one, and his face lit up with a smile. Three fingers raised. "And unlimited hookups."

I choked out a laugh. "Eventually, we all have to make sacrifices, Jax. You just haven't figured out what yours will be yet."

"Nah, Sidney. I've already got everything I want. Well, almost." Before another awkward silence could settle in, he looked at our stuff spread over the table and rubbed his hands together. "Time to work on winning that bet."

An hour into studying, bouncing questions off each other, we'd gotten into a groove. We had been ticking through all the major components of our syllabus, our seats slowly moving closer until we were sharing the same book. Jax was freaking smart. It was way sexier than I wanted to admit. He was flying through his work and breaking everything down into easy bite-sized pieces. Maybe studying with him wouldn't be so bad.

"You're good at this."

"Surprised?" He narrowed his gaze as he adjusted in his seat. A wall went up behind his eyes, making him closed off and defensive while his hands fiddled with his book.

"No, Jax. It's seriously impressive." I tried to infuse sincerity into my voice.

His shoulders visibly relaxed, and his eyes briefly caught mine. How many people had made the mistake of underestimating him? His arm grazed mine, drawing all my focus to where we were touching. I had been inching closer to him as the night went on, reading over his meticulous notes and listening as he explained. When I asked questions, he listened attentively, never getting distracted.

A zing of energy had been growing between us, like a magnetic pull forcing me closer. My gaze drifted down to his mouth, so close it would be easy to lean into him for a taste. These weren't library-appropriate thoughts, but come on, who could blame me? And this was why I needed rules because, without them, I would be falling all over Jax Ryder.

His phone vibrated, but he didn't look at it.

We were both breathing a little too hard, caught in this trance. All of his attention was on me, and it was intense. I was a moth to a flame. That thought gave me pause. The story didn't end well for the moth.

I broke first, leaning back, and reached into my bag for my water. "Aren't you going to get that?"

"Nope. Not important."

He didn't even check it. Did that mean he thought I was important? My cheeks heated, and I turned away, hoping he didn't catch it.

"Hey, Jax. I didn't expect to see you here." A beautiful blonde perched her hip against our table. She came out of nowhere and positioned herself with her back toward me. My anger rose when Jax seemed to recognize her. Who was this girl acting like I wasn't even here?

Jax was quick. "Sid, this is Stacey." He gestured his hand toward me.

Was it? No one had ever called me "Sid" before. Jax was studying me. His eyes narrowed in a challenge to see if I would correct him on his little nickname.

Her smile fell as she reluctantly turned to face me. Her eyes took in my simple attire and basic makeup. "Nice to meet you... Cindy, is it?"

Ha. Funny…

"I'm pretty tired. Want to call it a night?" I asked Jax quietly.

"You sure?" Jax's expression darkened. If I didn't know better, I would've thought he was disappointed.

"All of that studying has my mind fried. I'm not going to be able to fit anything else in anyway." My words came out awkward and stilted while I went through my phone, setting up my Uber. The car was nearby, so it wouldn't be more than a few minutes.

"I hear you on that one." Jax nodded, and he gathered all of his stuff. He was practically ignoring Stacey, who stood there, mouth agape.

Once I was ready, Jax looked over at her. "I'm going with her."

She made a huffing sound, but I turned to leave, letting him deal with that. I walked straight out of the building into the crisp night air, and I scanned the parking lot. I didn't realize how long we'd been there. It was nearly black outside.

"Come on, I'll walk you to your car."

"Actually, I walked here."

His sharp gaze found mine. "In that case, I'll drive you home."

A car pulled up.

"That's okay, my Uber's here. Have a good night, Jax." I got into the car, straining all my muscles not to look back. *God, a girl could get caught up in him.*

EIGHT
SIDNEY

"YOU KNOW your dad doesn't care what you wear, right?" Mia stood in my doorway while I pulled on a different shirt. I was on my third outfit change of the morning.

I was dressed more professionally than my normally eclectic attire, with a crisp white shirt and long pencil skirt. My hands ran over my hair, flattening the invisible flyaways, and I huffed out a breath. I really was acting crazy. "I know, I know. It's just been a while, and you know how he can be. High expectations and all that."

Being a coach in the NHL came with a lot of responsibilities, and my dad always expected the same effort out of me as he did his players. My dad had bailed on our last three meetups, and no matter how many times I told myself it was his loss, I still missed him. I hurried to pull on my shoes. He would be here to pick me up any minute. I was already walking out the door when my phone chimed.

Dad: Hey kiddo, I'm sorry I have to cancel breakfast. We won a big game last night, and I couldn't bail on the celebration. Promise I'll reschedule soon. Love you.

My eyes stung, and I sniffed in a breath, refusing to cry over this. Hockey had always come first, and I had been an idiot to think that was ever going to change. I typed out a quick reply and headed back to my room to get changed into something more comfortable.

Me: Of course. Enjoy your win. You deserve it.

Luckily, he couldn't hear my tone through the text. Mia took one look at me and wrapped me in one of her signature warm hugs. "He canceled again, didn't he?"

"Yup." I popped the *p*, trying to add more levity than I actually felt.

"He's an asshole. You know that, right?"

I walked through our apartment and grabbed a bottle of water from the fridge. Our home was big enough to fit three bedrooms, a kitchen, and a sitting area but small enough to walk from one end to the other in less than twenty steps. It was built in the early 2000s, giving everything a slightly dated look that was still functional.

Mia handed me a coffee, and I greedily took a sip, letting the comforting liquid warm me from the inside. "Can we talk about anything else?"

She paused and looked me up and down for a few moments before nodding. A slow, devious smile curved her mouth. "Sooooo, how was your non-date date?"

Anthony chose that moment to come out of his room and leaned against the doorframe. "Yeah, Sidney. How was your *date*?"

"It wasn't a date. We aren't a thing. He's not mine or anything like that," I said a bit too loudly. *Where the hell did that come from?*

Anthony choked on a laugh, and Mia squealed.

"That's not exactly what I meant, but now I'm curious. Are you catching feelings, Sidney? I wouldn't blame you if you were. That guy is *hot*." Mia fanned herself, and I rolled my eyes.

"I had to watch some chick hit on him right in front of me like I was invisible."

"Wait. Jax acted like you weren't there?" Anthony's voice was laced with anger.

"No, he didn't seem that interested in her, but… still," I replied, not quite meeting their eyes.

"You're telling me he turned down a willing hot girl for your study date?" Mia smiled so wide she looked like a cat who ate the canary.

"Drop it, please. You know I don't do hockey players."

She laughed and cheered with her coffee mug. I

headed back to my room, listening to her shout, "You're in so much trouble, girl."

I collapsed on my bed. Was I attracted to Jax? Sure.

The problem was I knew firsthand what happened when a player goes pro. After my mom died, my dad showed up, making promises about how I was the most important person to him and we were going to be a team from that point on. I thought he was my knight in shining armor, and we were going to live this happy life together. *I was so wrong.*

The first few weeks were perfect. I moved into his enormous house, which reminded me of a castle. We played cards, stayed up late eating ice cream, and watched scary movies.

I didn't realize he had time because of the off-season, and as fall got closer, he started to pull away. His "you mean the world to me" promises didn't last. He found me a modern-day version of a governess, packed his bags, and took off, telling me he loved me and would see me soon. I'd only seen him a few dozen times since.

I was too young to understand he was a selfish prick who went back to his career over me. Since then, I'd seen countless of his players do the same thing. I swear, at the rate they get divorced, it was a competition. Don't even get me started on the cheating. The takeaway was, under no circumstances was it a good idea to get involved with hockey players. They were literally heartbreak walking.

When I got to class, Jax slammed into the seat beside me, rocking the entire table and nearly spilling my coffee everywhere. I snatched the cup just in time and glared at him. He missed it completely, his baseball cap pulled so low it covered his eyes. He was completely rigid in his seat; a deep scowl formed on his lips, and a muscle worked in his jaw.

"Well, good morning to you too." My voice came out with more emotion than I wanted, but he didn't notice.

He gruffed out, "Morning."

I tilted my head to get a better look at him, watching as he turned away. I couldn't help the pang of annoyance ripping through me. That was it? No sign we knew each other at all.

Jax continued to be in full-blown thundercloud mode during class. He barely said two words to me, and he'd been staring a hole into the teacher's head since he got here. My initial thought was Jax was a complete dick, but as I watched him, I could see his jaw clenched and his hands were fisted, making white creases in his knuckles. He held himself so tensely that I worried he would crack a rib. He looked miserable. No, miserable was the wrong word. He looked stressed. Leaning over a bit, I tried to make eye contact. "You okay?"

His flat, gray eyes met mine. He must have thought it had been long enough for me to get his "don't talk to me" hint because he faced forward again.

"Soooo, I didn't know they let five-year-olds into

college," I said, looking directly at him, refusing to shift my gaze.

He went rigid, then took a deep breath in and a deep breath out. Slowly, I could see a crack in his wall, and his lips tipped up on the side. Victory! I inwardly fist pumped. A feeling of euphoria filled me, knowing that I had put it there.

"Six, actually. I'm sad you can't tell I've matured." A hint of amusement was audible in his words.

I couldn't help the pride I felt knowing that I did that. I lightened some of the anxiety plaguing him this morning.

"You played rough last night? I heard you were good at that sort of thing." Oh. My. God. *Please* tell me I didn't just say that. I meant his practice. I could feel the heat climb up my neck, covering my cheeks. He chuckled, and his dark gaze skimmed across me, pausing on my mouth, taking his time before meeting my eyes. He was clearly thinking about what I'd just said and everything I'd implied. His tongue darted out, and he licked his lips. I was struck again by how intense it was to have all of his attention on me. There was something irresistible about him, and it wasn't only the attraction.

"Something like that."

The air whooshed out of me all at once as his deep rumble rolled over me. I wanted to know exactly what "like that" meant. Shaking my head, it was my turn to stare straight ahead. This conversation had gotten me nowhere good. For all of my "hockey players are the worst" pep talks, it sure didn't take him long to break through my resolve.

He turned his head forward and went back to his grumpy demeanor, his pen rattling against the table as he flipped it from side to side. All the tension returned to his body like he wasn't smiling seconds ago.

By the time the class was over, I'd had enough of his attitude. I was going to snap him out of his mood, and I knew exactly how to do it. I grabbed my stuff and stood too quickly, causing me to lose my balance. His hand darted out and caught my wrist, stabilizing me.

"Careful," he said, fingers still wrapped around my arm.

The spot we were connected tingled under his touch. This was my opportunity to make "Operation Relax Jax" a go. I pushed all the hesitation to the back of my mind.

"Come on. I've got something to show you." At the risk of looking like a complete ass, I shifted our hands and closed my fingers around his, gently tugging. I wouldn't put it past him to resist, but he surprised me by sliding from his seat, grabbing his bag.

"Lead the way." Rough calluses moved against my smooth skin before he laced our fingers together, stroking his thumb over the pad of my palm. The feel of the barely there touch sent tingles through my arm. He was staring at my mouth, and I bit my bottom lip. He took a step toward me, but I stepped back, needing a little space between us to breathe. Neither of us let go of each other's hand, and I turned toward the door, dragging him behind me.

I smiled, knowing I was going to fix whatever was eating at him.

NINE
JAX

"COME ON, LET'S GO." Sid looked back at me, piercing hazel eyes searching mine. I was more than happy to follow. She was like a lifeline, dragging me toward the surface.

At this point, she could lead me off a cliff. I was that curious about what she had in mind. She looked at me with determined eyes, and the corner of her lips tilted up. She was definitely up to something. "Where are you bringing me? I'm in a shit mood, Sid."

She didn't slow down. If anything, she pulled harder, laughing. "I know. You were a sour ass for the entire class. Get over yourself for a minute, and trust me." She gave my hand a firm squeeze.

"Fine, but don't expect good company." Grumbling under my breath, I followed as she led me out of the building but didn't head to the parking lot where I expected. Instead, we cut across the soccer field and headed for an eight-foot-tall chain-link fence.

"I'm not sure if you looked at yourself lately." I gesture to her already short skirt. "But I'm not sure hopping fences is the right idea." I was a fucking idiot. If she wanted to climb this fence, my only response should've been thank you.

"Sounds like wishful thinking on your part." She lifted the corner of the green chain-link closest to the pole. The end folded up like a flap that she easily climbed under.

I eyed it. "Bit small for me, don't you think?"

"You can always try climbing."

I groaned and crouched so low my knees felt like they were in my armpits as I shuffled through. I went to stand, only to be yanked back hard. My shirt caught on one of the sharp ends, pinning me in place. I tried to detach it, but it was just out of reach. "A little help here?"

Sidney was only a few feet ahead of me, hands on her hips. "I don't know. I kinda like you tied up like that."

I shot her a dark look. "That can be arranged, but for now, get me loose."

She didn't move, and I groaned. "Please."

"Since you asked so nicely," she said with a smirk. God, all the ways I could make her pay for that.

My thoughts were cut off when her hand slid down my back, leaving a trail of heat. With a few quick tugs, I was released and stood to my full height, shifting to stretch myself out. "Over. I definitely should've climbed over."

"You think you'll live?" She raised a brow.

I ran a finger over the hole in my shirt. "Whatever you have planned, it better be worth it."

"Don't you trust me?" she said, mischief in her voice.

I let out a quick laugh. "Not really."

"Relax. I've got you."

We walked a couple of blocks in silence until the pressure was creeping back in, pushing down. A bit of fresh air wasn't doing anything for my mood.

Up ahead was an old junkyard. The sign on the front read, "You Ditch Them. We Wreck Them." It looked dilapidated, even by junkyard standards. "What are we doing here, Sid?"

She ignored me, giving a familiar smile to the attendant. He stared at her, eyes traveling from her feet to her head as he reluctantly buzzed us in.

"You know you aren't supposed to bring a guest. That isn't part of the deal." He eyed me like he was trying to size me up. Nice try. I had at least sixty pounds on this guy. Turning back to her, he went on in his high-pitched voice. "Fred's not going to be happy about this."

She put on a winning smile, and her hands clasped in a *please* gesture. "You aren't going to tell him, are you?"

His eyes softened as if he couldn't say no to this enchanting girl. *I feel you, man.* He waved us in, and even though I had no desire to be here, I found myself just as enthralled as he was.

We walked by tall piles of junk. Nothing looked salvageable. Again, I wondered how this place stayed open; it was small and nothing like the city-run operations.

As we rounded a corner, she gave me a shy grin. There was a sofa in the middle of a clearing overlooking more trash. I wouldn't call it scenic, but at least it was interesting. "I can't say anyone's ever brought me to a junkyard before."

She waved me over, taking out a clean blanket she had stashed in a plastic bin, and stretched it across the sofa. She pointed at the cushion.

"Sit." Her tone gave no room for argument. Sitting down, I found it surprisingly comfortable. There was a little tarp overhead to protect it from the elements. She had a solid setup. "You come here a lot?"

"Enough." She rolled out a cart full of glass vases, a pair of safety glasses, and a large wooden bat.

"Smashing things? Really, Sid?"

She raised a brow and set a vase on a long bar. "Got something better to do?"

The idea definitely held some appeal. "Nope."

I swallowed hard and tracked each of her movements as Sid rolled her shirtsleeves, adjusting her skirt higher so she could separate her legs. She gave me a cocky grin, bringing her bat elbow-high, and she swung through with such force it disintegrated the glass in front of her. Her laughter overtook her and filtered into me until I couldn't stop my own. I clapped while she mockingly bowed.

"Your turn." At my skeptical look, she huffed out, "Trust me, it will help."

"Sure it will." I would rather watch, but she looked so fucking hopeful. I stood and grabbed the safety glasses and bat while she set everything up.

I swung through half-heartedly, barely playing along with her game.

"You call that a swing?" Her warm hands landed on my back, positioning herself directly between my legs, and she moved my fist down the bat. I didn't need her help with my form, but I was sure as shit not going to stop her. Screw batting. This was what I needed right here.

She stepped away as if she could hear my thoughts. "Swing through. Don't stop when you hit the vase." Her bossy tone had me smirking. I usually liked to be the one in charge, but her confidence was sexy as hell.

She walked around the cart, pulling out an enormous vase and setting it up before taking a seat on the sofa a safe distance away.

Something about her got to me, and I felt my walls lowering with the intensity of her attention. The last few days were rough. Rocky, my dickhead agent, was all over me about my image. I was still reeling after that last call. He was pissed about Sid and my little race in the halls. Said that I need to control my image better. When I refused, he laid the guilt on thick and went on and on about how it was important to build recognition for my brand and how I needed to be seen as a safe bet.

Frustration built in my chest, and I followed Sid's directions, swinging through, and connected hard with the vase. All the pressure transferred from me to the shattering glass, and a smile lit up my face.

"You like it?" Sid sounded unsure, and I didn't like the hint of doubt in her voice.

"Yeah, Sid, I like it."

She clapped her hands. "My turn."

She rolled her shoulders, preparing to bat next, bringing attention to the skin just above her collar. Her scar barely peeked out, and I wanted to run my fingers across it. I stepped away before she could notice where I was staring.

Over the next hour, we chatted about unimportant things and settled into a rhythm as we set up more glass to break. There was an easy way about her that was as contagious as it was addictive. Most people peppered me with questions about hockey and my future playing in the NHL. She let me talk about it at the pace I wanted. She talked about her plans and how she couldn't wait to get her career started, and how she thought her mom would be proud.

I sat beside her on the old couch. "Of course she'd be proud, Sid. You're doing amazing."

There was a soft pink hue to her cheeks that she tried to hide from me, but I was paying attention. She reached into her bag, and my gaze caught on the bare skin where her shirt escaped her skirt's waistband.

Fuck, I wanted to run my thumb along that strip, but my thoughts were cut off.

"It's not much, but something to take the edge off." Sid handed me a protein bar, oblivious to my thoughts. Her words took on a different meaning in my head. The pressure was gone, but there was something else growing here.

She didn't ask what was up with me, but there was a question in her eyes. I rolled my shoulders and tried to explain the thing that was eating me alive. "Do you remember six years ago when a high school kid died street racing?"

"Yes, it was all over the news." Her voice was soft, barely a whisper.

"He was my best friend, Marcus." I took a deep breath, calming the ache that built in my chest. "Not only did we play together, but he was the reason I got into hockey."

She didn't push me, just waited for me to continue.

"After he—" I closed my eyes. *Breathe.* "After he died, I decided I would do whatever it took to fulfill his dreams of making it to the pros. Since I was on the second line and practiced a lot with Marcus, I naturally took over for him. Sometimes it feels like I'm living his life for him, and I'll never amount to who he would've become. You should've seen him. The way he could skate scared the shit out of guys in college." I rubbed my trembling hands over my face and raked them through my hair. "I've been struggling with my game lately. I've got to figure it out before people start to notice—"

Her soft hand slid over my jaw and tipped my gaze to meet hers. "It's beautiful that you're honoring your friend... but Jax, you're your own person. Don't get so caught up in living his dream that you forget your own." Her eyes were bright with unshed tears, but there was no pity there, only understanding.

Sidney pulled her legs onto the sofa, and her shoulder leaned further into mine. She was right. This was exactly what I needed, but I couldn't help worrying about why she needed this place to begin with?

TEN
SIDNEY

THERE WAS a big A on my computer screen.

"I won the bet, Sid. Pay up." Jax's voice was low near my ear, and I had to fight back a shiver. I slid a small piece of paper toward him and caught my breath when my finger ghosted across his. My pulse thrummed when he pulled away, opening and closing his fist.

His voice was barely above a whisper. "That's rule number three. How long do you think your other rules will last?"

I rolled my eyes, not bothering to respond to that.

He looked at the paper and smirked. I jotted down my number in purple ink and the words *Don't abuse it* on the note.

His breath fanned out against my neck once more before he finally took a deep breath and leaned back in his chair. He gave me the thumbs-up gesture, shocking a laugh out of me and effectively breaking the tension.

I stage-whispered, "I wish I'd have gotten that on camera. Could've gone viral on Instagram." That earned me a full-belly laugh. The sound had my heart stuttering—

"Ms. King, what are your thoughts on positive intermittent reinforcement?" Dr. Carter's voice broke me from my daydream.

Jax's head snapped up, seeing me flounder, mouth opening and closing like a guppy out of the water. "She was just explaining growth hacking and how intermittent reinforcement hacks people's psychology just like gambling."

As soon as the professor's attention turned away, I slumped in my seat, my heart still trying to beat out of my chest. I looked over at Jax and mouthed, "Thank you."

His hand slid up the back of my neck and squeezed—all of my attention instantly concentrated on the single point of contact. He wrote on his notepad before sliding it toward me.

We're a team now, Sid. I won't leave you hanging.

He brought his face closer, gaze boring into mine before writing something more.

Right?

I grabbed the notepad, jotting down my quick reply.

Right.

Jax shifted beside me, finding a comfortable spot for himself, but he didn't remove his hand from my neck. I relaxed into his touch, and his gravitational pull drew me toward him.

His other hand moved rapidly over the paper.

Thank fuck we studied. Looks like half the class is depressed.

Students' heads were down with a dejected look about them. There was a girl in the corner with tears rolling down her cheeks, but her eyes didn't move from the professor, furiously typing as he spoke. We all knew missing a single beat could cost us.

I took the notebook. *Yeah, lucky for you, I helped you out.*

He choked off a laugh before replying.

That's not how I remember it.

Not my fault you have a terrible memory.

Jax's hand slid down my neck, fingers brushing my collarbone, and he exhaled a quick breath. Was he as affected as I was? My heart beat for an entirely different reason. There was undeniable chemistry but also something more. Everything was just so comfortable with him.

Who was I kidding? He was ridiculously attractive. It should be a crime to be both that smart and attractive. Women didn't stand a chance. I turned to my bag and pretended to look for something to put distance between us. He hesitated like he wanted to argue, but he removed his hand.

I needed to rein it in. I knew firsthand what it felt like to come in second. To be left behind by someone you love, and it wasn't something I ever planned on doing again.

Class winded down, and I put my things away, trying to fit everything in my bag proved to be a game of Tetris. The zipper got caught, and it split open, spilling pens on the floor.

"I got it." Jax lowered, helping me pick them up. He reached for the same pencil as me and inhaled sharply. He stared at me, his mouth slightly open, and his breaths came out hard. I took a moment to realize my blouse was hanging low, and there was absolutely zero chance he didn't see right down my shirt. He handed me my pencil, and then a wicked look took over his face and the slow grin that curved one side of his mouth. He shrugged as if to say, "What did you expect?"

Great...

He looked away from me, giving me privacy to fix myself. He tapped his hands on his legs, saving me by changing the topic. "I told you I could get you that A."

"Uh-huh." Looking at him sideways, I headed for the door. "Thanks for your help."

"What do you say we make it a more permanent situation?" He followed me into the hall but wasn't making eye contact. Was *the* Jaxton Ryder nervous? I should put him out of his misery, but where was the fun in that?

I brushed my arm against his, ignoring the spark of energy from the simple touch. "You think? I was thinking one of the group studies might be worth a try."

His head snapped to me so fast it was clear that

for all his being awkward, he fully expected me to say yes. For a second, I wanted to keep going to see how far I could push him, but I gave him a big smile. "You still good with Thursdays?"

The first emotion that flashed across his face was relief, but it was quickly followed by him looking like he wanted to throttle me. "What the hell, Sid? You are so much fucking trouble."

I couldn't help but let out a full-hearted laugh at his serious face.

His eyes narrowed, and I felt pinned by his stare. So caught up in him, I was nearly plowed over by another student. Jax gripped my hip, tugging me out of the way just in time, and growled, "Hey, fucker, watch it."

The guy looked at him with wide eyes before scurrying off. Jax's chest rose and fell rapidly, breathing as hard as I was. I sucked in my lower lip, and his eyes tracked the movement. A tortured rasp slipped from him. We stared at each other, and I grinned when a smile broke across his face, and he winked at me. I closed my eyes, trying to catch my breath and take in the lightness of this moment.

Jax cleared his throat, bringing my gaze to him. "Yeah, Thursdays work for me."

I took a second to remember what he was talking about. "Cool, I'll meet you at the library—"

Jax looked away as he cut me off. "Or… if you're comfortable with it, would it be okay if you just come over to my place? That way, I could grab some food and not have to rush so much."

Did I want to go to his place? Maybe a little too much. "What's in it for me?"

His eyebrow rose in surprise, then eyes quickly narrowed. "Well, you'll have amazing company."

Grinning at his expression, I countered, "I'd have that at the library."

A cocky smile slid over his mouth. "So, you admit it's amazing?"

"What's amazing?"

"My company."

"Is Jaxton Ryder searching for compliments? Oh yes, you are the most amazing, the amazingest. No one knows just how amazing you are." Jax threw a crumpled piece of paper at me, and I laughed so hard a snort escaped. Which made me laugh harder.

"Laughing suits you." He stared at me, and a broad smile crossed his face. His voice turned playful and drew all of my attention. "What if I bring home a chocolate milkshake?"

I held my hand out. I meant to shake on it, but I was so distracted that I gently ran my fingers along his, and a ripple of sensation went through me. Taking a deep breath, I close my fingers around his, locking our hands. "Deal, but only if you make it strawberry flavor instead."

ELEVEN
JAX

I OPENED the playbook and adjusted myself on my bed, determined to get them memorized tonight. These past few weeks had flown by, and I couldn't afford to fall behind in my game. The couple of PR events Rocky set up had bombarded me with new press.

Which I knew was the point, but I was tired of seeing my face everywhere. I had this constant inkling that I should talk to Sid about it, but there was a distinct part of me that wanted to keep her out of it.

I spent the next hour immersed in studying, but I couldn't stop picturing the feisty brunette currently running circles in my brain. Just being near her calmed the restless part of me. The part that thought I would never be enough. She was addictive, and it was more than just the challenge of her ridiculous rules. Now all I wanted to do was figure her out.

Her pouty lips and her smart-ass mouth had been the star of an embarrassing number of my fantasies. She had drive, tenacity, a stubbornness that nothing and no one could get in her way. She reminded me of Marcus. I bet she saw her dreams as a "when" and not an "if," just like he did.

Of course, with all the girls chasing me, she had to be the one pushing me away. Oh, she was attracted, sure, but she put as much space between us as possible. Last week, I thought she was going to fall out of her chair because she leaned so far away.

I should've been insulted, but for all of her attempts to look unaffected, her eyes still drifted back to mine. Sid showed me she wanted me, whether she knew it or not. When she concentrated on her notes, her body slowly listed my way, as if she was being drawn into the same current I was. Then there was the way her cheeks flushed pink when I brushed against her.

I caught myself paying more attention to her than the class. She did this thing where she pulled her hair up with a deep red elastic, revealing the smooth column of her neck, or pushed it all behind her shoulders, filling the space with her citrus scent. Then there was the way her teeth gnawed her bottom lip as she fought for every second of concentration. And when she laughed... Fucking bottle that shit up and sell it to all the lonely men out there because it felt like coming home.

Unable to resist, I reached for my phone and sent her a quick text.

Me: You're wrecking my concentration.

Staring at my phone, I watched as the little bubbles danced at the bottom.

Trouble: I'm ruining your concentration? You texted me.

Me: There's that sass I love.

I paused, not knowing what to say, but I didn't want to stop talking to her.

Me: I'm tired of running through plays and now I'm bored.

Trouble: Sounds like a YOU problem.

Me: Come on, don't be like that.

Trouble: Fine. Read something.

Me: Like a book?

Trouble: Yes, genius. A book.

Me: Yeah, ok not my smartest answer.

Me: What kind of book?

Trouble: IDK anything you like. You have read books, haven't you?

Me: Yes, Sid. I've read books.

Trouble: Alright... What did you like?

Fuck, what did I like? I didn't know. I liked *Game of Thrones*, but I lost interest after the third book. *Dune* was an... experience. Not one I was down for diving back into. When the hell was the last time I read anything good?

Me: What do you like?

It took so long for her to answer I thought she'd left me hanging.

Trouble: You're not going to like what I like.

Me: What? Why?

Trouble: Because guys don't read the type of books I read.

Me: Well, now you have to tell me.

Trouble: Yeah, I don't think so.

Me: Why the fuck not?

Trouble: Because, no.

My mouth twisted in a grin. Now I needed to know exactly what books she liked.

Me: What are you afraid of?

No reply.

Me: Are you reading dirty books, Sidney?

Bubbles appeared and disappeared as she typed. When they stopped and nothing else popped up, I sent her another message. I sounded desperate, but fuck it. I wanted to know. Something about getting my hands on a book so filthy she was embarrassed to tell me about it had my entire body vibrating.

Me: Tell me a book to read and I'll tell you how much I like it.

I dropped my arm and ignored the pounding in my chest. Fuck. Did I push her too far? Did she think I was some kind of perv? I typed out, "just kidding," but her message appeared before I hit Send.

Trouble: Sin & Sinners, but we are not talking about it.

Me: Sure we aren't.

Trouble: Goodbye, Jax.

I paused in front of the mirror. A huge, ear-splitting grin covered my face. Something about her pulled all of my strings. There was nothing I enjoyed more than getting under her skin.

I hit Dial, pacing the room, and slid my left hand into the pocket of my jeans. It kept ringing. What the fuck? The fucking balls on her.

The click of the connection on the other side cut off my thoughts.

"You know I can revoke your phone privileges for calling me, right? No one calls anyone anymore. Strictly impersonal texts. Maybe some memes. You crossed an invisible line with this whole calling thing. Like, when you were a kid and you didn't show up to someone's house at suppertime. It's just not done." Sid's voice was light, with hints of laughter behind it. Her feistiness had my mouth tipping at the corner.

"Were you really going to ghost me on this call?" I tried to sound serious, but I couldn't help the small laugh.

"I wouldn't call it ghosting, but sure, yeah, I was thinking about not answering," she said playfully.

"Ouch, that hurts."

"Don't worry. A little humility will be good for your big ego."

"Uh-huh, *sure* it will."

"What do ya need, Jax?" There was rustling in the background, and I could barely make out the squeak of her bed when she sat on it. Suppressing a groan, I took a long breath in. The image of Sid lying on her bed had blood flooding to my dick. *Get it together, man.*

"Okay, I'm going to be up-front with you. I don't normally call anyone. I wasn't kidding when I said you're stuck in my head, and I need to concentrate, so I just wanted to talk to you. You know, to see if that helps." There was such a long, awkward pause I thought she might have hung up. Her breath was soft through the speaker, and I sat back on my bed. She hadn't hung up, so I would wait her out.

"What's your favorite food?" she asked.

I did a silent fist pump victory dance. "My hometown pizza. Hands down, the best. You can't convince me otherwise."

"I bet there's a bunch of people in Italy, Boston, and New York that would disagree with you."

"They'd be wrong. They don't know what they're missing." My cheeks hurt from smiling, but it was just her. It was what she did to me.

"For me, it's warmed-up chocolate croissants." She moaned a little, and I tensed as a shiver ran through me. This girl was going to be the death of me.

"What's your favorite movie?" I asked, adjusting until I was lying flat on my bed.

"Hmmm, I'm not sure I have a favorite movie, but I'm dying to see *Hamilton*." I noted that fun fact and filed it away to look up later.

"If you weren't the next sports star, what would you be?" She was getting into this.

"Easy. Homeless." That startled a laugh out of her, which had me chuckling. The more we talked, the more relaxed I got. "Here's one: Would you rather fight one horse-sized duck or one hundred duck-sized horses?"

"What?" Her surprised laughter rang through the phone. "I don't want to fight either."

"Not an option. Come on, Trouble, answer the question."

"Trouble, huh?" She paused for a second but continued. "Hmm, if I have to choose, I'd pick the giant duck. At least it would be faster than thousands of tiny bites from tiny horses."

"Oh, morbid. Didn't expect that." I found myself sprawled out on my bed, listening to her talk about her plans after school. She was strong and determined, and it was sexy as hell. Sid was unbelievably easy to talk to. It was like slipping into a dance we'd done so many times our bodies had it memorized. Her voice was soft, and I tried to talk as little as possible to not distract her, giving just enough so she knew I wasn't bored.

I didn't notice the time until she yawned. She was barely awake on the other end. It had been a good five minutes since either of us had spoken. Realizing she might have actually been asleep, I whispered, "Sidney?"

It was past 2:00 a.m. "Uh-huh?" Her voice was sleepy but clear.

"I'll see you tomorrow, alright?"

"Are you trying to be my friend, Jax?"

I couldn't stop my grin. "No, not really."

TWELVE
SIDNEY

"SORRY I'M LATE." I panted, hurrying to the empty spot beside Mia, and dropped my books on the long table with a loud thump. The cafeteria was packed this time of day, everyone buzzing in and out between classes. The room was painted a stale gray, with row upon row of tables. At least the left wall was lined with windows letting in the morning sun. There was an almost food-truck-like kitchen where they served a bare-minimum menu. At least what they did serve was delicious.

I tried to take my jacket off, but my arm got stuck, leaving me hopping around to release it from the sleeve.

"What's gotten into you?" Mia snorted, making me pause in my struggle.

"My class is clear across campus. I practically had to run to get here. You know how I feel about running." I escaped from the torture device that was my coat and huffed, trying to catch my breath.

Mia piled her blonde hair high on top of her head, and her green eyes were bright with laughter. "Good thing I grabbed you breakfast, huh?"

She pointed to a heaping plate of pancakes and an extra-large cup of coffee. I was starved after my morning class, and there was barely time before my next one.

A sigh escaped me as I squeezed into the seat to her left. "You know I love you, right?" My voice was muffled as I shoveled pancakes into my mouth. "I don't know what I would do without you."

"Probably starve," she responded and pulled a water bottle from her bag, sliding it my way.

I took a bite of a deliciously syrupy pancake and moaned in approval.

A massive guy sat down directly across from me. He was built like a brick wall, with thick, corded muscles, and his teal-colored T-shirt popped nicely against his deep brown skin.

I snapped my mouth closed, and he gave me a devilish smirk.

"Don't stop on my account. Nothing wrong with a bit of vocal enjoyment."

I rolled my eyes. *Dear lord, who is this guy...*

Another guy sat to the right of him, directly across from Mia. He was equally large and equally gorgeous. His hair was jet-black and styled in a deep undercut, like he was some extra from *Peaky Blinders*.

He was all sharp lines and had an edge to him I couldn't pinpoint.

There was a full plate in front of him, but he was too busy staring at Mia to notice. When he saw me watching, he looked away. *Puh-lease, you're totally busted.*

"You're Sidney King, right?" he asked, taking a monster bite of his breakfast sandwich and licking the sauce from the corner of his mouth. The sound of Mia's quick intake of breath had me glancing in time to see her blush before she turned away.

"Um, yeah?"

Mia elbowed me in the ribs, and I sent a silent *I have no idea who they are* look her way. What the hell was happening?

"I'm sorry. Who are you?"

Both guys look at me, confused. Then two matching mischievous grins cross their faces. "We're friends of Jax."

"Uh-huh."

The guy across from me started introducing himself. "I'm Lucas."

"Um… hey, nice to meet you," I said, still having no clue what was going on. It was clear these were Jax's teammates, but I still wasn't sure why they were here.

Lucas continued his spiel, pointing at the guy across from Mia. Now this guy looked like he was up to no good. "This here is River. He hates to talk. Good luck getting two words out of him."

"Two words," River said, voice deep, mouth tipping up at the corner, causing a grin of my own.

"Oh-kay…" Mia's voice stretched out the word, and she looked at them with curious eyes. "So, what exactly is happening here?"

Lucas turned toward me. "We wanted to meet the infamous hallway girl."

I blinked. "What?" What did he call me? I looked between them for some kind of clue, but it was Mia who answered.

"He's talking about Twitter. I'll show you later." She smirked, then checked something on her phone.

River's gaze caught on her smile. He looked like he wanted to devour her, and a shiver ran down my spine. God, to be looked at like that. Ten bucks, Mia got him in the sack. He falls madly in love with her, and she drops him within a month. If anyone understood my need to keep things light, it was her.

The guys were looking at me expectantly. "Um… this is Mia, my roommate. She's pre-med."

Lucas and River asked her questions about her major, genuinely interested in her becoming a doctor.

She lit up when she talked about her future. Damn straight, it should impress them.

River's head ducked with a near-invisible smile. He caught me looking and shrugged.

Mia choked on her drink when a familiar face sat across from us. We hadn't seen Alex since that night at the club, and from the way Mia explained it, they'd had a damn good time. She didn't get embarrassed, just gave him a smile. "Hey, Alex. Didn't know you went here."

He lifted a brow at her. "That's because you ghosted me."

She scrunched up her nose. "Sorry about that. Busy and all."

I caught the look in Mia's eyes as she stared across the table at Alex. It was a mix of annoyance with a healthy dose of desire. He was staring back, and I sure hoped he knew what he was doing because she would eat him alive. Turning, I caught River watching them, a muscle ticking in his jaw. Shit. I made a mental reminder to talk to her about it. These guys no doubt meant the world to each other. It wasn't worth getting between them, especially with such a short time before we graduated.

My phone vibrated, signaling a new notification. An account I didn't recognize had tagged me in several Instagram posts.

Everything went quiet, and I froze in place. Students rushed by in a blur as my vision tunneled in on the screen. My hand tightened on my phone enough that my knuckles turned white as I flipped through the images. They were all pics of Jax. He was smiling at the stunning Selena Patronne. She was an up-and-coming tennis star making a name for herself at the college level. She looked back at him with what could only be described as sultry eyes and bit the corner of her lip. They stood close enough that both of her arms were resting on his chest, and they looked like the perfect couple. My stomach clenched, and a feeling of nausea rolled over me as I stared at them.

I rubbed my hands over my face and berated myself for being ridiculous. We were nothing to each other. Study partners. That was it. Then why was a rock forming in my stomach, and the more I clicked through the pictures, the bigger it grew? It felt dangerously close to jealousy.

"Jesus, Sidney, you look like a ghost," Lucas said, surprised.

Alex hit him. "What the hell, man? Do you have no filter at all?"

I just flipped him off, too distracted by my screen to care.

Lucas shouted. "Hey, Ryder, we're over here."

I turned in time to see Jax walking toward us. His hair was in the same mussed state as the other day, and he was dressed casually in a plain black long-sleeve shirt that hugged his chest. His sleeves were bunched up, showing off his thick forearms.

He pulled up a seat next to me and flushed around his neck when our arms touched. I was quick to recoil. Not sure I could handle casual touches right then.

Alex piped in, eyes roaming over Jax. "You're late."

"Yeah, I got caught setting up an event." I couldn't help my snort, and Jax looked at me, brows raised. "What's up with you?"

I struggled to make my face go blank. *What's up with me? Nothing I'm going to admit out loud.*

My pancakes tasted like ash on my tongue, and I dropped my fork to my plate. Giving up on my meal altogether, I stood, grabbing my stuff.

Mia's brows furrowed, but I waved her off before heading down the hall too fast to look natural. I was filled with an overwhelming need to get away from Jax. Like he was hurting me even while my rational brain knew that was impossible.

Quick footsteps came from behind, and a strong hand clamped over my arm. "Hold up." Jax panted, trying to catch his breath. I stopped and crossed my hands in front of my chest, feeling the sudden need to hide myself.

He let go of my arm, sliding his hands into his front pockets, and rocked back on his heels. "What's gotten into you?"

"Nothing. I'm fine." *It's fine. I'm fine. Everything is fine.*

His brows pinched in concern, and he took a step closer. "No, you're not. Tell me what's wrong?"

I straightened my shoulders and took a step back, putting some much-needed space between us. "Like I said, I'm good." But I couldn't help the edge of my voice when I said, "How was your *'event'* this morning?"

He lowered his head, and a smile formed on his lips. "Are you jealous?"

"You wish."

"Uh-huh." His smile broadened, and rage seeped under my skin, causing it to flush. What the hell was he smirking at? His grin only grew at my expression.

"Well, even though you aren't jealous"—his tone said he didn't believe me for a second—"you should know our agent's been setting me up on PR dates with Selena Patronne. It's an act to get more publicity, that's all."

My stomach flipped, some of the tension unraveling. "Why could you possibly need publicity? You're already drafted to Boston."

He shrugged. "Teams like to see that onboarding players are 'steady.' No one wants someone on their team who's going to fuck around."

I swallowed down a bad taste. "So, she makes you steady."

He stepped in close to me, forcing my gaze up. "None of it's real, Trouble. It could all be gone in a second if…"

"If what?" The question escaped before I could stop it.

Jax lowered his mouth until his breath fanned over mine. His fingers cupped my jaw, and he coaxed, "If someone *real* wanted to take her place."

The world spun around me, all my concentration on the barely there space between us. I searched his clear gray eyes before my gaze dropped to his full lips, and shivered when heat rushed between my thighs. All it would take was lifting onto my toes, and I could taste him.

My breath hitched. "I… I can't."

He nodded. "Right, your rules."

"Right."

For the first time, I hated my rules.

THIRTEEN
JAX

MUSIC POUNDED IN THE CLUB, and Alex hung off my shoulder, drunk off his ass, his speech slurred when he said, "Fucking great game tonight. That goal was epic."

"Thanks, man." I guided him to a stool and propped his back against the wall in hopes he didn't tip over. We'd just finished our third away game in an undefeated series. My heart was still pounding from my tie-breaking goal. The entire team was at the bar, and puck bunnies lined up everywhere, hoping to take a player home.

I just wanted to get the fuck out of here. If it wasn't for the guys insisting, I'd be in my hotel, bugging the shit out of Sid right now.

A girl stepped into my side at the same moment my phone rang. I picked up the second I saw Trouble written across the screen.

"Hey," I shouted over the music but couldn't hear her reply. "Sorry, it's hard to hear in here."

"I said great goal tonight." Her voice was strained; she must be practically yelling.

My thumb rubbed over my bottom lip. "So you watched, then?"

I thought I heard her laugh, but it was hard to tell. I was already walking toward the exit to hear her better when the girl beside me squeezed my arm.

"Hey, do you want to come to my place?" She was raised on her toes, so close she practically spoke directly into the phone.

I pulled it away from her and told her to back off. The last thing I wanted was some random hookup. I didn't stop walking until I was in the night air behind the club.

"Hey, Trouble. Can you hear me now?"

"Yeah, I can hear you. I was just calling to say good game tonight. Enjoy your win. You deserve it." Her voice was strained, and a radar flashed in my mind that something was wrong, but she'd already hung up before I could say anything.

"Hey, buddy. Where the fuck did you go?" Lucas held open the back door, looking at me expectantly.

I shot off a quick good-night text to Sid before answering, "Had to take a call."

Lucas gave me a knowing grin. "Sidney."

"Fuck off, man."

"Hell, no. I'm enjoying every second of this."

I headed inside but couldn't shake the feeling that something had changed. I headed back to the hotel before the guys and sent Sidney another text, but she didn't answer. She was probably just asleep. I told myself that again before I passed out.

I hadn't seen Sid since she saw the posts about Selena. Fuck, it might've made me a bad person, but I loved seeing the jealousy written all over her. It took everything in me not to kiss her and break her fucking rules right there in the hallway.

Anthony's black Volkswagen Golf that Sid had been borrowing pulled into our driveway, but she didn't get out right away.

My fingers tapped against the windowsill. "What's she waiting for?"

"Talking to yourself, man?" Lucas asked from across the room.

"Fuck off."

When it became painfully clear she was debating ditching me, I jogged to her car and tugged her door open.

"Hi." She lifted herself out, looking anywhere but at me.

"You're late." My voice was rough as I took her in. I stepped closer until my toes brushed hers and waited until she met my gaze.

Her eyes danced between mine and my mouth. I ran my tongue along my top teeth and watched her throat bob with her swallow. God, this girl was hard to resist.

"Yeah, I took a wrong turn and ended up going in circles, but here I am." Her voice was high, but she stood straight and walked forward, forcing me back. I plucked the bag from her shoulder, noting her tight jeans that showed off her strong, lean legs and a knitted sweater hugging her curves. Clearing my throat, I led her into our house.

"Hey, Sidney," Alex said as he walked in from the other room. His voice was playful. "I hear you're here to tutor our boy."

She laughed as her eyes met mine. "You've got it backward."

"Fuck, I would've gotten a tutor if she'd been half as hot as you."

I smacked Alex on the back of his head. "You can fuck right off."

"Careful, your jealousy's showing." Alex shot me a knowing smirk.

Lucas came up to us. "My girlfriend, Piper, told me you were in the same class together a few years back." He slid his hands in his pockets, continuing. "She said you helped her out with some notes, but she wasn't sure you'd remember her."

I sucked in a breath as a full-blown smile took over Sid's face. "Are you kidding me? She's the sweetest. Tell her hi for me." The way she said it, with such genuine enthusiasm, had us all nodding.

"Will do." Lucas beamed. He was easy. Compliment his girl and he was a pushover.

I liked her being around my friends. Instead of giving her space, I took two steps into her until the side of her body touched my chest. I sucked in a breath when Sidney leaned against me, and her scent surrounded me. I was sure it would be years before I could smell an orange and not think of her. Wetting my lips, I slid my hand down her arm until my fingers threaded through hers. Her hand twitched, but she didn't pull away.

"Good to see you, Sidney," River shouted and waved from the couch, barely taking his eyes off the game. Meanwhile, I couldn't move mine away from her.

"You can't just squirrel her away in your room," Lucas said, clapping his hand on my shoulder.

"Watch me."

"Bye, Sidney. You let me know if he gives you any problems," Alex winked.

Her palm was delicate in mine as I led her up the stairs. My room was nothing special. There were hockey posters on the walls, a rack with medals on display, and notepads stacked on the desk corner.

Stopping at the threshold, she hesitated to come in, and her teeth gnawed on her bottom lip. I held back a groan and pictured running my finger along her mouth to release her lip.

I dropped her bag on the bed, breaking the tension, and started pulling out binders. "Relax, we're just studying. I promise to stay on my side."

Sidney looked between me and the bed and shrugged. "Yeah, okay."

She backed herself against the wall with her legs tucked under her, taking up the least amount of room on the bed as humanly possible.

"Put this behind your back." I tossed her a pillow,

and she caught it before it collided with her face, eyes round with shock. She mocked throwing it back, but she placed the pillow behind her and wiggled a bit to get more comfortable. My mouth watered. She had no idea what that little wiggle did to me.

I turned on my playlist, about to get started when Lucas barged in with a tray of drinks. "You guys are actually studying? I'm a little disappointed."

I grabbed the tray and pushed him out of the room. "Thanks, man. Now fuck off."

I shut the door in his overeager face, and I turned, walking back to a now smiling Sidney. "One strawberry milkshake, as per our agreement."

She took it from me and moaned, tilting her head back with the first sip. "Hmm, so good."

I froze, staring at her. She looked utterly blissed-out, which had me thinking of other ways to keep her looking like this. It was only made worse by having her on my bed.

Mentally giving my head a shake, I sat facing her and propped my elbows on my knees, using one hand to support my head and the other to hold my chocolate shake. We were mirror images sitting this way.

"So you guys are all lined up for playoffs."

"Not yet. Still a few games to earn our spot. Wait? How do you know that?"

Her cheeks turned cherry red.

"You've been watching?" I couldn't help the surprise in my voice.

"You wish" was her feisty reply.

"Yeah, I kind of do."

After a few hours and several chapters later, we were completely laid on my bed, our heads beside each other, surrounded by books and papers. I hadn't been this relaxed in a long-ass time. She was barely awake, eyes blinking at a slow speed, and she gently rested her head on her arm as if she might drift off.

She looked so fucking exhausted. "Do you want to sleep here? I can sleep in the other room."

She shifted into a seated position and yawned while shaking her head. "That's okay. I can drive." Her eyes were still droopy, giving her a kiss-drunk look.

"I'd prefer it if you stayed. You're barely holding yourself up."

She looked at me, deciding that I was sincere and not just horny, and gave me a nod.

"Is there anyone you need to let know where you are?"

Sidney took out her phone and sent a quick message. "All good."

I handed her my softest shirt and gym shorts. "You can wear these."

"Thanks." Her eyes searched for me, and the slightest hint of a smile curved her lip, and then she headed to the bathroom to get ready. I grabbed my spare blanket and a pillow before freezing on the spot. She walked in looking damn good in my clothes. The shirt slid to the side, exposing the soft skin over her collarbone, making me want to lower my head and run my tongue in the dip. She held on to the tangled short strings, not paying attention to me. The shorts were obviously too big for her, and they would have to be tied if they had any hope of staying up. I hummed at the back of my throat at the thought of them sliding down. Her eyes met mine, and I couldn't resist the draw she had on me. I walked closer, dipping my head to bring my lips just shy of her ear.

"You look like you could use some help."

Sidney's skin pebbled along her neck, and a shiver ran through her. "It's stuck."

I slid my hands down her arms, moving her hands, and I took the strings in mine. She sucked in a breath as I worked at the knot, quickly opening it. My knuckles grazed across her soft skin. Burning for her, I had to swallow hard to stop from groaning. I pulled the strings tight, riveted by the goose bumps forming under my touch, and my fingers drifted over her skin one last time before I tied a bow.

Sidney was breathing as hard as I was. Her eyes were hooded, and I followed them as they dropped to my mouth. She bit her bottom lip while leaning closer to me.

My thumb ran along her bite mark, pulling her lip free. "You have no idea how many times I've thought about soothing this spot with my tongue."

A shiver rolled through her with my words, and my body tensed, mouth watering. I wanted to close the distance between us so fucking bad, but it had to be her. I paused, my mouth hovering over hers, and strained every muscle not to move.

Come on, Trouble. Break your fucking rules.

Her pupils filled her eyes until there was only a golden rim surrounding them. They flicked between mine, searching for an answer while her fingers dug into my chest, pulling me closer while attempting to push me away. I tried to breathe, but it got stuck in my throat, waiting for her. *Fuck, baby. Please.*

She slowly raised on her toes, her lips barely grazing mine, and she hummed in the back of her throat. I couldn't stop my hands from closing around her waist and holding her to me, but I didn't move to close the distance.

She made a needy sound, and my whole world tipped when Sidney pressed her lips against mine. She dug her fingers into my hair, pulling me closer, and deepened the kiss. Her moans evaporated any hesitance felt, and I bit down on her bottom lip like I'd pictured doing a million fucking times before. It was everything I thought it would be but also so much fucking more. I could get lost in the way she tasted, in the small sounds she made when I sucked on her tongue and the way her hips pushed against me, searching for the friction she desperately needed. She gasped, trembling in my arms, and my control broke. I gripped her jaw, tipping her head back to capture her mouth completely, and took over the kiss. Her fingers dug into my hair, tugging me closer, and I rocked into her, eating up the needy sounds she made. Fuck, I wanted her to be mine so badly I thought it might kill me to stop. But I wanted more than a kiss, and I wasn't fucking this up.

I pulled away and grinned at her frown, walking backward toward the door. "That's rule number one. Three to go."

FOURTEEN
SIDNEY

"WHO THE HELL'S SELENA?" The second I walked into our place, Mia showed me several Twitter posts.

A tightness I had no right to feel tugged at my chest, and I didn't meet her probing eyes. "Jax's agent set them up. He had to look steady. Basically, junior hockey players had a poor reputation, and the league wants him to look 'settled down.'"

Posts about Jax running around with two girls were definitely going to have the opposite effect his agent wanted. I rubbed my palms over my face and took a deep breath, trying to shake off the feeling he didn't need Selena at all.

I reached for Mia's phone and flipped through the pics until my gaze landed on one of Selena tucked into Jax's arm. Their faces were so close they were nearly kissing. A sinking feeling started in my stomach and plummeted to the floor. This didn't look like fake dating. A sharp pain compressed my chest, and I struggled to take my next breath.

Mia peeked over my shoulder. "Doesn't that bother you?"

I shrugged and did my best to clear the emotions from my face. "Why would it? We aren't dating."

Her brows rose, looking at me with skepticism. "Don't lie to me. You might not be officially dating, but—"

I cut her off. "I knew this was going on. It's a common part of the industry."

"Just because you understand why it's happening doesn't mean you have to be okay with it."

"Yeah, well, there's nothing I can do about it." I ignored the dip in my stomach as the truth of the words sank in.

"You sure about that? Have you talked to him?"

I put on my best imitation of a smile. "It's fine. Really. Alright, change of subject." I plopped down on the couch. "How was last night's date with the guy in your class?"

She sat down beside me. "He spent the entire time talking about himself and his mother, of all people."

I made a disgusted face at her. "Gross."

"The guy's a lost cause. So, if he asks, tell him I'm swamped. I'm hoping to ghost him until he gets the point or moves on."

"So what you're telling me is you don't have plans tonight?" I asked, trying to sound innocent and in no way desperate.

She raised a cautious brow. "What are you up to? You never want to go out."

I dropped my head back on the cushion and groaned. "I lost a bet with Jax, and now I have to go to his game."

Mia squealed. "Oh. My. God. Yes. Yes, I want to go." She was already off the couch and rushing toward her bedroom but stopped at the door. 'What are we going to wear?"

I couldn't help my devious grin. "You'll see."

"There's more people than I thought there would be."

By the time we got here, it was a half hour before puck drop, and the arena was filling with people. Mia's arm hooked mine as she pulled me through the sea of people to stand at the top of the stairs overlooking the ice. There was row upon row of seating, all leading down to the rink in the center, where the guys were already warming up. I swallowed hard when I spotted Jax weaving through his teammates before shooting on the net. He moved like he was made for this. I watched the opposing team. They looked good. It would be a hard game. "They need to win this game. If the Huskies lose, they'll be knocked back in rankings."

"Of course you're secretly following them." Mia shook her head at me.

Before I could reply, an arm bumped into mine. "Hey, you're blocking the way." The man's face was painted blue and yellow. He was looking me over, and a large vein pulsed in his forehead.

"Shit, sorry," I said before he could make a big deal about me wearing the other team's jersey.

"Let's go before your gawking creates an angry mob." Mia laughed beside me and tugged me down the stairs, ignoring the grunt of protest from the painted man as we cut in front of him.

"I wasn't gawking." *I totally was.* "I was just figuring out the arena."

"Sure you were. You look like a kid at Disneyland."

I hopped down the stairs behind her, trying to keep up. "It's just bigger than I expected."

The corner of her lip raised at my words, and I cut her off. "Whatever you're about to say, just stop."

"You're no fun." She stopped at the bottom row, practically pressed up to the glass, and glanced at our tickets. "Row 1, seats 2 and 3. This is us."

A young security guard hurried down the stairs. "I'm sorry, girls, but you can't sit here."

Mia looked as confused as I was. "*O-kay.* Why is that?"

"This row is player-reserved seating only. There should've been a sign on it," she said, looking down the aisle as if she thought it would magically appear. "I'm not sure what happened to it." Her voice came out stronger. "I'm sorry, but you really can't sit here." Her hands wrung together in front of her, and her eyes shifted with discomfort.

A loud thump came from the glass behind me,

and I turned to face a scowling Jax. His gaze was pinned on my half-turned back. When his gaze met mine, I mouthed, "What?" but he just shook his head.

The security guard piped up, attempting to speak loud enough for him to hear her through the quarter-inch gap between the protective glass panels. "I'm so sorry, Jax. I was just telling them that the team holds these seats on reserve for friends and family."

"It's okay, Steph. They're with the team. From now on, treat them like they're one of us."

Shock registered across her face. It was clear she wasn't expecting that. She gave me a sidelong glance, obviously trying to size me up, and then a moment of recognition crossed her face.

Great…

Steph left, glancing back at us a few times before snapping a pic of me with her phone. I was about to say something, but Jax knocked on the glass again and gestured to me to walk toward the back of the rink.

I followed him to the last bend in the rink. He pointed down to a steel handle on my side of the boards. Realizing it was a door, I shoved down on the handle, and it swung in toward me.

Jax didn't give me time to move out of the way before crowding me and ripping off his helmet.

"Off, now," he commanded, glaring at my jersey.

I glanced around, but there was no one this far back in the arena. "Jax, it's a bit cold to not have a jersey."

He raised a brow. "Do you have a shirt under it?"

I nodded in response, trying hard to keep the smile off my face. I knew he'd be pissed about the jersey, but this was so much more.

"Good. Take it off."

A thrill rolled through me, and I fought to keep the tremble from showing. He was even taller wearing his skates. I smirked. "What if I don't want to take it off?"

"Sidney, do not fuck with me right now. Take. It. Off." He growled the words, and tingles traveled down my spine.

I lifted the jersey over my head and immediately wrapped my arms around my chest from the chill. Jax reached back and pulled his jersey over his head, leaving him in just his pads. I swallowed hard and took it when he pushed it into my hands. "You don't wear anyone's number but mine."

I sucked in a breath, doing my best to ignore the thrill his words created, and my skin pebbled for an entirely new reason. Not sure how to react to his display of possessiveness, I tugged it over my head and let his jersey engulf me. He leaned forward, close enough that all I had to do was lean in and we'd be kissing in front of everyone, but he wasn't looking at me. Instead, he patiently rolled up each of my sleeves, revealing my wrists.

Jax leaned back, giving me an appreciative look, and his tongue wet his bottom lip. "You look good wearing my name, Trouble."

Instead of acknowledging his words, I scrunched

my nose up at the smell of his gear. That didn't stop me from taking another breath. "You smell gross."

He hauled me into a tight hug and buried my face in his chest, ignoring my pitiful attempt to break free. "You like it."

He was right. I kind of did. He was warm in the chilly arena, and his salty scent was doing all kinds of things to me. I still said, "You're entirely too sure of yourself."

He leaned back and tilted his head to the side, gaze boring a little too deep into mine. "Not as much as I'd like to be."

What exactly did that mean?

I tugged at my sleeves. "Won't you get in trouble for this?"

He smirked. "Worth it."

He tightened his hold momentarily before releasing me. "I have to go back and get ready. Lucas's girlfriend, Piper, should be here any minute. She'll sit with you." Jax stepped forward and leaned his head down, so close his mouth brushed my ear. "I'm happy you came, Trouble."

He released me, grabbed his helmet, and got back on the ice, shutting the door behind him. He caught me watching as he was about to go into what I assumed was the locker room entrance and his gaze roamed over me, before slipping through the door. Heat pooled in my stomach, washing away the chill in the air.

Mia bumped my shoulder with hers. "Girl, you've got it bad."

A few minutes later, Piper arrived with an enormous smile. She had long golden-blonde hair with beachy waves and stunning clear blue eyes. She looked like she'd just moved here from California. "Hey, guys, I'm excited to finally have someone to sit with. I was ecstatic when Jax called and said you guys were coming."

I rolled my eyes. "It was under duress, I promise."

Piper sat, effectively blocking my escape. "Well, now that you're here, let's have a bit of fun, shall we?" She looked between us, waiting for an answer.

Letting out a big dramatic breath, the corner of my mouth kicked up into a grin. *"Fine."* I drew out the word as long as I could. They both laughed at me, and Mia hit me with her mitten.

Piper rubbed her hands together. "First food!"

We chatted about nothing while we got our snack, then headed back to our seats, arms filled with food. The second we sat down, we dug in, blissfully eating the first few pieces.

Piper licked her fingers and said, "I could never do this with Lucas. He would have it all devoured in seconds."

"Are you going with Lucas this summer?" Mia asked, curious.

"Oh yeah. I'll stay near his training camp, but then I start school in September, so that'll make it tougher." Her voice was light, but she held herself a little tighter. "What about you and Jax?" Piper asked in between mouthfuls of food.

"What about him?" I replied, a bit guarded.

"Cut it out. You literally slept there last night," Mia chimed in while she tossed a chicken bone in the bucket.

"Yeah, 'slept' being the operative word." I didn't dare mention the kiss.

Piper nearly spit out her drink. I had to pat her on the back until she got her breath back. She looked at me in shock. "You're telling me you not only got invited to their place, but you spent the night?"

"Well, technically, it got really late, so Jax asked me to stay instead of driving home tired." Okay, even I could hear how weak that sounded in the light of day.

Piper leaned forward, eyes alight with excitement. "You don't understand what a big deal this is. I've known him longer than I've known Lucas. He never invites anyone over there. The man's not a saint. He takes advantage of what's offered to him, but they're not allowed to stay the night." Her smile turned wicked. "That is until now. Tell me, did you study in his room?" She must've read my expression because she clapped her hands together, getting more and more excited with every question. "Wait! Did you sleep in his bed? Did he give you something to wear?"

Mia spun to look at me with a devilish grin.

"I'm sorry to crush your hopes, but I've got other plans for after school. Getting into something right now would not be a good idea." *No matter how great he is.*

"Oh honey, what you're saying implies you get a choice in this matter." Piper put her arm around me. "I get it, though. I have big goals, and Lucas would never hold me back."

Mia raised her cup something deeper passing over her expression. Too quick for me to make out. "Cheers to men not holding us back from our dreams!"

All three of us clinked our plastic cups and took a long drink.

"Okay, what did you guys do to my girl? I left her, and she loved me, and now I snuck back to see her and she's toasting to singlehood?" Lucas had a floppy smile on his face, and his eyes were pinned on Piper's.

"Hey, baby!"

These two were too cute for words.

"You know I love you. I was drinking in solidarity with Sidney."

Lucas's brows pinched together, and he shifted on his skates. He took a long look at me, and his eyes searched mine, trying to sort something out. "Well, I better get back. Just wanted to give you a kiss before we got started."

A few minutes later, the lights went down, and the announcer called out each player's name as they skated out from behind their bench. The crowd's roar became deafening when Jax's name was called.

He did a lap around the rink before stopping abruptly on the other side of the boards, kicking up snow with his blades.

I jerked back on reflex, then raised a brow. "Show-off."

"Wish me luck, Trouble." His voice was barely audible over the noise. He placed his glove-covered fist to the glass and gave me an expectant look.

Mia smiled. "He wants a fist bump."

I bumped my hand against the glass. "Good luck."

He held it to his chest and played like he was swooning.

Piper giggled from my side. "You're totally screwed."

Nothing could've prepared me for watching Jax play. He danced around the other players like they weren't even there. Like he was in control of every second he was on the ice. Hell, he was practically a god out there.

There were only thirty seconds left of the tied game, and I sucked in a breath, heart pounding in my chest when Alex passed Jax the puck. He took it straight up the middle, but he didn't see the defenseman charging right at him. I jumped up from my seat and screamed at him to watch out. My body yelled at me to somehow magically protect him, but all I could do was watch as Jax's opponent lowered his shoulder, going in for the check. At the absolute last second, Jax deked out of the way, and the asshole player went flying across the ice. I couldn't believe I used to like that team.

Jax made the goal look easy, and his teammates wrapped him up in a huddle. Jax escaped his teammates, and his eyes found mine. The floor dropped out of my stomach while my heart tried to escape my chest. I wasn't sure how I would be able to look at him again. Hell, how was I going to complete full sentences when he was around after this?

Piper knocked her shoulder against mine, smiling. "Right?"

Not moving my eyes from Jax, I smiled back, cheeks flushed. "Right."

FIFTEEN
JAX

THE BREWHOUSE WAS where everyone hung out after games. It was an older bar with wood tables, perfect for getting together with friends. After tonight's win, it was packed with cheering fans, all vying for our attention, but all I cared about was getting to Sid.

Lucas led the way through the crowd to get to the girls' table. "You ready?"

"For what?"

He wrapped an arm around my shoulder. "To see your girl after she's watched you play?"

"Fuck off, asshole." I shrugged him off and walked toward the table, ignoring the little thrill his words evoked.

He called from behind me, "We'll see."

A tight feeling of possessiveness filled my chest when I spotted Sidney. She was stunning, standing in front of the high-top wood table, completely relaxed while everyone talked over each other. My fingers itched to run through her dark hair. It was perfectly in place, and everything in me wanted to go over there and mess it up.

A low growl formed at the back of my throat when Johnsy stepped to her side. He was in his rookie year and had already made a name for himself as a man whore. Sidney had to tilt her head to look at him, and the fucker leaned in closer. Fire burned through my veins when his fingers slid over her waist, shifting her out of the way of guys piling into the bar.

Fuck this.

My feet ate up the space between us, and before I could think better of it, I wrapped my arms around her waist and tugged her back against my chest. "How'd you like the game, Sid?"

Her body tensed for a second, but she relaxed into my hold, turning her face to look at me, eyes full of curiosity.

"I liked when that huge guy landed a punch," she said, her voice teasing.

A loud buzzing coursed through my body when Sidney smiled at me, a little awe shining in her eyes. It looked like my girl enjoyed watching me play.

My chest rumbled with my suppressed laugh, and I tightened my arms around her waist, drawing a squeak from her. "Of fucking course you saw that. I thought you'd pay more attention to the hat trick I scored."

Johnsy cleared his throat, looking between us. "Uh, sorry, Ryder. I didn't know."

"Know what?" Sid cut in, but I didn't let him answer. God, I fucking knew she'd be pissed if she caught me staking a claim on her. Didn't stop me from doing it, though.

"Now you fucking do." I stared down at him until he shifted his weight from foot to foot.

"Yeah, alright. Um, yeah, have a good night, Sidney." He disappeared through the crowd faster than should've been possible.

"What was that?" Sid asked, accusation clear in her voice, and pulled from my arms.

"Nothing." I smirked, and she rolled her eyes. She turned her attention to Piper, who was currently wrapped in Lucas's arms, but her eyes kept drifting my way. That invisible magnet caused constant tension between us.

"Move over." Alex sat on the stool beside Mia. Beside them, Lucas had lifted Piper onto his lap. Piper caught my eye when she leaned into his chest and winked at me. I didn't like her all-knowing look since I wasn't even sure I knew what was going on between Sid and me.

Sid glanced between the last stool and me. "You can take it. You played tonight and all."

Piper smiled wide. "Just sit on his lap. There's no reason for you to stand. It's not like he's going to bite you."

I sank my teeth into my bottom lip to prevent myself from saying I'd do just that and sat down. I slid my fingers through Sidney's belt loops and pulled her between my knees. "You look good with my jersey on, Trouble."

She tucked her head, and her teeth gnawed on her lower lip. I grazed my lips against her ear, and the smooth column of her neck erupted with goose bumps. All I was able to think about since we kissed was the way she tasted and the bite of her nails when they dug into my hair.

She paused and searched my gaze, her chest lifting with each hurried breath. I wanted to say fuck everyone and take her home, but my girl wouldn't like that. Instead, I grazed my fingers up her waist and lifted her onto my lap so she was situated on my right thigh and her legs hung between mine. Her eyes were fiery, and they slowly moved lower, fixating on my mouth. I suppressed a groan when she trembled in my arms. We had an unspoken understanding to keep whatever was happening between us quiet for now, but if she kept looking at me like that, I was going to say fuck it and haul her ass on the table so everyone knew.

I suppressed the urge to do just that and smoothed her hair behind her shoulder, twisting a silver streak between my fingers. "I'm glad you came tonight."

"Don't look so proud of yourself. I was coerced." She flashed me that sassy smirk I loved so much.

"Worth it to get you here." I winked. We stared at each other for who knows how long. She looked away from me when someone coughed, but I could see a blush turning her neck and cheeks pink. A quick glance revealed everyone was watching us with I-told-you-so smiles on their faces.

She took a deep sip of her fruity drink, then another. It looked like we were here for the night. A thrill went through me at the prospect of being with Sid for the next few hours.

"So, Sidney, what are your plans after graduation this spring?" River asked her, but he flicked a look at me as if saying, "Pay attention." He didn't have to worry. I knew all about her plans.

"I've got an internship lined up in Ottawa." Her voice tipped up at the end with excitement.

River smiled at her, nodding. "Impressive. Here I thought we were the ones that were heading for success."

"She's been working on getting this internship for years," Mia chimed in from across the table, practically beaming. "She has an entire strategic game plan on how she's going to be the youngest accepted member of parliament. This job's only the first step in her career. Before you know it, even famous hockey players will talk about how they knew *her* in school."

I brushed my hand against Sidney's. "I already knew you were special."

A slight pain formed in my chest. I was playing with fire, and I knew I was the one who would get burned. I gulped my beer and tried to let that go. I would never try to stand between her and her dream, and I already knew she wouldn't try to block me from mine.

Sid swallowed and whispered, "Thanks, Jax."

She leaned her weight into me, head resting on my shoulder, and laughed when Alex yanked Mia onto his lap. River glared daggers at him. There was something going on between them, and I just hoped they didn't fuck it up.

Alex ignored River and asked me, "Why do you look like you knew that already?"

"Because I know pretty much everything about her."

She made a strangled noise. "You do not."

"I know you, Trouble."

She huffed, shaking her head. "Please. Barely."

I paused until the weight of my gaze pulled hers to mine. I was dead fucking serious. "Try me."

"What?" Her brows pulled together so hard I'd think I'd thrown her off if it wasn't for the deep flush crawling up her neck.

I'd been paying attention, and it was time she knew it.

"I *bet* I can answer any question about you."

The table went silent around us, but all my attention was on Sid.

She tilted her head, trying to read me. "Is everything a game to you?"

"You aren't."

She sucked in a breath and bit into her lower lip. This girl better be careful, or I would kiss her in front of everyone. She gnawed on the delicate skin before saying. "What do you get?"

"If I can answer all of your questions, you have to call me 'King' for a week."

She barked out a laugh. "Yeah, no."

"Oh, come on, Sidney," Lucas taunted. "Are you worried he'll win?"

Her eyes snapped back to mine.

"Yeah, Trouble. You worried?" *Come on, Trouble. Take the bait.*

Sid studied me for a minute, then shrugged. "There's no way you're winning this."

"Watch me."

"Fine. Three questions."

"Deal."

Everyone leaned toward us, now the most exciting thing in the bar.

"What's my favorite color?"

"You'd think I'd guess blue because of your coat, but it's really the deep plum you get all your binders in."

Her eyes went wide. "How did you…"

"I told you. I've been paying attention. That's one."

She drummed her fingers on the table, trying to think of something harder. Mia piped in instead. "What's her favorite food?"

I checked with Sid, and when she nodded, I answered, "She'll eat pretty much anything, but her favorite is chocolate croissants." It was a guess, but it was right.

Sidney took what felt like forever to come up with the last question. When she had it, she faced me, her tongue poking into the side of her cheek, trying to hold back her smile. She thought she had me. "If I was an animal, what would I be?"

Fuck. I should say something cute, like a fox. She was definitely sly like one, but that wasn't what she'd call herself. No, she liked to stay inside, curled up, and not move for hours. That was how she got her best work done. Hell, it was even what she did for fun, plugging into a book for hours at a time. What fucking animal did that? A slow smile pulled at the corner of my lips. "A sloth."

As soon as I said it, the table erupted, and everyone gave me shit for my answer. But disbelief filled Sid's face, and I knew I'd won.

"Okay, you win, Jax." She rolled her pretty green eyes, trying to look unaffected, but she was snuggled in closer, and her fingers tightened into my shirt.

"He what?" Alex and Mia shouted, but I ignored them.

I slid my fingers along her jaw and tilted her face to mine. "What was that?"

When she didn't automatically say it, I thought she was going to fold, but she surprised me when she lifted, bringing our lips closer, mirroring the seconds before she kissed me, and said in a low, seductive voice that went straight to my cock. "You win, *King*."

Fuck. If we were anywhere else, I would've had her laid out in front of me. She said it like a challenge, but she didn't know I picked King because I wanted to be called by her last name.

Several hours passed, and we were all a little glassy-eyed, winding down from a night full of laughter. I looked at Sid, who was still leaning against me. "I really liked you being at my game tonight."

"You were pretty spectacular out there." There was a little wonder in her voice, and she nestled into my chest. She was spinning her red hair elastic I wore on my wrist. She'd left it at my place the other night, and I'd been wearing it ever since.

"Yeah, you think so."

"Don't push it." She pinched my side, making me jump.

I didn't want to call it a night, even though it was long past time to leave. Everyone else was already up and getting ready, but I took note that Sid was in no hurry to go either. I idly drew circles on the soft skin of her forearm before slowly sliding my hand down until my fingers grazed hers. Goose bumps crawled up her arm as I worked my fingers back gently, interlacing them with hers—

"Alright, hot stuff, let the girl go," Mia said with a laugh. "She and I have to get back before our cab turns into a pumpkin."

Sidney moved away from me, no longer in the trance that held us both here. She smiled when she noticed I was still looking at her, making me want to drag her back to my side. Instead, she grabbed onto Mia's hand and turned in the exit's direction.

"I'll walk you out." I scrambled from my stool

and placed my hand over the base of her spine, not ready to let her go. Our gazes met a little too long, but her eyes turned serious, and she glanced away. Disappointment flooded me when their cab was already waiting for them outside. Talk about a lesson in wanting something you couldn't have. Taking a deep breath, I let it out, but before I could say anything, Sidney lifted on her toes and kissed just next to my lips. "See you Monday, *King*."

Monday had never sounded so appealing or felt so far away. Piper came up beside me as I watched them leave. She was practically bouncing with repressed excitement.

"Don't start." I gave her a warning glare, but it just made her smile wider.

Fuck, I was utterly and completely screwed.

SIXTEEN
SIDNEY

THE CLOCK FLIPPED from 1:59 to 2:00 a.m. I'd gotten home hours ago, but every time I closed my eyes, I swore I could feel Jax's lips pressed against mine. It was like he was seared permanently in my brain. He hadn't tried to kiss me tonight, instead slowly flaming the fire growing within me. He did it with the smallest of touches, making me come undone. I felt every nerve ending come alive. I'd wanted to get as close as possible until his body melded into mine, but I had to settle for adjusting myself on his lap. The scruff of his two-day-old beard against my neck sent shivers down my spine when he pressed his nose into my hair, inhaling deeply. If we weren't in public, I would've straddled him, pulling his mouth to mine. I squirmed, unable to get comfortable, the buzz of excitement keeping me awake. I groaned and flipped over, covering my head with a pillow.

Just go to sleep.

My phone vibrated on the nightstand. It was late, and fear lanced through my chest at the late hour, but I knew Mia and Anthony were already home.

Jax: Caleb is an asshole.

Oh my god, oh my god. Oh my fucking god. My neck warmed, realizing Jax was reading my favorite book. I thought he was kidding when he'd asked me about it. My cheeks flamed as I tried to breathe through my embarrassment. It was okay—there was nothing to be ashamed of. Smut was perfectly normal, empowering even. No guy was going to tell me differently. But he was not saying anything bad. He was actually freaking reading it. A thrill bubbled in my chest as I pictured him in his room, flipping through the pages.

Jax: Sid?

Shit. I'd waited too long. He was probably worried that it freaked me out or something. Well, I was freaked-out, but not because he was reading it.

Me: That's kind of the point. Bad boys and all that.

Jax: If anyone treats you like this, I'll fucking kill him.

I ignored the tingle that traveled down my spine. It was at this moment that every feminist molecule in my body died because I freaking loved that. Overprotective, possessive, jealous popular hockey player? Yep, sounded like my type of guy.

Me: I promise to only like book assholes.

Jax: He handcuffed her to the bed, Sid. And not in the kinky way.

My grip tightened on the phone, and I kicked the sheets off my hot skin. I honestly didn't think he'd read it, and if he'd gotten that far, he'd passed... Jesus. I stared frozen at the screen, having no idea what to write back, and startled when another message popped up.

Jax: I was sitting next to Alex when it got to the shower scene. Could've fucking warned me.

Images of Jax hard on the couch, reading next to his friends, had an ache burning low in my stomach. The shower scene had her on her knees, swallowing the main male character's cock down until tears pooled in her eyes. I wanted to feel controlled like that when I read it. Owned like that.

Me: Where's the fun in that?

Jax: You don't have to reply to this, but... I've never been so hard in my fucking life. You and your favorite book did that to me.

Heat flooded between my thighs as I reread his text. I did it? Was he thinking about me when he read it? I wanted him to tell me. Tell me exactly what he thought of the scene.

Me: Do you like it?

Jax: Yeah, I fucking do.

My lungs burned with the force of my sucked-in breath. This was new and dangerous territory. After everything that had happened between us... this needed to end, but I didn't want it to stop. My body begged me to block out my mind. Just this once.

Me: Tell me.

Jax: Fuck.

I swore I could feel how turned on he was through his messages.

Jax: I like the way she spreads her legs apart and her panties are dark where she's soaked through them.

I could hardly breathe reading his messages. Thank god he didn't need a response to keep going.

Jax: How the smooth skin of her thighs feel under his palms as he brings his hand to her cunt. Would you be wet for me, Sid?

Lust lanced through me and sent my heart beating out of my chest. A needy ache built between my thighs, and I slid my hand under my panties to cup myself. My fingers were instantly coated wet, and my eyes rolled back as I slid one finger over my sensitive skin. I held my breath, waiting for his next message, but nothing came through. Shit. Before I could chicken out, I hit Dial, and he answered immediately, his harsh breath coming out in pants.

"What did he do next?" My words were practically a plea for him to keep going. To not question this.

He groaned, and his voice was rough. "You're killing me." The line was silent except for the sound of his breath for several seconds. "He pulled her panties to the side and buried two fingers into her until she fucked herself on them."

I bit back my moan so hard I could taste the metal tang of blood, but that didn't stop me from sliding my fingers inside, wishing they were his. "What does his other hand do?"

Jax's low reply, mixed with the distinct sound of rhythmic skin on skin, had my toes curling. "He wraps it around her neck and pins her to the bed. Do you like that part, Sid?"

"Yes," I breathed. My fingertips swirled around my clit before thrusting deep.

"You are such a good girl, Sidney. I bet you like when he licks her cunt and bites down on her clit. Was that your favorite part? Because it's fucking mine."

Images of Jax between my thighs, hand gripping my throat as he devoured my cunt, flooded my senses. A cry broke from my mouth as my orgasm shattered through me, followed by Jax's groan.

Jax's rough breathing filled my ear as the world came back into focus, bringing the reality of what just happened with it. Jax's low voice rumbled, "Good night, Sid."

Shit. I hung up before I could say anything stupid. What the hell did I just do, and why did I want to do it again?

"Come on, where is it?" I yanked the cushions off the sofa and searched for my laptop. For the hundredth time, I checked my watch and let out a frustrated groan. I only had five minutes until I would definitely be late for class. I knew for a fact I'd had it last night. Going to my room as a last-ditch effort, I reached my hand behind my bed and felt something smooth and metallic pinned there. "Gotcha!"

"Thank the lord," Mia sighed. She was standing in pineapple-patterned sleep shorts, a thin white shirt, and a sleep mask pushed up on her forehead. She looked exhausted, with dark circles under her eyes, and her usually glowing skin was ashy.

"I'm so sorry. I'm running super late and couldn't find my laptop."

"You stay up all night talking to a sports god, and now you're running around in a tizzy. I'm onto you, Sidney King." Her grin washed away some of the tiredness there.

"Keep dreaming. I'll see you later," I said as I finished packing my bag.

She looked around our destroyed home and shot back, "You owe me, girl."

I sent her my most apologetic smile and rushed out of the house, practically jumping down the stairs, which I was definitely not coordinated enough to pull off.

I flew out the front door and crashed right into a solid chest. My weight tipped and braced for impact, sure to hit the ground.

"Easy now. I've got you." Strong arms wrapped around me, and I drew in a fresh, woodsy scent.

"What are you doing here?" my voice snapped out before I could stop it.

Jax tilted his head, and the corner of his mouth twitched. "So, not a morning person?"

That was an understatement.

"Sorry, I was just surprised to see you. Good morning," I said, trying to give him my most innocent look.

A half grin curved his lips. "That's okay, I can take it."

Jax looked good with his cap pulled low, gray sweats, and a dark blue hoodie. He looked soft, welcoming, sexy, and I wanted to curl my entire body against him. He cleared his throat, drawing my eyes back to his. His gaze was dark as he leaned forward, and his lips barely skimmed the shell of my ear. "I'm here to drive you to class."

A shiver ran all the way through to my core. "It's a few blocks. I could've made it."

"Wouldn't be able to make it now, though. Come on, get in." He pointed over to a black truck parked at the curb. "Let's get moving. Don't want you to be late."

I wasn't sure if he was saying that to himself or me as he ever so slowly broke contact, taking in a deep breath before stepping back. I fixed my eyes on his, precious seconds ticking by as we were caught in this trance.

"Hey, Jax," some guy shouted from down the road, but Jax didn't turn from me. Instead, he held out his hand and guided me to his truck. He opened the door like a gentleman, crowded in closer when I sat, and reached over, buckling me in.

He tapped a finger under my jaw and said, "You look good in the morning, Trouble," before shutting my door with a click.

My stomach flipped, and I checked out his truck as a distraction. It smelled fresh, with a soft undertone of pine. There were notebooks in the center console and a gym bag in the back seat, but it was also clean. Not a speck of dirt, pristine condition. Jax was someone who liked to take care of his things.

With that thought, my eyes caught on his smiling face as he got into the driver's seat. He had that crooked, cocky smile you'd expect every star athlete to have, but on him, it was almost impossible to escape. His smile grew at my blatant appraisal, and he raised a coffee. I gasped in excitement as I took it from him. "Oh my god, thank you."

"You should see your face right now. Fucking perfect." He burst out laughing, but I was too busy taking my first sips to care.

"You got it the way I like it." I hummed in my throat as I took another sip. I could hear the reverence in my voice. This man had moved up into saint territory.

He turned onto the road, making the quick trip to the school, and last night's NHL highlights came on the radio. I switched the station, and his brows furrowed in question. One that I wouldn't explain.

His gaze turned back to the road, but he looked at me from the corner of his eye. "I remembered from the library." His voice was low, and his cheeks were pink. Maybe this wasn't the type of thing he usually did? If it was, he had all kinds of game. Women didn't stand a chance, and that might end up including me.

Get yourself together, girl. Guy gets you one coffee, and you fall out of your clothes? It was three. And the answer is, yeah, pretty much.

I twisted my hands in my lap, trying and failing to not be awkward. "So, do you make it a habit of rescuing people late for class?"

He raised his eyebrow, silently asking, *Seriously?* "No, I couldn't give a shit most of the time."

That sent a shiver down my spine. "But you give a shit now?"

I needed to learn when to shut up.

He cleared his throat, skipping my question. "How are your classes?"

"I have this one class that's ridiculously hard, and the guy that sits next to me is a practical storm cloud ninety-five percent of the time. So, there's that."

His grin was back, making him look boyish. "And the other five percent?"

The other five percent. He looked at me like he was going to eat me. And I sat there like I might let him.

"Barely tolerable."

My little rant won me a startled laugh from Jax, the smile softening some of his hard lines. He narrowed his eyes on me. "I should make you pay for that 'barely tolerable' comment." His voice deepened, and after last night, I had no doubt he'd make good on his promise.

Jax pulled up to the front entrance and put the truck in park. Not quite ready to get out, I fiddled with my bag. I still had to run, but now I had coffee! I leaned over and slid my hand up his arm. It was thick, hard, and deeply tan. My mouth watered as my hand traveled over him. He tracked my movements, eyes filled with heat, and I snapped my hand back.

"Thanks, Jax. It was… it was—"

"Thanks, who?" He lifted a brow expectantly.

I huffed out a breath. "King."

His dimple was on full display, and he bit his cheek. "My pleasure. Wait, I have something else."

He grabbed a white bag with Ellie's Bakery written across it. The smell of fresh pastry and chocolate filled my nose. I desperately tried to contain my moan, but from his bit-back groan, I didn't succeed. Jax might just be the sexiest man alive.

Opening my door before I did something especially stupid like ask him to marry me, I jumped out, being careful not to spill my coffee.

He leaned toward me and kept his voice low. "Sid."

A shiver ran down my spine as he watched me with dark eyes. "Yeah."

"I finished your book last night. I think there's a few things we should talk about."

I swallowed hard and slammed the door shut. The last sex scene in that book had her bent over a table, her wrists and ankles tied as he fucked her in the ass while a group of people watched.

His laugh followed me as I ran toward class.

SEVENTEEN
JAX

"FUCK, man. If you hustled half as hard on the ice as you do to get out of here on Thursdays, you'd be a first-round pick." Archer, our second-line defenseman, said from the row of lockers across from me.

"I'm already a first-round pick. Maybe you should start packing faster. You could learn something." I stuffed the last of my gear into my locker, thanking god we had an equipment manager who would wash them before tomorrow's game.

There was a round of chuckles from the guys, but the room went silent when our assistant coach, Matty, walked in. "Ryder."

"Yes, sir?" I had always liked Matty. He was good at practice and helped keep the bench organized during games. I didn't particularly like calling him sir, but for hockey, and only for hockey, I did what I was told.

"Coach wants to see you."

The guys winced in unison. It was never good when the coach wanted to see you after practice. I quickly ran through the drills in my head but couldn't come up with a fuckup big enough to be called in.

River raised a single brow in question.

I shrugged it off. *Who the fuck knows, man.*

Matty nodded toward the door. "Let's go."

"Yeah, alright." Any day but Thursday, I wouldn't give a shit, but I didn't like the idea of Sid waiting for me. Fuck. The sound of her breathy moans last night nearly did me in.

I left the rest of my gear on the bench. It would have to wait until whatever Coach had to yell at me about. River grabbed his bag as I walked by and moved closer to me than necessary, dropping his voice low so only I could hear. "I'll let Sidney know you'll be late."

"Thanks. I won't be long."

River gave me a knowing look. Depending on Coach's mood, I could be here for a long-ass time.

Luckily, Coach only wanted to talk about a few new plays, not to give me shit for some unknown reason, so I was only running a half hour late. Normally, I'd be all for a one-on-one session with him, but all I could think about was getting home to Sid.

The sight of her car in the driveway kicked up my heart rate and sent energy pulsing through my veins in anticipation of seeing her again. Her needy moans and delicious fucking whimpers had haunted me since our call.

I dropped my stuff in the entryway and went straight to the living room, where the guys were shouting. I was ready to give them shit for interrupting Sid but froze. She sat next to Alex with an Xbox remote in her hands, and River stood to her left, eyes glued to the screen. They were both laser focused on the latest NHL EA Sports game.

Lucas was practically giddy, counting down. "Ten, nine, eight, seven, six, five, four, three, two, one."

Alex yanked Sid into his arms and stood, twirling her around. "You're my fucking hero."

River stared at the TV, stunned, mouth dropped open. A slow smile curled my lips at the sight of her with my friends. She looked good, beaming in triumph. One of my sweaters dwarfed her; she'd rolled the sleeves up to show her wrists, and the bottom of her shorts was barely visible beneath. Girls were notorious clothing thieves. Shirts, hoodies, hell, even socks went missing. Klepto souvenirs. I didn't let them wear my shit *ever*, but Sid was different. A deep possessiveness warmed my stomach. I liked it when she wore my things.

I should say fuck it and stay down here for the night, but I was entirely too selfish for that. "Hey, Sid."

Flushed pink, she turned to me with an ear-splitting grin. "Hey, *King*."

The guys laughed, chirping her for losing the bet.

"Fuck, I forgot about that. I didn't think he had it in him to win." Alex grinned at her and gripped my shoulder, giving me a little shake.

Her cheeks flushed a beautiful deep pink.

"Your girl here just whipped River's ass, five-nothing." Lucas plopped down on the couch, looking at her in awe.

I fucking feel you, buddy.

I let out a low whistle. "Damn. I didn't know you were a secret gamer."

She chuckled, mouth twisting to the side. "I'm not."

"You hear that, River? You got crushed by a rookie." Lucas beamed.

Alex squeezed her again before patting River on the back. "It's alright, Riv. You eventually had to lose."

"You all lost too," River grumbled.

Alex kicked his feet onto the table. "Yeah, but she beat you. That's all that matters."

River turned his stunned gaze on Sid, lowering his remote from its frozen position in front of him. He looked deathly serious before a chuckle rumbled up his chest, and he held out his hand for a shake. "Nice work. Do you give lessons?"

She clasped it in her own, giving it a firm shake. "Not going to share my secrets, River. You're just going to have to figure out how you lost by yourself."

A chorus of excited "oohs" circled the room.

River handed her a remote. "Best two out of three?"

I grabbed it before Sid could and tossed it on the couch. "Alright, you guys. It's been fun and all, but she's got studying to do."

Sid looked at me for a second. Did I overstep? She was having fun. Who was I to break it up?

"It's probably best before I give these guys a complex. Wouldn't want River to lose multiple times in one night. I don't think he's ready for that. Maybe next time." She grabbed her bag and winked at me.

I lifted the bag from her shoulder. "Fuck, Sid. This has got to weigh fifty pounds."

From now on, I was carrying it for her.

We walked upstairs, and this time, Sid didn't hesitate to sit on my bed. She took out several books and tugged her knees up to her chest.

"You know Alex is never going to stop hounding you until you tell him how you won. I mean, the guy's been losing to him for years."

"Too bad for him, I have no idea. I think River was going easy on me."

"Doubtful."

He knew we would never let him live it down.

Sid was surrounded by books, and my chest collapsed in a dejected sigh. There were slight blue smudges under her eyes. She'd worked several extra shifts the past few weekends, and I wasn't sure how she managed to balance out her schedule. She covered her yawn, but I could see she was barely hanging in there.

"You hungry? I thought about ordering some Thai."

"Yeah, that sounds great," she said and adjusted to be comfortable against the headboard.

"Okay. I've just got to grab a quick shower. I didn't get one at the rink."

She wrinkled her nose. "I wondered what that smell was."

"Smart-ass."

"Well, one of us has to be smart."

I grabbed a change of clothes and called the Thai place as I headed toward the bathroom and made quick work of my shower.

After throwing some pants on, I walked back into my room, already talking to Sid.

"Hope you don't mind, I ordered a few of my favorites for you to try." Tossing my dirty clothes in the bin, I searched through my bag to find my pencils before saying, "They said it will be pretty fast, twenty minutes-ish."

Realizing I'd been met with silence, my eyes drifted up. Sidney stared at me; her mouth was open, eyes hungrily tracing over my tattoos, taking in every detail. My skin heated as her gaze roamed over my chest, and her tongue darted out, wetting her bottom lip. I moved slowly, trying not to disrupt her gaze. My girl was so caught up by my naked chest she wasn't thinking straight.

A groan rumbled in the back of my throat, and she looked away. I crossed the room in a few steps and slid my fingers across her jaw, guiding her gaze back to mine. "You like what you see, Sid."

My fingers tightened, and a shiver rolled through her, leaving goose bumps in its wake. Fuck. I lowered myself until my lips were barely an inch above hers, and an overwhelming need to kiss her took over my sanity.

She pulled back, putting much-needed space between us that I fucking hated, and examined my chest. "Do your raven tattoos mean anything?" Her voice was soft, barely above a whisper, still caught in the moment we shared.

She didn't know how much that question dug into me. There was nothing she could say that would snap me out of my daze better than bringing up Marcus.

I sat beside Sidney, needing her close before I answered, and ignored the reasons why. I cleared my throat and tried to explain. "Did I tell you that Marcus is Piper's brother?"

Her eyes went round with shock. "I had no idea."

"We all grew up together. His mom used to scoff at us, 'You two are too smart and too much trouble for your own good' She always softened it by saying it was in our nature. 'Two little ravens who can't wait to fly.' Marcus was born for bigger things. I always felt like he was leading me to places I'd never have reached on my own. When he died, I got the tattoo of two ravens so I could keep a part of him with me while I reached for his dreams." I sucked in a choked breath.

Her eyes never left mine, full of understanding, not pity. Her fingers intertwined with mine, and calm washed over me as I gripped her hand.

"You know, you remind me of him."

Her eyebrow lifted with that.

"He was always so driven. He always knew where he was headed and what he wanted. His steadiness grounded me."

I searched her eyes. Did she catch on that she grounded me? No one could ever replace the friendship he and I had built on years of scratched knees, video games, and shared dreams. But there was something here that could grow into that same deep connection. The tension between us grew thick, and her pulse was visible in her neck.

She sucked me in, and I was helpless to the fall.

Her chest rose and fell at double speed, and something filled her eyes that I couldn't decode.

My phone buzzed beside us, breaking the tension, and she pulled away.

I checked it, needing the distraction. "Food's here."

Throwing on a shirt, I headed to the front door and gave the driver a nice tip for being early. I set up the food for us and divided the plates on the floor in front of the bed, inviting her to sit with me. She devoured her food, and her hum of satisfaction sparked heat in my chest. I wanted to be the one who made her sound like that. Mouth full, she gave me a thumbs-up, mumbling, "Really good."

Within a few minutes, she leaned against the side

of the bed with her head tipped back, looking as content as could be. All I wanted to do was lean in close. Instead, I cleaned up around us and let her relax before we got back into it.

Fuck it, I was taking a chance. "Sid?"

"Mhmm."

"Can you answer a debate between Alex and me"

Her eyes were still closed, but she nodded.

"I'm trying to figure out what a girl's doing when she tells a guy she's clearly into that she doesn't want him."

She laughed, eyes still closed, and gave me a big smile. "She's lying."

She was on her side, and I was on mine, facing her. I could feel my eyes drooping, but I kept asking questions. Just a few more, and I would get up and go into the other room.

I woke up a few hours later, and Sidney was softly pressing against me. I was wrapped around her, hugging her to me, and took deep breaths of her citrusy scent. Unable to resist, I traced the long column of her neck with my nose, gently kissing the base of her jaw, and groaned when Sid made a soft whimpering sound. My dick instantly hardened, and my muscles strained not to grind it against her perfectly placed ass.

Sidney stiffened, and I held my breath. It might kill me to leave this bed, but I would fucking make myself if she asked me to.

She shifted back until her ass pressed against my cock.

Fuck.

I didn't even try to stop myself from thrusting forward. She moaned, and I rubbed my length between her cheeks, cursing the layers of clothes between us.

I shifted until my cock pressed against her cunt and fucking ate up her hungry, needy sounds. Her hips rocked against me, urging me on, and I took it as my sign to keep going. I thrust steadily against her, my dick straining in my pants, and placed wet kisses where her shirt slipped over her shoulder. "Fuck, Sid."

Her nails dug into my thigh, and my mind blacked out with lust. I flipped her onto her back and bracketed her head with my forearms, keeping my weight off her.

Her pupils were blown wide, her heart pounding against mine, and I breathed against her mouth. "You're beautiful."

She ran delicate fingers across my cheek and raked her nails into my hair, drawing my mouth to hers. I groaned, a shiver running down my spine, running straight to my cock with the first taste of her sweet mouth. I got lost in the kiss before pulling back and nipping her mouth. "Fuck, you taste good."

She searched my gaze. "Shut up and kiss me."

She didn't have to ask me twice. I dropped my lips to hers, taking it in a hungry, messy kiss. I wanted to consume her, own her, and by the way she grabbed my hair, holding me closer, she felt the same way.

I shifted until one of my legs rested between her thighs and the other on the outside. She gasped into my mouth when I pressed my leg against her sweet, needy cunt while rocking my pulsing cock against her thigh.

She moaned and lifted her hips, giving me a better angle to thrust against her. It had been a long fucking time since I came in my pants, but I was so fucking close already.

Sid's teeth sank into my bottom lip, and I tasted the metallic tang of blood when I ran my tongue over it. I broke our kiss, sinking my weight into her, and removed her hands from my hair, pinning them above her head with one hand.

She squirmed beneath me but didn't try to escape my grasp. I gripped her jaw with my other hand, forcing her mouth open, and ran my thumb along her bottom teeth. Her eyes were near black as she sucked my thumb between her lips, swirling her tongue around it. *Fucking christ.* I groaned, my eyes rolling back, and I thrust hard into her thigh. Fuck, that was hot.

I pulled my thumb out of her mouth, growing impossibly hard with her whimpered protest, but I wanted to know just how dirty my girl was. I widened her jaw with my fingers, and a low rumble vibrated through my chest when she tilted her head back, giving me more access. Spit pooled in my mouth, and I let it slide off my tongue into her mouth. Her eyes widened, and she rocked her cunt against me, chasing the friction.

I dropped my mouth to hers and spoke against her lips. "You like that, needy girl."

Sid moaned and shook beneath me. I ground my teeth against the urge to strip her naked and fuck the shit out of her. Every fiber of my being wanted to make her mine. But she wasn't ready for that step yet. It wouldn't stop me from marking her. I trailed open-mouth kisses down her neck before sucking hard and biting the skin. Her neck was covered in deep purple bruises where I'd marked her. A wide smile formed on my lips, loving that everyone would know someone owned her. Even if she wasn't ready to tell them it was me. She kissed me and sucked my tongue hard into her mouth, working it over like she would my cock, and I was so fucking close to nutting against her.

I ripped my head back. "I'm too close."

"Me too."

Shit. I lost control with her admission and ground hard against her cunt, listening to her sounds and finding the perfect rhythm. "If you're going to make me come in my fucking pants, you're sure as hell going to come in yours."

She whimpered in response, riding against my leg, and I slid my hand between her legs, pressing my palm into her cunt. I braced myself so she could rock against me. "That's it. Take what you need."

Her entire body vibrated, her legs squeezing against my thigh as a cry broke from her mouth, and

I quickly followed her over the edge. I collapsed against her chest and took a shuddering breath and lay there for several moments before rolling off. I hesitated before meeting Sid's gaze, worried about what I'd find there.

Her eyes were hooded, and her skin flushed as she watched me back with a small smile. "That was unexpected."

I laughed. That was the furthest thing from unexpected. I'd imagined some version of that since the first day we met. Instead of admitting that, I gestured toward my pants, now discolored with my cum. "I'm going to clean up. I'll be right back."

Sid leaned forward, moving to get up, and there was panic in her eyes. I wrapped my hand around her wrist.

"Do not fucking move, Trouble. I expect you to be in my bed when I get back. We'll figure everything else out later." I raised my brow, pausing before getting up.

She nodded. "Okay."

I leaned down, kissing the tip of her nose before grabbing a shirt and jogging pants and heading to the washroom. I quickly washed off in the shower and got dressed. My eyes caught on my reflection in the mirror, and I smirked at the scratches she'd left on my neck. She'd marked me too. A twinge tightened my chest. I was completely fucked.

She was mostly asleep when I climbed in beside her, satisfaction coursing through me that I'd worn her out. I grinned against her neck. This was the second time she was sleeping in my bed, breaking rule number two.

She rotated, curling into my chest, and I pulled her in tighter, sliding my fingers through her hair. She hummed softly and snuggled in closer, her fists clasping my shirt like she was unwilling to let go. Her voice was heavy with exhaustion, barely awake. "I'm not going to fall in love with you when you have to leave."

Fuck. My chest caved with the ache of her words. I tucked my face against her neck and took a deep breath in, waiting until she was deep asleep to reply. "I can't promise you the same."

EIGHTEEN
SIDNEY

JAX'S BREATH fanned over the side of my neck with each exhale, and the heat of his body wrapped around mine and warmed me through my core. My ribs squeezed, and I snuggled deeper, burying my face into his chest, allowing myself a few seconds of indulgence in this quiet moment. I was warm, comfortable, secure, and an overwhelming sense of safety had my breath hitching. I'd broken rule number two last night, the one that was supposed to keep me from catching feelings. The one I should've known better. I couldn't hold on to Jax, but he'd quickly become an addiction I wasn't sure I wanted to break. At least not yet.

I worked my way from under his arm, not ready to face that thought head-on, and gathered my things as quietly as I could. Still fully dressed from last night, I was able to escape quickly down the stairs.

Lucas, Alex, and River were already awake, and they gave me friendly hellos with knowing smiles.

I fought down the blush threatening my cheeks. "Morning."

"Want some pancakes?" Alex asked, gesturing to the full plate on the counter with his spatula.

"I've got to take off, but thanks, though," I answered, making my way to the door, where Lucas stood with his hands in his pockets. He wore a crisp white T-shirt and a ball cap with the Huskies logo on it.

He greeted me with a grin, but it didn't reach his eyes.

"Everything okay? How's Piper?"

He shook his head. "She's great. Everything is great."

I wasn't sure I could believe him with how he stared at me. "Spit it out, Lucas."

"I just don't want to see this all fall apart at the end of the year."

"Are you worried I'm going to be hurt?" I tried for my most nonchalant cocky tone.

"No, I'm terrified *he* will be."

I took a step back, not prepared for that.

Lucas held up his hand. "You've got to understand Jax has been closed off since Marcus died. Sure, he's messed around, but you're different. You've opened something in him we've all noticed."

All the guys nodded.

"But..." Lucas paused.

"But Jax's leaving." My voice was quiet. "What are you asking of me, Lucas?"

"Fuck if I know." He shook his head. "If I had a single clue how to go about this without the disaster coming at you in the end, I would tell you."

I patted his shoulder and tried to act more confident than I felt. "Don't worry. I've got this."

His eyes still looked unsure, but he nodded and gave me one of his signature grins. "You better, because I'm not dealing with his mopey ass in the changing room."

All the guys laughed, but I couldn't help staying quiet. I didn't want to hurt him—we were playing a dangerous game, and neither of us could stop.

I got home, and Anthony and Curtis were sitting on our sofa, smiling at me. They both wore pajamas, and Anthony's sandy-brown hair was sticking up, no doubt from his boyfriend's fingers last night.

Anthony sipped his coffee and smiled. "Spill. I need all the deets."

"There are no deets. I crashed at Jax's place because it was late."

"You can't even look at me when you say that. Now, tell me everything."

I gnawed on my lower lip and sucked in a breath. I wasn't ready to analyze what had happened last night or what it might lead to.

Curtis took pity on me. "Leave her alone, Anthony. Poor girl just got home."

"Thank you," I said, giving him my brightest smile.

"Plus, you look like you got thoroughly laid, so we can easily guess what happened," he said, looking over the rim of his coffee.

I scoffed. "We didn't have sex."

"You did something" was his quick reply.

When I didn't deny it, Anthony made a whooping sound. "'Bout fucking time."

"Remember, I'm avoiding relationships? I literally have rules."

"Sounds like he's enjoying breaking them. Tell me. How many have you crossed so far?"

I huffed out a breath. He wouldn't stop until I gave them something. "Three, okay? Kissing, and, well, last night was the second time I've slept over."

"Wouldn't you say four's broken? You know, since he's a hockey player," Curtis said, enjoying this entirely too much.

"Whatever."

Anthony barked out a laugh. "Sidney, that's literally the only one that had any actual backing. You know, with your dad being in the NHL."

He wasn't wrong, but it turned out I wasn't immune to the allure of hockey players. Lucas's words of concern filtered through my brain. I had to remember to keep distance between Jax and me. Because whatever was happening would end when we graduated. That was one thing I wouldn't budge on. "Just drop it. Okay?"

Anthony tilted his head, and Curtis sank into the

crook of his arm as they both watched me. "Sure, Sidney. There's some coffee ready if you want some."

I grinned. "You should've led with that."

I sat cross-legged studying on my bed when my phone vibrated with a video call. I answered it on my computer, and my dad's smiling face popped up on my screen.

"Hey, kiddo."

He looked put together and professional, as always. Ever since he became a head coach, his wardrobe had comprised tailored suits and freshly pressed dress shirts.

"Hey, Dad. How's..." I took a second to remember what city they were playing in. I tried not to follow them. "Ottawa?"

"Cold." He chuckled. "How's my favorite daughter?"

I rolled my eyes. "Only daughter."

"Still my favorite."

I hated these conversations. Where he pretended like everything was fine and we were actually close. When reality was we barely knew each other, he was so wrapped up in his career.

"You going to come visit soon?" I left the fact he'd skipped his last two planned visits unsaid.

"Yeah, the team's got a break coming up. I'll be able to fly in then. I miss you, kiddo."

He wouldn't miss me if he'd just show up now and then. I ignored the pain in my chest, pushing it down to where I couldn't feel it anymore. I knew better than to trust the words of someone who put hockey in front of me. "I miss you too."

His eyebrow rose, but he let my tone go. "What's new? How's class going?"

This time, my smile reached my eyes. "I got the internship!"

"That's amazing. Way to go, sweetie." Pride filled his voice. "See, all that hard work paid off. I'm proud of you."

My mom wasn't the only one who preached hard work and sacrifice growing up. What else could I expect from a dad in pro sports?

"Yeah, I guess." I turned my face so he couldn't read my expression.

"You still not dating. You know, I've always thought that was going a bit too far."

Said the guy who abandoned his family. Thoughts of Jax invaded my mind, and the question of *what if* snuck in. I wasn't quick enough to hide it from my face.

My dad smiled. "Oh, you are? Does he go to school with you? What's his major?"

"Kinesiology." The second I said it, I knew it was a mistake.

His brows pulled together. "He's not in sports, is he?"

Lie, or don't lie. That was the question. Unfortunately, I was a horrible liar. "Yeah, he is, but don't worry, we aren't serious."

My dad's voice lowered, anger building. "What sport does he play, Sidney?"

I hated when he called me that. I took a deep breath, bracing myself, and got it over with. "Hockey."

"Did you not learn anything from me and your mother?" his voice boomed, just shy of yelling.

"It's different. We're different. We're not even dating."

"Listen to me, Sidney. I loved your mother, but everything changes when you get to the NHL."

"It's not like that," I protested.

"It's always like that. I've been in this business for twenty years. First as a player and now as a coach, and one thing stays the same." He leaned into his screen and stared me down. "Every rookie is a jackass, and hockey will *always* come first."

There it was. There was the reminder I needed. I locked down the pain his words created, even their existence, proof that I let this get too far. "I've got it under control."

"You better, Sidney. I promise you this. You'll regret it if you don't."

The rest of the conversation was tense, and I broke it off early, using the excuse of needing to study. He gave me a quick I love you and hung up before I could say it back. I let the air whoosh from my lungs and dropped my head back on my pillow. Today really said, *You're making a mistake.* Then repeatedly nailed it home.

My dad was right. I needed to throw the brakes

on with Jax before I screwed everything up. I groaned, lifting to pull my computer onto my lap. The Human Behavior midterm presentation was in two weeks, and even though Jax and I had studied, I was still terrified I would fail miserably. I needed that recommendation more than I needed anything else. It was the last hurdle standing in my way.

An hour into studying, my phone vibrated.

Jax: You took off this morning.

Shit.

Me: I had to get home. Studying and all that.

Bubbles started and stopped on the screen for several seconds before his text finally came through.

Jax: Is everything ok?

Me: Of course.

Lie. I sucked in a breath, fighting back the burning in my eyes, and turned off my phone.

NINETEEN
JAX

I GOT TO CLASS EARLY, hoping to corner Sid, only to find her seat empty. A sinking, oily feeling turned in my stomach. She was avoiding me. I'd texted her a few times, like the desperate ass I had become, but I'd gotten a bunch of bullshit one-word replies.

Frustrated, I collapsed into my seat, not even bothering to take out my laptop. I understood she was freaked-out. We'd crossed an unspoken line. Hell, I was freaking out. I pressed my palms into my eyes and released a strangled groan.

My head had been assaulting me with images from Thursday night. Every touch, feel, gasp had been playing on repeat. Hell, she was infiltrating my dreams in the best ways possible. When her mouth found mine, everything started clicking into place.

I called Rocky first thing Friday morning and told him all bets were off. No more fake dating, no more

PR stunts. He could get one of the other guys to do it. He went into a rant about how getting into a relationship now would be stupid. But it was too fucking late.

Sid had slipped her way into my life and infiltrated my thoughts. It was in the little things, like when she laughed with her entire body, making everyone around her laugh too, or how she tapped her foot to a silent beat during class. The way she bit her pencil and tucked her hair behind her ear while concentrating or her overwhelming love of coffee and strawberry milkshakes. She was intoxicating.

Everything that encompassed her had sucked me in for weeks, and I wasn't even trying to resist the pull anymore. I craved her even in my sleep, waking up wishing I could recapture the dream. I didn't just imagine her grinding herself against me. She was right there with me on the edge. I closed my eyes at the picture and let out a low groan. The way she responded to my every touch made everything ten times hotter.

Therein lies why she was MIA. She knew I knew what was up.

I didn't understand how she was able to resist this pull between us. I was barely able to be near her without pinning her to the wall and kissing the shit out of her.

I'd replayed her words that night, over and over.

"I'm not going to fall in love with you when you have to leave."

The truth of her words had wrapped me up for

days. We both knew I was a horrible bet. Countless women would jump at the chance of being *Jax Ryder's* girlfriend, but they didn't get *me* like she did. All they wanted was a piece of fame and money. Fisting my hand in my hair, I looked back at Professor Carter. I might as well not be here for how little I was paying attention.

His voice droned on, "The connections formed…" Pulling out my laptop, I took notes for the two of us. She might be freaking out enough to skip class to get away from our new reality, but I wouldn't let her fall behind because of it.

Sid was apprehensive about being involved with a pro athlete. I needed to show her I was worth the risk because I knew that she was worth it. There was something special here. Maybe the heartache was inevitable, but not meeting this head-on to see how it played out would be a regret we'd hold for a lifetime.

I was jolted from my thoughts when a slim hand with long red nails reached over my desk. When I followed the arm up to its owner, I found a bubbly brunette with bright red fuck-me lips tipped up at the side, sitting in the seat directly in front of my desk.

"So, where's Sarah?" Her voice was soft, breathy, almost alluring, but it left a sour taste in my mouth.

"It's Sid. Sidney to you."

"She's been hogging all of your time." She shifted closer, expecting my attention.

I turned my head toward the professor and iced

her out. It didn't take long for her to gasp. Like she couldn't believe I would ignore her. *Believe it.*

She was huddled with her friends, and words traveled up to me even though she spoke softly. "He's a stuck-up, soon-to-be washed-up hockey player. I can't believe I was going to waste *my* time." Her voice held a defensive edge, and she was covering it up with her ridiculous statement.

I leaned over my desk so I could speak near her ear, and her sharp intake of breath filled the air. She leaned back toward me, a blush trailing up her throat, and her chest was immobile, waiting for my words.

I made sure to speak loud enough for her friends to hear. "Don't lie. We both know you would kill for me to waste *my* time with you." I pulled back from her and left that to sink in.

She huffed when she realized I wasn't coming on to her. Instead of bitching that Sid was brushing me off, I could've taken her up on her offer, but even the idea of it turned my stomach.

"Fuck." I slammed my helmet into my locker. I'd played like shit at practice, and I'd be lucky if the coach didn't bench me for it. The guys were giving me looks, but no one was stupid enough to comment. I hadn't played this badly since I'd tried to start with the flu. My brain had been all kinds of fucked-up, and there was only one person who could fix it.

I stripped out of my gear and dragged my ass to

the shower, where I stayed under the endless hot water, letting it pelt against my skin. This girl fucked me up. I turned off the tap, wrapping my towel around myself, and headed to my locker.

"What the hell happened out there?" a voice asked from around the corner.

I nearly tackled the guy before realizing it was Lucas. "You gotta fucking death wish? It was just an off night."

He ignored me. "So, what are you going to do about your Sidney problem?" His normal sarcasm was missing from his voice.

Of course, the nosey bastard couldn't stay out of it. I rubbed both hands over my face and let a long breath out. "I don't know. I really don't know."

He stood next to my locker, his voice serious. "You ever think you might love her?"

My gaze snapped to his, and my breath whooshed out of me. I closed my eyes and pulled on my hair until my scalp hurt, hating the words I was about to say. "Wouldn't matter if I did. She's been loud and clear about where this is going."

He shook his head. "Never took you as someone who would just give up."

That earned him a backhanded slap across his stomach.

"Oomph." He gave me a disbelieving look. "What the hell was that for?"

"For giving me a hard fucking time."

He rubbed his stomach and turned away from

me. "Whatever, man, but if I were you, I'd be fighting for that."

Intrusive thoughts tried to seep into my mind, and I dragged my hand over my face, working out my frustration. Sid's unwillingness to try was a constant presence in my thoughts. I knew she was off to start a big career, and our schedules would be a fucking disaster. But knowing how I felt and what I would give to be with her, I couldn't understand why she didn't want to risk it. There was something I didn't know, something more stopping this that she hadn't told me.

I pushed the thoughts down and suppressed them the best I could. An overwhelming need to get away took over me, and I grabbed my bag, leaving without saying goodbye.

It was impossible to change everything that was happening. I knew that, but damn, what Lucas said sounded good. If I could just convince her to let go a little, to be open to the idea of reaching out into the unknown. The hope slipped from my chest, knowing asking her to be with me wouldn't be fair. Her plans for her future didn't align with mine, and I'd be a conceited asshole not to understand that.

I grabbed my phone, firing off a text.

Me: Your place or mine?

Bubbles appeared and disappeared on the screen. *Come on, baby. Don't shut me out.*

Trouble: Mine

Damn right you are.

She was mine for now, and I was going to take

advantage of every single second of it. Walking into the parking lot, I headed to my truck. Nothing was going to stop me from getting to her.

I could feel the hollowness in my chest when I pulled up to her place, still struggling to suppress what my heart wanted versus what our reality was.

Me: Come for a ride with me?
Trouble: Be down in a min

Sid got into the truck and took one look at me. "Hey, what's wrong?"

She was all bundled up in one of my enormous sweaters. Sweater stealing would typically be a capital offense, but she looked damn good wrapped up in it. Did it smell like me?

"Nothing. Just a hard practice." Her brow raised, not believing a second of my bullshit. But I couldn't talk to her about it. Not without pressuring her into something she didn't want. Or worse, freaking her out and losing her for good. Instead, I slid my fingers through hers. "I just need to drive. Okay?"

She squeezed my hand and flipped the center console up, converting the front of my truck into a bench seat. She tucked herself under my arm, fitting perfectly against my side, somehow knowing exactly what I needed. She drew small circles over my arm and turned her hair elastic that was ever present on my wrist. "Want to talk about it?"

I kissed the top of her head. "Not tonight."

She nodded, snuggling in closer, and we drove

together through the night. I pulled up to her place just as the sun pinkened the sky. The air was thick with everything that stood between us. Putting the truck in park, I cupped the sides of her face, running my thumbs over her cheekbones. "Don't disappear on me?"

Her eyes went wide. "I didn't."

I dropped my forehead to hers. "I don't need an explanation. Just please don't disappear on me."

She sighed, her fingers twirling her hair elastic around my wrist, and whispered, "Okay."

We took a deep breath together, neither saying anything, instead feeling the current sucking us under. We were a train wreck waiting to happen, but neither of us would get off the tracks.

TWENTY
JAX

"I DID IT, I did it, I did it!" Sid squealed as we exited the class. Her presentation was fucking flawless, and I knew I wasn't the only one watching in rapt attention. Hell, even Professor. Carter looked caught up in her. I'd be jealous if she hadn't watched me the entire time. Her eyes never left mine until the last few lines. Pride filled my chest, and I wrapped my arms around her, swinging her into the air. She squealed when I spun and tipped her head back, completely trusting me.

The other students filed out of class, bumping into us in their rush, and I guided her backward until she was protected in the hall's corner. My broad shoulders concealed her from all the students, no doubt watching our public display.

My jaw clenched, and I raised a hand to her cheek. "You did fucking amazing, Sid."

She watched me with shining eyes, and I nearly

caved into her. I lowered my head to the curve of her neck, breathing in her citrus scent and smiling when goose bumps appeared. "I'm blown away by how good you were up there."

Sid laughed it off, but I was dead serious.

She pulled back and giggled, practically giddy off the high of her presentation, and gave me an ear-splitting grin. "We nailed it, didn't we?"

"Hell yeah, we did." I searched her gaze, palmed her face, and a little thrill ran through me when she turned into it. "You're amazing, Sid. You can do anything you want to. The world is at your feet."

She laughed it off again. This girl needed to learn to believe me. "Says the guy who's about to go on and become Boston's hockey golden boy. Pretty sure people already have posters of you there."

I shook my head, needing her to understand how proud I was of her. "It's not more impressive than what you've accomplished."

She buried her face into my chest and wrapped her arms around my waist. "Jax, you can do anything. You're biding your time with us regular people."

My brows pulled together as I grazed my thumb over her cheekbone until she looked at me, and I tried to infuse my voice with sincerity. "You'd be surprised how wrong you are."

She looked down but said, "We need to celebrate."

"What do you have in mind?"

"I could go for a week off studying. My brain feels like it's about to pop."

I stiffened and looked away. I needed to come up with a different reason to see her, or it would be a hard-as-fuck week.

She didn't notice my apprehension and continued. "We may be the only ones who actually passed that presentation after all." Her fingers curled into my shirt. "If it wasn't for you, I wouldn't have made it. Thank you—"

I covered her mouth with my hand. "There will be none of that. You helped me just as much as I helped you. We're a team, and we fucking rocked."

Her lashes lowered, and looked away. With the presentation over, would she want to study together? Because I wanted a lot more than that.

"There's a big game this weekend. If we win, it'll secure our playoff spot. I *might* know someone who knows someone that could get you and Mia tickets." I winked, and a wolfish smile played across my face. "Then we're all heading to Offside. There's a pretty big DJ playing."

She leaned in, whispering like she was sharing a secret, "Ahh, I don't know. I heard the starting forward's kind of full of himself."

My arms circled around her waist, squeezing a squeak out of her. "Is that so? Well, I heard he's what your fantasies are made of."

If she only knew how many of my fantasies she starred in. I wet my lips at the thought, but she cut in,

"Don't you know you shouldn't believe everything you read on the internet?"

I let out a shocked laugh. "You are so much fucking trouble, Sidney King."

"So, is your girl coming tonight?" Lucas asked, tying his skates. There were only a few minutes before the game.

I saw him out of the corner of my eye. We both knew who he was talking about when he said, "your girl."

"Who told you?"

"Piper ran into her," Lucas said, his cocky grin aching to be punched.

"What are you getting at?"

"You guys are getting pretty serious. Are you preparing her for what pro-hockey life is going to be like?"

I rubbed my chest as a sharp pain pierced through it. "She'll be long gone when we leave for training camp." Even as the words came out, I could hear the ache laced through them.

He eyed me thoughtfully for a few beats before nodding and moving to walk away but stopped, turning to look at me. "Be careful that you know what you're doing." With that bit of nonsense, he left the locker room.

It wasn't long before the building was echoing with our school chants, sending shock waves of energy through me. My blood pounded in my veins as my heart beat in my chest. I tipped my head back and breathed, a smile breaking through. A Cheshire grin crossed Lucas's mouth as we shared a knowing look. There was nothing quite like the high I got from playing with the home crowd.

I spotted Sidney sitting beside Mia in the players' seats. Her sultry eyes met mine, trapping me to her. She bit down on her lower lip, and my tongue rolled over mine, wetting her phantom bite. Rocky could go fuck himself with his PR bullshit. This girl was mine, and it was time she knew it.

Alex tapped my back with his stick. "Focus, man, before the coach catches you."

I dragged my attention back to the game and set up for the face-off. The guy from the opposing team crowded into my space and overlapped our sticks. It was legal but an asshole move.

"Fuck off." I flipped his stick off with my own and took a quick look at him before the puck dropped.

He nodded toward Sidney. "Your puck slut's hot. Wonder if she'd take me for a ride?"

My gaze flashed white, then black, as rage pulsed through my veins. It was only Alex's bumping my shoulder that stopped me from taking him down right here. I chuckled, but it was dark and laced with malice. "You're fucking dead."

Alex cut in. "You're fucked now, buddy."

The second the whistle blew, the guy took off from beside me, running fucking scared. But this was hockey, and there was nothing stopping me from taking him out. My blood pulsed in my ears, blocking out all sound as I skated across the rink directly toward him. I crashed into his side with all my momentum, driving his body into the boards directly in front of Sid. I winked at her, and her cheeks flushed. "That's for you, Trouble."

The ref called me on a five-minute major, but I was more than happy to take the penalty.

TWENTY-ONE
SIDNEY

WATCHING Jax was like seeing the devil incarnate. The way he moved was both like he could kick someone's ass or take someone on the table. He was sucking down water in between shifts, and I couldn't help but watch the way he moved on the ice. He was made for this.

Jax gave me the attention that every other girl begged for. Even when he wasn't looking at me, his body drifted toward mine. We were being tugged toward each other, and I couldn't slow it down. Truth was, I didn't want to.

When Mia and I got to Offside, the DJ was already set up.

"You look pretty starstruck." Mia's smile took up her entire face.

"Don't even start."

"I'm just saying there's something between you two. He couldn't keep his eyes off you, and he was playing a freaking hockey game."

"I'm not talking about this," I deadpanned.

Mia linked her arm with mine, effectively letting me off the hook. "Drinks?"

"Drinks!" I was going to need something to take the edge off after watching Jax play.

A round of shots later, Mia led me out to the dance floor.

My eyes closed, and I let the house music move through my body. I loved dancing, the way it took over every thought and allowed me to let go.

Thick arms wrapped around me from behind, and I leaned back, expecting to smell Jax's now familiar scent. Instead, I was met with the reek of stale beer.

"Let go of me, asshole." I pushed against his arms, anger building in my chest.

"Hey, don't be a bitch. We're just dancing. Come on, sweetheart. You know you want to." His voice was slurred, and his arms tightened, pushing the air out of my lungs. Fear settled in as I struggled to get him to let me go, and I fought in earnest to get him off me.

"Let her fucking go." Jax was in front of me, ripping the drunk guy away. He lifted him by his collar, his rage pouring off him.

"Man, she was dancing up on me. It's not my fault your girl is a slut."

"Wrong fucking answer." Jax's fist collided with the guy's nose and crunched as it broke with the impact. Blood dripped down into his teeth before he covered his face with his hand. "What the fuck? You broke my fucking nose."

Jax gripped his collar tighter, yanking him close, and I could barely make out his voice. "Don't touch her again. Do you fucking understand me?" His voice was low and cold. It left no doubt that he meant exactly what he was saying. It should scare the crap out of me, but my nipples were already getting hard.

A part of me desperately wanted to see how far he'd take this, but people were staring. If Jax went any further, he'd put his NHL career at risk. I ran my hand up his back. "Let him go. He's not worth it."

Jax gave him one last shake before shoving the guy away. "Fuck off. Before I change my mind."

I barely registered the guy taking off, all my focus pinned on Jax as he stepped closer, thumb running over my cheek. "You okay?"

I placed my hand on his chest, needing to feel him. "Yeah, it was nothing."

"It wasn't nothing." His low growl vibrated my palm. "He fucking touched you without your permission."

I shrugged. "Nothing every girl isn't used to."

His body tensed, and his eyes darkened. "Never again, Sid."

I bit my bottom lip, and a thrill went through me as he tracked the motion. "Thank you."

"You don't have to thank me for that." He palmed

my waist, tugging me closer until his inhales brushed against my neck. "I should've been here sooner."

Rationally, I knew there was no way for him to know some dick would rub against me. That didn't stop my core from tightening as his possessiveness washed over me. Everything about him called to me, the overwhelming sense of falling becoming more familiar.

"Dance with me." Jax's deep voice was rough in my ear. He was so close his lips brushed my skin. Goose bumps spread across my arms as the warmth of him coated me. The alcohol and heat of the dance floor had me in a dreamlike state.

His arm lowered to cover my hips and guided me against him. His chest heaved against mine, and I could feel his heart pounding out a rhythm that matched my own. A gentle graze of his lips on the shell of my ear sent shivers down my spine. Heavy, broken breaths skated against the delicate skin, and all of my nerve endings came to life. I dug my nails into his shoulders, holding him, not wanting this to end. He nipped my earlobe, and the slight pain was mixed with pleasure. I moaned, and he did it again.

Needing to touch him, I lifted my arms, wrapping my hands behind his neck, and buried my fingers in his hair.

"You're fucking perfect." He groaned and yanked my hips harder to him. His other hand trembled as it rose, grazing my skin. It was a slow, torturous ascent that left me desperate. It traveled up my stomach underneath my loose shirt, stopping just below my breast, waiting for my permission. I held my breath, paralyzed with the need to feel him, and he lifted his hand, barely brushing the soft underside exposed to him with no bra as a barrier. He groaned, and my lips tipped in a wicked smile.

"Fuck, you're hot. You're made for me, baby." He pressed his mouth to my neck in open-mouth kisses, sucking hard enough to leave marks in their wake. Each touch was a direct line to between my thighs.

He let me go, grasping my hand before I could protest, and dragged me into a dark alcove created by a triple-stacked row of speakers that only had room for the two of us behind it. He went in first, guiding me backward until my ass was against his cock. I made needy sounds, and he wrapped his hand around my throat, squeezing gently.

"Quiet. You don't want anyone to hear you."

His words set me on fire. The chance of anyone seeing us was slim to none, but it didn't stop the thrill of what we were doing. He slid his rough hand down my stomach. His fingers stopped just below my waistband, where he drew small circles with his thumb.

"Please." I tried to swallow it down, but it came out in a plea.

He popped the button on my jeans, and I moaned when he cupped me over my panties. The sound encouraged him, and he moved the fabric to the side, gliding his fingers through my folds. He growled in my ear, "You're so fucking wet. Is all this for me?"

I moved my hips, chasing his fingers. "Yes. Only you."

His teeth grazed my shoulder, and he sank two fingers into me without warning.

"Fuck." I screamed the word with the intensity of his touch.

He nipped my ear. "You like the idea of being caught, don't you?"

Lust pulsed to my core, soaking his hand. "Yes."

His laugh rumbled against my back. "I want to get caught. I want them to see you fucking yourself on my fingers so everyone knows you're mine."

That should be the last thing I wanted, but right now, I didn't care. "Please."

"You're going to come when I tell you to," he demanded. His hand tightened on my neck, and I struggled to take a breath.

Shit. My arousal pooled between my legs, and I soaked his hand.

"That's my girl." He bit my shoulder and swirled his fingers around my clit before thrusting into me, repeating the motion in a steady rhythm, building tension until I was hovering on the edge of an orgasm.

"That's it. Take what you need. Fuck my fingers."

I moved with his encouragement and dropped my head back onto his shoulder, my fingers clenching into his thighs. Emotions filled me, stretching my skin until I could explode from within. I wanted all of this, but I wanted more. I wanted everything he could give me.

"Now, Sidney. Come for me." His low command had me coming apart as the tension broke over me in waves, as my orgasm threatened to pull me under. My knees went weak, and he held me up with an arm banded around my middle.

"Fuck, Sid, the things you do to me."

Hearing him say my name was like having an ice-cold bucket of water dumped on my head, snapping my dreamlike state. The reality of my feelings separated me from him. I didn't just want him to make me come. I wanted things I couldn't have.

I couldn't separate my feelings from what was happening, and he was leaving. Not to mention he was in some kind of weird PR relationship with a tennis star. I turned in his arms to face him. His eyes were dark with lust, and I had to force myself to shift away. I didn't get far—instead of letting me go, his arms tightened around my back, and he took deep jagged breaths, dropping his forehead to mine, trying to regain control. His hands cupped my jaw, fingers trembling against me. "Stay."

"I can't, Jax…" My voice broke around his name. "I can't."

Jaw clenching, he nodded, loosening his grip, and I slipped out, leaving him there, even though my entire being wanted to go back. I glanced at him through the crowded dance floor. He looked at the ceiling, his muscles clenched like he was holding himself back from following me.

What the hell had we done?

TWENTY-TWO
SIDNEY

I KNOCKED on Jax's door and pulled my jacket closer against the chilly night air. The look on his face when I'd walked away from him was all I could think about. I should've stayed; I should've done so many things. Instead, I ran. Truth was, I was terrified. Terrified of what was happening between us. Terrified that my dad was right, and this really was hopeless. Terrified that if we started this, like really started, I wouldn't survive Jaxton Ryder.

My dad's words rang in my head over and over again.

"Every rookie is a jackass, and hockey will always come first."

"I've got it under control."

"You better, Sidney. I promise you this. You'll regret it if you don't."

It was a lie. I'd never been more out of control than I was right now.

The door swung open, revealing a pissed-off Jax. My eyes caught on his low-slung joggers and socked feet. He stilled and crossed his arms over his chest. His normally open face closed, and pain lanced through my chest at his cold tone. "Why are you here, Sidney?"

"I... I just... I just wanted to apologize for tonight. I shouldn't have left."

He rocked back and gave me the same look he gave all the other girls. "Of course you should have. You got what you needed from me." Hurt flashed behind his eyes before closing off again.

No. No. No. I went to put my hand on his chest, but he flinched under my touch. My eyes burned, and my voice came out broken. "I'm sorry. I freaked out. I wasn't supposed to like you so much. It wasn't supposed to get this far."

He stared at me for several moments before the wall dropped from behind his eyes. He blew out a deep breath, and his hands cupped my face, sending relief crashing over me. "You're overthinking this, Sid. Let go for a bit."

Let go for a bit? How was I supposed to do that? How could I possibly let him go once I let him in?

Jax's knuckles tipped my face to look at him, and I traced the line of his jaw. His head leaned into my hand, turning to kiss my open palm while his hands skated down my arms. He tightened them around my wrists and brought them both behind me, slowly backing me up into the door, pinning them there.

Dipping his head, Jax gently nipped at my lip.

"What's holding you back, Sidney?"

Self-preservation came to mind.

I forced a laugh. "What do you think Selena would think about this conversation?"

"I haven't seen her since the day you brought it up. She was never important." He gestured between us. "This is important."

His words sent warmth down my spine, but what could I say to that?

He lowered his gaze to mine, chest expanding against my chest as he breathed me in. "Are you afraid that I'll just take off on you? I'm not. I want to see where this goes."

My heart skipped at his words. "You *are* leaving."

Jax's fingers grazed my skin as he tucked a strand of my hair behind my ear. "We don't have to be over just because I'm going to Boston."

He would be literally a country away. My eyes burned, and I fought back tears, wishing I didn't know exactly how that story ends. I swallowed hard and pushed my words out. "I don't want to make this into something that it can't be. I want to be friends."

Jax lowered his mouth to my neck. "We both know that's not true."

His dark voice sent a shiver down my spine. This time, he noticed the shiver that ran through me and gently grazed his fingertips up my bare arms. "I know you, Sid. I know you don't want to walk away. Say it."

He leaned back, searching my eyes, and waited for my answer.

The dangerous part was he was right. This fire was threatening to consume me. I stepped into him and nodded, not quite ready to speak. He grabbed my coat and held out his free hand, guiding me to his room. He held the door open at the top, forcing me to duck under his arm, and it reminded me of when we first met, racing through the halls, opening every door we could. He smiled, tapped under my chin with his knuckle, and stepped inside.

I stiffened when he sat on the bed, but he pulled me to him, sliding me over his lap to the other side of him. My legs remained draped over his, and my body was tucked into his chest.

I tried not to dwell on the normalcy of being here like this. There was nothing changing our future. We were two trains heading toward each other until their inevitable crash. Unable to stop, no matter how hard they break, the impact leaving the wreckage of us. My chest ached at the thought.

Sensing my emotions, he gently guided my eyes to his. He placed a light kiss between my brows and moved back, eyes boring into mine. "It'll be worth it, Sid. Whatever it is you're thinking, it's worth it."

I cuddled deeper, knowing that no matter what was coming, there was no getting off this track. I just hoped he understood what it would cost us.

He tilted my head, waiting until my eyes met his. "What's going on in that head of yours?"

"I like you." I tried to shrug nonchalantly, but I ruined it by looking away.

His chest pressed against my side as he took a deep breath. "I see… I like you too." His fingers brushed over mine, and I tightened my jaw, suppressing the urge to entwine them.

"So… what exactly is the issue?" His voice was raw and hesitant.

"You know in movies where they do this 'let's just be friends' thing?"

His brows furrowed, but he nodded.

"Well, everyone knows that doesn't end well. They end up catching feelings and spend the whole time pretending they didn't until they inevitably end up together."

"We can skip all that bullshit in the middle."

My throat burned as I pushed out the words. "Except we can't because we won't end up together, and developing feelings for you and then trying to pretend that we're friends after sounds horrible to me."

He swallowed and nodded. "You think if we have sex that you'll develop deeper feelings?"

"Pretty much," I said, giving him a quick nod, still not meeting his gaze.

His fingers traced my jaw as he lifted my face. Pausing, he waited until my eyes met his. "Yeah, well, me too. I'm not exactly following here."

"Jax, you're going to Boston. I'm so happy for you… but can't wait around for you to pop in and out of my life. I can't live like that."

"So, what you're telling me is"—he pointed back and forth between us—"when I leave, it's done? Is that what you're saying?"

Pain radiated from my chest, and I looked up into his sad eyes, nodding.

"I get right now. Then it's over?" His voice grew aggravated. "You've got to be kidding me, Sid."

"Jax, you have to know this won't work." I put conviction in my voice that I didn't feel and had to remind myself that I had years of history backing my decision up. Years of coming in second.

"Don't make assumptions of what I fucking know. I'm willing to try. I'm telling you I fucking want you, Sid. Not just right now."

I sucked in a raspy breath, trying to blink away the tears threatening to form. "I can't do that. I just can't."

Jax raked his hands through his hair and stared at the ceiling before meeting my gaze. "Fine. We're together. We stop fucking pretending that we don't care. Eat it up, go full out, and when school ends, it's over. No texts on birthdays, invites to parties, no checking up. Total radio silence." Jax's voice was charged with anger, but it was sliced with pain like the words burned as he said them. His rough, calloused fingers brushed over mine before raising them to palm my face. His eyes were filled with agony as he said, "Will being with me until I leave hurt more? That damage was already done, whether you say the words or not."

I went to object, but his words cut me off.

"If I can't have forever, please don't take away right now."

My mouth wobbled as I stared up into his eyes. I went to speak, but the words wouldn't come out. I nodded my head without looking away.

"You're fucking killing me." He stared at the wall for several beats before his eyes met mine. "We can do that, Sidney, but the cost will be all of you now."

His mouth crashed against mine, and I met him in desperation. For weeks now, I'd been waiting for this. I pushed it down but was unable to stop the fire. His mouth nipped mine, and a sharp desire flickered through me all the way to my core. I moaned as his lips continued to my ear, licking the sensitive shell and sucking on the soft bottom lobe. Strong hands gripped my hips as he lifted me over his lap, settling my legs so I straddled him. We were chest to chest, and my hands moved up his body, feeling each of his muscles contract at my touch. Digging my fingers into his thick hair, I dragged his mouth to mine.

He broke the kiss to remove my shirt, and his breath hitched, seeing my bra-less breasts. A deep raspy groan rumbled through him as he leaned back, taking me in.

"You're mine." Jax's voice was rough, and his gaze roamed over me. "Do you understand that?" His grip tightened on my jaw, forcing my gaze to his. "I know because I'm yours."

Eyes searching mine, he waited for my nod of agreement before capturing my mouth with his.

We devolved into desperate touches, trying to

soothe the insistent pull between us. The electric current always present had multiplied tenfold since the first touch of our lips, as if it knew it was close to what it wanted most. It was driving an overwhelming need to touch, feel, taste. Lips dragging, teeth biting, tongues stroking, mouths gasping for breath. I rocked myself against his hard length through our clothes, trying to get closer, to ease the ache. A thrill went through me at his quick intake of air.

My needy hands yanked Jax's shirt over his head, and my breath caught as I took in his tattooed chest and the dual ravens covering his pecs. He roughly yanked me against him, and we both groaned as his hard-muscled chest pressed flush against my breasts.

"Sidney—"

My head tipped back as his heat seeped into my bones. As if driven mad to taste every inch of me, he took advantage of the angle, searing a greedy trail of open-mouth kisses up my neck. My mouth opened in a silent cry, and a shiver flew through me as he ran the tip of his tongue over the curve of my neck. I hissed as his teeth clamped down. Whispering his approval, he banded his strong arm around me as he leaned me back for easier access. He made a wet trail of kisses from the hollow of my throat down to my sternum, and my skin prickled as his rough, calloused hands cupped my breasts, weighing them. He murmured something unintelligible before squeezing them into each other. I swallowed down my breath in anticipation of his next touch.

His mouth dipped in low, grazing my skin. The warmth of his breath fanned over my sensitive, exposed breast. He paused until I squirmed in his lap. Slowly, his tongue reached out, lapping along the seam between them, and he hummed at the back of his throat. My skin burned from the contact, radiating outward through me, and each lick sent a mental picture of what he'd do to my core. He pulled back, lips curving on one side in a sinister smile as he took in my naked chest. "*Fuck.*" His voice was rough and breathy.

I arched into him as he swirled his tongue around one nipple, then the other. Carving my fingers into his hair, I moaned as he used his hand to knead one breast with strong, deep strokes while he worked his mouth over the other. I tugged hard and forced him to look at me. Molten eyes met mine. His pupils were blown wide, only a hint of gray. Never looking away, he slowly ran his flattened tongue along the underside of my breast. *Fuck, that's hot.*

My fingers contracted in his hair as he slowly sucked my nipple into his mouth, taking long greedy pulls that connected directly to my core. Panting, I held on to him, writhing in his lap.

A primal sound left him, and he bit down on my nipple, heat flooding between my thighs. I frantically bucked, crying out at the need pouring through me. He wrapped his hand around the back of my neck, tilting my head back and holding me in front of him, fully exposed.

"Jesus Christ, baby." Overwhelming need

consumed me, and my hips ground in circles, uncontrollably searching for friction. He crashed his mouth over mine, thrusting his tongue, owning my mouth in a frantic, dominating kiss. I raked my nails down his back in answer, and he dragged his hands down my waist. His firm grip pushed my hips down as he lifted his into mine. I moaned at the pressure finally meeting the ache.

"You're driving me fucking crazy." He sucked in my bottom lip, biting it gently before lifting me to flip our positions and move me below him.

He was propped up on his elbows on either side of my head, denying me the friction my body craved. Slow, languid kisses, gentle nips, his tongue licking against mine. His gaze bored into me, eyes going wide with a glimmer of realization before his hips descended between mine. Simultaneous groans filled the air at the contact. I pressed my breasts against his hard chest, drawing a moan from deep within my throat.

He pulled back, moving his weight to the side as he slipped his hand down between us. His fingers barely grazed my skin as he ran circles over my navel and painfully, slowly worked his way down. My heart pounded out of my chest, and I sucked in my breath as his hand pushed beneath my leggings. His gaze found mine as his fingers ghosted over where I needed him most.

His touch sent a devastating need rippling through me. I tried to lift my hips into his hand, but his arm had me pinned to the bed.

His head lowered to my ear. "Breathe, Sid." His voice was a command, and I took a deep breath in, surrendering control to him.

He shifted my panties aside and groaned into the hollow of my neck. "So fucking wet."

His fingers dragged the wetness from my entrance up, barely touching me where I needed him most. I couldn't stop my whimper as my hips bucked into his firm arm, still holding me in place.

"Please…" My voice came out as a plea.

"Tell me you're mine." A seriousness took over I didn't want to face. I bit down hard on my lip, silently begging him to touch me. "Tell me you're mine, Sid."

"I'm yours," I answered, my voice barely audible.

His teeth bit down on my shoulder, and his body trembled over me. Waves of pleasure flowed through my body as his fingers rubbed against my clit. His mouth found mine, and he inhaled my cries.

I wanted to touch him; no, I *needed* to touch him. I pushed my hand under his waistband and sucked in a breath as I wrapped around his length, stroking him from root to tip. *Mine.*

His body bucked involuntarily into my hand, and a thrill of power coursed through me. Letting out a primal sound, he snatched my hand in his, pinning it above my head.

My body trembled as his fingers filled me with one smooth stroke. *Fuck.* Crying out at the fullness, I bucked when he increased his speed, drawing whimpering needy sounds from me. His thumb pushed sharply into my clit and worked a tantric rhythm. Tingles worked up my back, and my body clenched around him until he swiftly pulled his fingers from me.

"No," I cried out, pleading.

Jax's dark eyes bored into mine, his voice strained. "I know... I know, Sidney. I need to taste you first."

I shuddered as my body responded to his words. He released my wrist and dragged his mouth unhurriedly down my body, stopping to take in each peak of my breasts and sucking hard, nearly painfully, then soothing them with soft licks. I was coming apart with need as he circled my navel, and my core clenched at its hollowness.

Jax sat up on his knees, dragging my leggings and panties off and discarding them on the floor. He spread my legs with his hands and nestled his shoulders between them. His gaze was hot on my core as he stroked a finger through my slick folds. "Beautiful, so fucking beautiful."

I moaned and watched him look his fill. A rumble went through his chest, and he lowered his mouth to my mound. Jax licked from back to front, pausing just above my clit, and my breath stuck in my throat, barely contained in anticipation.

His lips closed around me, sucking hard, and my hips unabashedly ground against his face with an all-consuming need. He smiled against my clit and pushed his fingers inside me agonizingly slowly. I moved, desperately needing him to move them deeper. He denied me the pressure, waiting for me to still my movements before continuing his aching path. When his fingers finally seated deep within me, I cried out his name. He bit the soft flesh of my thigh, dragging them in and out, and my hips rotated with his rhythm. He sucked on me at the same pace, stoking the fire within my veins until he took over every thought, every ounce of my consciousness.

Our bodies moved in sync, and his fingers curled inside me, sending flashes of pleasure until my toes curled and fists clenched as he held me on the precipice. Making a low humming sound in the back of his throat, he bit down on my clit, sending shards of electricity out in waves. My body arched off the bed as I yanked his hair, taking everything I needed from him. Trembles ran through me as my greedy core clenched around his fingers, drawing every second out.

I sucked in a breath as he kissed his way up my stomach. "Fuck, Sid."

"Off, now." My hands desperately pushed at the waistband of his pants, thanking God that I'm on birthcontrol.

He made quick work of stripping down and smiled against my lips. "I like it when you boss me around."

His playfulness was cut short when I guided his cock to my entrance.

He gripped my throat, forcing my chin up. "Eyes on me."

I didn't look away as he entered me with agonizing slowness, his dark gaze never leaving mine. My chest swelled with each of his thrusts with something so much more than lust. I wrapped my legs around his back, pulling him deeper, and he groaned against my mouth. "I've been fucking dreaming about this, but they didn't come close to this."

The reverence in his tone made me feel worshiped, and I dug my fingers into his hips. "I need more, Jax."

"*Fuck.*" He rocked into me with a force that would've had me shifting up the bed if he didn't have me pinned in place. Each stroke felt like he was cracking my chest after I'd tried so hard to protect my heart.

Jax thrust, shaking with his release, and he growled against my lips. "Mine."

Warmth flooded through me as another orgasm stole my breath.

He rolled over, tugging me so I was half lying over his chest and one of my legs draped on his. His arm wrapped around me, and he lazily stroked my hair. Only one thought drifted through my mind: *I'm his.* He kissed the top of my head, and the warmth from his body slowly lulled me to sleep.

TWENTY-THREE
JAX

SID: **I'm not feeling well. Going to stay in tonight.**

I barely registered Alex and River's bickering. I was so caught up in her text. I reread it for the tenth time, and my thumb hovered over the Send button, my response dangling in limbo.

Me: *What the fuck, Sid?*

It had been three days since we'd committed to being together. Three days since I'd been laid bare, and she'd offered back scraps. Scraps I'd taken and would take again. Tipping my head back, I stared at the stucco ceiling, kneading my fingers into the muscle between my neck and shoulder. I took a deep breath in and exhaled, puffing out my cheeks. Seriously, Sid, what the fuck?

I clicked my phone off and left my message unsent. I wasn't expecting her to set a ticking time bomb on our relationship, but I'd accepted it anyway.

She swore to be mine until the end of the semester. Then boom, radio silence. I was busy. She was busy. Fair enough, but three days without seeing her?

I dug my palms into my eyes and let out a low groan. My girl was freaking out, and if I didn't stop her, she'd make a run for it. I stood abruptly, and Alex and River looked up at me with matching wicked grins.

Alex started in. "What's got your panties in a bunch? Not used to being ignored?"

I looked between them with a scowl and landed my jab. "How's Mia doing?"

They both looked down in unison, not meeting each other's gaze.

I smirked. "That's what I thought. If you poke my soft spots, I'll start poking yours."

They ignored me, sitting in a heavy silence that had me taking another look between them, but I had enough to deal with without taking on their issues. "I'm going out."

Unease sat like a stone in my gut when I parked in front of her house. One part of me didn't want to pressure her, but the other wanted to shake her senseless. I dragged my hands down my face and let out an exasperated growl. *Don't be such a pussy and go talk to her.*

I knocked on her door, calling out to her, "Sid, open up." *Rap, rap, rap.* "Sid, you can't avoid me forever. Answer the door."

The door swung open, and I found Mia's eyes shooting daggers at me. "Shhh, she's asleep."

I shouldered my way inside. "You lack creativity today. Where is she?"

Mia pushed a palm to my chest, making me pause. "You are such a conceited ass. Why are you here?" Her tone had my head tilting, taking an extra second to look at her. She was wound tight, lips pressed in a firm line.

I threw my hands up in exasperation. "I'm sure she told you what went down between us, and now she's fucking ghosting me."

Mia's eyes widened, and her mouth dropped open.

"She didn't tell you?" Knowing how close these two were, it pissed me off that she was hiding it.

Hurt crossed Mia's expression at the same realization. She huffed out a breath before continuing. "I don't know what any of that is about, and it does kind of... and I mean only *kind of* explains this dumbass display of assholeness, but she really is sick."

My guts rolled at the thought of her being sick enough that she couldn't answer my texts. "What's wrong?"

"She's rocking a high fever and only wakes up to cough. This is the longest she's slept since yesterday."

"Where is she?"

"She's in her room, but Jax, I'm serious. So, god

help *you* if you wake her." She looked downright intimidating, staring me down.

I didn't wait for any more threats and headed right to Sid's room. She was bundled up in her covers, sound asleep. There was stuff everywhere. Her books and clothes were on the floor. As if she'd gotten home and was too exhausted to do anything but dump it where she stood. There was a small garbage bin beside the bed, overflowing with tissues, and her nightstand was covered with cough syrups, Halls, and ibuprofen. I sat as softly as I could to not wake her and palmed her forehead. *Jesus Christ, she's hot.*

I pulled out my phone and started googling what to do with a fever, but it basically said to take some ibuprofen and wait it out. Carefully, I eased off the bed, and shame created a pit in my stomach. When I should've been taking care of my girl, I'd been cussing her out.

I'm a fucking asshole.

Not sure what to do with myself, I picked up her things, sorted her books neatly like she liked, and organized her pens in that precise way of hers. I moved on, collecting the clothes from her floor and throwing them in the hamper, then walked into the kitchen. Ignoring the look Mia sent me, I grabbed a garbage bag and strolled back into Sid's room. I changed the garbage near her bed and carried the laundry bin out, slowly closing the door behind me.

Mia grabbed the bag from my hands and tossed it into the kitchen's larger one. "How's she doing?"

"She's burning up but asleep." I tugged my hair with my free hand. "Why didn't she tell me?"

Mia frowned, but I could see the corner of her mouth tip. "I'm sure she did, but you went off into your own pigheaded brain. Glad you've pulled your head out of your ass." She nodded toward the basket. "What are you doing with that?"

"What does it look like?" I shifted the basket to my hip.

She gave me a skeptical look. Damn, Mia had a good poker face. She finished sizing me up. "We go to the laundromat down the road."

"I'm bringing them home. Text me if she wakes up."

She smirked and gave me a small nod of approval.

I'd already fucked up the last few days when Sid needed me. I wasn't messing around now.

Lucas sat with me as I folded Sid's clean laundry on our couch. We both carefully ignored the fact that her underwear was now layered in a neat pile. I had no idea how to fold her thongs, and hell would freeze over before I asked Lucas for help.

Lucas's brows pulled together, and his jaw tensed. "So… you gonna tell me what's happening between you two?"

The laundry should've been proof enough, but I knew he wouldn't stop until I said something. "We messed around. We're…" I paused, searching for the right words for what was happening. "It's complicated."

"Seriously?" Lucas snorted. "Yeah, 'cause that ever works."

I shot him a glare, effectively wiping the grin from his face. "It's fine. We're leaving soon, anyway." I was careful not to admit that I wasn't fine with this arrangement either. Softening my voice, I asked, "How's Pips holding up?"

I knew it was hard for him to admit, but I could see how he looked at her when she wasn't looking. Like he was terrified he would lose her.

"We're good. We've got it all sorted." He tried to pass it off like it was nothing, but we'd been friends far too long for that to fly.

I sighed, leaning back. "You know, it's natural to worry when there's a big change, but she loves you. You've got to know that."

Lucas looked back at me and visibly relaxed. "Thanks, man." He reached out and started folding one of Sid's shirts.

A few hours later, I popped back into Sid's place. I sent a text to Mia and Anthony before I got there, and Anthony was already waiting at the door. I lugged the laundry bin in with me. "How's she doing?"

"Okay. She's woken up a few times, but she's back out as soon as she's done coughing."

"Thanks for taking care of her," I said and stepped past the couch to get to Sid's room.

Anthony reached out, grabbing my arm to halt me. "Shouldn't I be thanking you?" His brows lowered as he got serious. "I don't know what's going on between you two, but watch yourself. She's serious about not getting into a relationship."

I took an involuntary step back. His words registered like a slap. "We both know it's limited."

He nodded, letting go of my arm, but his brows pinched in worry. For Sid or me? I didn't know. "I'm not trying to be an ass here, Jax. My instincts tell me there's something more happening between you. She's a special girl."

"I know, man," I said and walked around him into Sid's room.

"Jax?" Sid's voice was weak between coughs.

"Hey, Trouble." I sat on the edge of her bed and passed her the water I'd brought in earlier. She took a few sips, getting her coughing under control. I checked her forehead and breathed a sigh of relief: it was cool. Her fever was gone, but she still looked exhausted. "You've been having a rough go." I tucked her hair behind her ear and waited until she looked at me. "You should've called me."

Even in her tired state, she rolled her eyes. "Sure, I'll remember that the next time I'm bedridden with the flu."

I helped her lean forward and stuffed a few pillows behind her so her head was elevated when she slept.

"Stay." She was drifting off again and grasped my hand in hers, pulling it to her chest in a possessive motion.

I got in the bed beside her and gently ran my fingers through her hair until she was asleep.

After Monday's classes, I picked up some things on my way to Sid's place. Mia let me in, eyeing the Ellie's bakery bag.

"Don't worry, I got something for you." I handed her two sandwiches. "One of those is for Anthony. How's our patient doing?"

Swallowing a large bite, Mia responded, "She's been awake for a bit but still in bed. She's doing mostly better, though. Not really coughing anymore."

"Thanks." I grabbed Sid's food and headed into her room.

She covered her face when she saw me. "Jesus, Jax, you can't be here."

I grinned, pulling the covers from her head, seeing her crimson cheeks. "And why's that?"

She gave up trying to hide under her covers and sat against the headboard. "Mia told me everything you've been doing. Thank you."

"You haven't seen nothing yet." I hauled out her soup and a little bun. "Ellie assured me herself this soup can cure anything that ails you."

She moaned as she took the first sip, eyes closing, and hummed around her spoon. "So good."

Glad she felt well enough to eat, I pulled my laptop from my bag. I was extra careful with my notes this morning. This was the second class she'd missed, and I didn't want her freaking out.

"I stopped to get notes from all of your classes. A few of your professors had them available, but I cornered whoever looked the smartest for your others."

I took advantage of my fame to get it done. I usually avoided doing that like the plague, but I was grateful for it this morning.

She let out a gasp, looking at all the notes, eyes wide, mouth open. "Jax, you didn't have to."

"Forget it. What are *friends* for?" I elongated the word. "Feel up to watching some TV? The new *High Tide* episode's out." Without waiting for her answer, I crawled onto the bed, careful not to spill her soup, and flicked on her TV.

When Sid finished with supper, I wrapped my arm around her and tucked her against my side, feeling her melt against me. She smiled at something happening in the show, but I wasn't paying attention. This was precisely where I was meant to be.

TWENTY-FOUR
SIDNEY

RAIN CAME DOWN HARD, drenching the sidewalk and everyone daring enough to go out in it. Unfortunately, that would be me in a second. I'd waited the last fifteen minutes in hope it would let up, but if anything, it rained more. It wasn't a long walk to my house, but there was no way around getting soaked. I pulled my jacket collar up, disappointed that I'd just switched to my spring one. I was going to miss having a heavier coat once I was soaked through. There was nothing to be done now. I had to suck it up and get it over with. I took a deep breath and pushed through the doors just in time to see Jax's black truck pull up.

He lowered his window, wearing his signature cocky smile.

"I thought you might need a ride."

"We're going to have to make a run for it," Jax said, parking behind his place. Lightning crashed through the sky, and my body hummed in response. There was something exciting about a storm. I undid my seat belt, and Jax met my gaze with a sinister grin on his face. Eyes holding mine, he raised a finger, signaling between us.

Three.

Two.

One.

Go.

We both burst out of the truck, racing to his house. Luckily, the door was unlocked, so we pushed our way inside. Laughter bubbled out of me while I gasped for breath. I looked over to Jax in his soaked-through clothes, and I knew I was the same. I froze when he stepped into me, eyes dark with need, and raised his hands to either side of my neck. My breath hitched as the rough pad of his thumb skimmed over my cheek and coaxed my head back. My eyes followed the water dripping from his hair down his face, and without warning, his mouth crashed over mine.

I moaned into his hungry, greedy kiss.

A playful grin tipped the corner of his mouth. "Last one to the shower buys dinner."

He knocked me to the side, trying to get a head start, but I wrapped both hands around his middle, slowing him down until I could put one foot in front of him, racing up the stairs first. "Cheater." His voice was raspy and full of laughter.

"Nuh-uh, you cheated first," I shouted as I ran full speed through his room, charging into the bathroom. Our laughter echoed through the space as he followed me in. He came closer until my back touched the wall, and his hands tightened on my sides as he took my mouth in a searing kiss, sending warmth pooling between my thighs. My fists clenched his shirt, and I pulled him into me.

He groaned into my mouth and nipped my bottom lip. "Shower first. Don't want you getting sick again."

He kissed my nose and stepped back to turn the shower on. It was a large walk-in, almost double the width of a standard shower, with a rainfall showerhead. He faced me, and his soft gray eyes met mine as his hands slowly lifted my shirt off. My skin pebbled as his fingers grazed my stomach and skimmed the side of my breast as my shirt rose over my head.

His voice was rough. "*Jesus*, Sid, you're fucking killing me."

I waited for him to attack, but he dropped his mouth to the curve of my neck and placed gentle kisses there. A hum started in the back of my throat, and I lifted his shirt. "Take it off."

I felt his smile on my sensitive skin. "Bossy."

He pushed himself off me and jerked his shirt over his head, shucking off his pants and boxers. He shot me a cocky grin and watched my mouth pop open. My eyes tracked downward, over the patterns of his tattoos, the ridges of his stomach, further until my breath caught in my throat. I swallowed as my mouth filled with saliva, and my gaze took in every dip and valley before slowly rising to meet his eyes. Jax's cockiness was replaced with hunger, eyes wide, mouth open. He wanted to devour me, and I was happy to let him.

Heat flooded me, and I stepped closer until there was barely room between us. I gently traced the patterns of his intricate tattoos with my nail, and goose bumps covered his skin. His eyes tracked my movements as my finger hovered over the blue and black feathers of a raven over his heart, down the serpentine pattern snaking over his hip bone.

Heat and something more pooled in his eyes, and his voice was rough when he pulled on my skirt. "Take it off."

I immediately shimmied out of it and took my panties off, not looking away from his stare.

Jax groaned in the back of his throat, eyes devouring every inch of me on display, and dropped his head into the crook of my neck, growling as twin fists gripped my hips.

His voice was thick and raspy. "I'm never going to get used to this."

Jax reached into the shower to check the temperature before lifting me into the steam-filled alcove. He grabbed something from the drawer, placing it on a shelf nearby. Sucking in a breath, I closed my eyes, body alive with anticipation. He pressed his body against mine, and warm water streamed between us as his hard length branded my stomach. A groan of pleasure rumbled through his chest, and his hands skimmed up my arms, over my shoulders, cupped the sides of my neck. He tipped my head back into the warm water, and his fingers gently massaged the back of my neck, drawing a moan from my lips. My heart stuttered at his tender touch, and I met his gaze, full of unsaid emotion. I placed my hand over his chest, and his heart beat a rhythm that matched my own. He gave me a small smile before pouring shampoo into his palm. I moaned when he kneaded it into my scalp, starting at the base of my neck and working up to the crown.

My eyes rolled back. "*Jax.*" It came out as a plea for more.

He moved his way over my temples, and I practically purred at his touch. His hands gently cradled my face, and he tilted my head back to rinse my hair. My nails dug into his shoulders, pulling a groan from the back of his throat.

Wrapping his hand around my hair, he slowly tugged my head back before he softly applied the conditioner through the ends, his gentleness sending warmth through me. He loosened the strands with his finger under the water until my hair was slicked down my back. We watched each other, not daring to look away. His eyes were molten with need, and his hand tracked down my side, cupping my ass, while the other tightened on my neck in a possessive grasp, sending electricity through me. He took his time with his kiss, owning my mouth and murmuring filthy things against my lips.

I wanted him to take what he needed, take everything. Our bodies did what our minds couldn't demand more from the other. Ending the kiss, he rested his forehead on mine and released my neck. His chest rubbed against my breasts as we both tried to catch our breath.

Picking up a fresh cloth, Jax dragged it up my body, barely skimming my breast as he reached over my shoulder for the soap. A familiar woodsy scent filled my nose as he lathered it.

Jax dragged the rough fabric over my skin, grazing along my collarbone and around the contour of my breasts. He lifted their weight in his hand, and he leaned down to suck the rivulets of water pooling off. He took long draws on it while circling my other nipple with his thumb and pushed down hard, sending pulsing heat to my core. I couldn't hold back the gasp that passed my lips from the sheer desire flooding through me.

He dipped his mouth, breathing on the shell of my ear, and pushed me until my back pressed against the cool tile wall. "Patience, Trouble. I've got you."

He dropped to his knees, and his hot breath fanned over me as his fingers slowly glided up my leg, causing all of my muscles to freeze in anticipation. We both groaned when he slipped his fingers into my wet, warm core.

"*Fuck,*" he murmured, and his mouth hovered over me, his tongue barely grazing my clit. He groaned against me, "Stay still."

My body rebelled with the need to explode, but I locked my legs in place, breathing hard in anticipation. He ran his fingers from my core to my clit and back, soaking every inch with my wetness.

Jax brought the cloth over my ass and kneaded the muscles in firm strokes before moving into the center. He paused just before sliding it between the crack and looked up at me with dark eyes. "Sidney, I want to touch you here."

I felt light-headed from not breathing, and he steadied me with one arm. My body burned from within as I slowly spread my legs wider in permission. He turned his head, biting into my thigh with a groan, and washed the rest of me. I was drenched by the time he dropped the cloth and slid his fingers all the way up my ass, covering me. He guided one slippery finger to my bud and gently pushed, not entering, just circling, creating friction and need. I pushed my hips back, driven to feel more of him, unable to think.

Jax hummed his approval and pressed his tongue hard against my clit, sucking and lapping at it. I cried out, unable to stop myself from grinding on him. His other hand rose between my thighs and pushed two fingers into my core while the other continued to slide up and down the seam of my ass, creating mouthwatering pressure. He matched the rhythm of his fingers with his tongue. His slow strokes drove me insane—it felt incredible, and a shudder ran through me when he sped his pace. Sucking my clit harder, he pushed his fingers deeper, and I whimpered at the contact.

He pulled them back from my core and placed a

third to my entrance. Rotating the ones inside me, he slowly pushed them in, stretching me. A long moan was pulled from me as I pushed my hips against them. *So fucking full.* Drawing in and out, he lapped lazily at my clit, slowly stroking the heat inside me until I was drawn tight with tension that built every time my hips rocked and his tongue licked or his mouth sucked.

"Fuck, yes, Sid." His low, gruff voice tipped me over the edge, and my head fell back as the pressure burst through me. My core clenched greedily around his fingers, every part of me coming undone. The release rocked me, and he held me up with his free hand as his fingers and mouth slowly milked the rest of my orgasm.

He stood slowly, placing a trail of kisses on his way up. I leaned into him, and he treated me to a slow, deep kiss as the fog of my orgasm faded.

"You're so fucking beautiful when you come for me," he growled and turned me so my forearms pressed against the wall. Jax's face tucked into my neck, and he traced my scar with his tongue, sending a shiver down my spine. He held me steady, and his heart pounded against my back as he gently stroked his hand up my side in a soothing pattern.

Jax stroked his length between my wet thighs, and I tightened them around him, drawing a groan from the back of his throat.

Mouth open, I dropped my head back to his shoulder as he slowly worked himself between my folds, against my sensitive clit, and ground into me.

Jax's movements were gentle, caressing, like he was savoring my body. He pressed kisses along my jaw. "Look at me, Sid."

Twisting my torso, I craned my head to look back, and his gaze pierced mine, full of emotion. He nipped my bottom lip, then caressed it with his tongue, hands sliding over my skin until every nerve ending screamed with need.

His hand guided the head of his cock to my entrance, circling, grazing, barely slipping in before pulling out, until an inferno grew inside me. With my upper body still turned, I held his gaze as he entered me in one fluid thrust. A tortured moan escaped from his lips as his eyes rolled back. The feeling of fullness overwhelmed my senses, and I squeezed around him with unconfined need.

His every motion was controlled, his body tight with restraint. He felt huge from this angle, stretching me, gently stroking me from the inside, and my heart clenched as he worshiped me.

His other hand moved down my stomach and rubbed two fingers over my clit. I dropped my head to the cool shower wall, and I rocked back hard into him. No matter how I moved, he kept the same slow, teasing pace. My body felt like it was fracturing as he thrust his length into my core. Jax shook as he drove in and out of me, building the pressure we were both desperate for. He gripped my chin, forcing me to look back at him, and his hungry, dark eyes ate me whole, our bodies owning each other's.

His fingers pushed harder against my clit, and his

hips just barely picked up speed. My body shattered against him, and I cried out with the force of my pleasure.

He paused, buried inside me, and gave me time to settle around him before he quickened his pace. His grip on my hips tightened, and I knew there would be bruises there to show for it. He was entirely too in control of himself, and I wanted to see him break apart with the same force as my orgasm. With a wicked grin on my face, I told him, "Stop."

"*Jesus, Sid.*" Jax's hips halted, and his voice sounded like he was in physical pain. I pushed off the wall, making him step back, and dropped to my knees in front of him.

His eyes lowered, and his gaze roamed over me as I took him in my hand. "I want you to finish inside my mouth."

A loud groan shuddered through him, and his fingers entwined themselves in my hair. I licked from root to tip and sucked the tip into my mouth, swirling my tongue. His thighs flexed as he tried not to rock into me, but I wanted him to lose control. I wanted to feel him shatter too.

"Jax, tell me what you like." I looked up with wide, soft eyes and slowly lapped the precum from his cock. His hips rocked forward, and a muscle ticked in his jaw.

"You're really living up to your nickname, Trouble." His eyes were practically black pools of need, and his smile had an animalistic edge to it, barely restrained.

I squeezed my hand around him. "Tell me."

"Fuck." His fingers tightened in my hair. "Squeeze harder."

I fisted him in my hand, hard but careful not to hurt him.

"Harder, Sidney. Come on, baby."

I tightened my grip until my hand shook, and he rocked through my closed fist, a growl escaping his mouth.

"That's it, baby. Now suck it."

I sucked him down, my nails digging into his ass, and pulled his hips toward my mouth. I repeated the motion until he lost control, thrusting in deep, unrestrained motions.

I looked up, meeting his eyes, as he drove his cock forward, deep into my throat, and that was all it took.

"*Fuck, Fuck, fuck.*" Jax's voice came out as a plea, and I worked him harder, faster. His fingers tightened in my hair as he kept pumping. Three more strokes and his body went rigid as he came. I swallowed him down, taking everything he gave me.

Dragging me up to his chest, he collapsed his back against the wall and kissed me delicately, cherishing my mouth, no doubt tasting himself too. The warm water coated our bodies, and his arms wrapped around me, pulling me tight. We rested together for several breaths.

Curved into him, I didn't want to move, but he unwrapped his arms, grabbing the cloth. He gently washed me again, this time barely touching my sensitive spots, then quickly washed himself. He kissed my forehead and guided me from the water. Goose bumps covered his sides, but he dried my body first, wrapping me in a fluffy towel and tucking the end in the front. Jax handed me another towel for my hair before grabbing a smaller one for himself.

He searched my eyes, and I knew he read the words unspoken.

"Come on." He pulled me into the room, directly onto the bed, and tucked me into his side, his arms wrapped firmly around me. He gently kissed my forehead as I kissed across his chest. We were wrapped in a cloud of intimacy that neither of us wanted to break. As I nuzzled in closer, my eyes drooped closed.

TWENTY-FIVE
JAX

I WOKE up to the sound of running water and hushed rustling noises from the washroom. Sid stepped into the room, fully dressed, looking sexy as hell. She pulled her hair into a messy bun, and my extra-large sweater hung off her. "You aren't running out on me, are you?"

She jumped a half foot in the air, eyes wide. "*Jesus*, Jax, you scared me."

She clutched her chest as if she was trying to hold her heart inside and took three calming breaths before speaking. "I was trying to be quiet so I wouldn't wake you. It's early."

"You were sneaking out on me?" I raised an eyebrow, waiting for her response.

"Sneaking out implies something nefarious. I was letting you sleep in. It's eight in the morning, and I'm pretty sure we didn't get to sleep until three last night." The slight pink tinge of her cheeks told me precisely what she was thinking about. I rubbed the sleep from my eyes, and my gaze roamed over her flushed skin.

Sitting up in bed, I swung my legs over the side. "Uh-huh." I tried to play it off like I wasn't buying it, but a smirk tipped my lips.

She moved within range, and I pulled her between my legs, her hands coming up to my shoulders as she dipped her lips down to mine. It didn't take much to move our kiss from a light morning touch to deep, hungry pulls.

She gripped my hair, and my head tilted back, bringing her head down beside my ear. Her teeth ran over the shell before nipping the soft bottom, making me groan in approval.

"You're going to make me late."

"Where are you going?" My hands glided up her legs, grabbing the firm globes of her ass. I was leaving to spend spring break with my mom tonight, and it sure felt like she was skipping out on me. I wanted to ask her to come, but my pride got in the way, not wanting to hear her say no. She was staying here over the week. She'd brushed off the question of why she wasn't going back home.

"I'm covering Mia's shift. I barely have time to get home for my work clothes. Then I'll be rushing to work." Her lips grazed my neck, and her soft breath fanned out over my skin. A shudder worked its way through me at her gentle touch. She shifted her gaze down to my noticeable erection that was barely covered by the sheet. Her tongue came out, wetting her bottom lip, and I squeezed her ass harder, stealing a moan from her mouth. I spread my hand over the side of her waist, and the other drifted up to cup her breast. "What time do you get done?"

She dropped her head to mine and let out a long breath. "Not until after you leave."

My grip tightened, not liking that this would be the last time I saw her for a week. "Call in sick."

She straightened, taking a raspy breath, and stepped back. "I've got to go."

I was sure she was trying to sound stern, but it came out breathy.

"Call in late."

She searched my gaze for several seconds before firing off a quick text, tossing her phone on the floor. "We've got a half hour. Think you can work with that?"

I didn't waste any time lifting her off the ground and pinning her to the bed beneath me. "Trouble, I'm going to use every second to make you remember exactly who you're waiting for." I kissed down the column of her neck, sucking hard, and bit the reddened skin, leaving marks all over her. That way, she'd think of me every time she looked in a mirror. She hummed in the back of her throat and tipped her head, making room for me. My girl wanted to be marked.

I pulled off her shirt, rolled down the cup of her

bra, and sucked her nipple into my mouth. She gasped when I bit the sensitive skin of her breast and left marks where only she could see.

"Jax." Her voice sounded desperate for release, and I made quick work of sliding my hand under her panties.

I groaned when my fingers slipped over her slick folds and dragged her arousal from her opening over her clit until she squirmed beneath my touch.

"You will not touch yourself when I'm gone," I commanded, pressing harder on her clit, and she whimpered, climbing desperately closer to her orgasm.

I removed the pressure, enjoying her cry of protest that I was keeping what she needed most away from her, but I had to hear it. "Your pussy is mine, Trouble. Now say it."

She squirmed under my hand, trying to chase the friction for herself, but I pinned her hips down with my forearm.

She glared up at me, anger mixed with frustration clear in her gaze. I nipped on her bottom lip, then soothed it with my tongue. I breathed against her. "I need to hear you say it. I need to know that I'm the only one who gets to make you come. Not even you."

Her breath whooshed out of her, and she bit my lower lip, sharp enough to leave a mark. "You're the only one that gets to make me come."

I growled in satisfaction and drove my fingers into her core, hooking them toward the soft spot at the front. I rubbed her clit in continuous circles and watched her climb closer and closer to her orgasm. Her eyes closed, just at the peak, and I groaned, "Eyes open, Sidney. I want to see exactly how you look when you come apart for me."

Her lids flew open, and she took in several deep breaths, so close she whimpered for me to push her over. I drove in a third finger, scissoring them to take up more room, and her pussy pulsed around my fingers as her orgasm broke through her.

I collapsed beside her and murmured in her ear. "You look so pretty when you come for me. I'm going to miss this sweet pussy of yours, and you're lucky you have to go to work because I would've fucked you until you couldn't walk if we had more time."

She made an incoherent sound, and I kissed the top of her head, blowing out a breath.

"I'll walk you out."

Sidney made a sound of protest but climbed off me, adjusting her clothes into place, and her eyes rounded as the sheet dropped, and my cock bobbed at her attention. A wicked smile crossed my lips, but I grabbed a pair of sweats, watching her eyes as she stared until I was fully covered. I ran my tongue along my top teeth, satisfaction coursing in my veins at the deep purple bruises collaring her neck.

She looked up at me, unable to hide the disappointment pinching the corner of her eyes.

"Don't look at me like that." I circled her with my arms. "You're the one who's going to be late."

She huffed but took my hand, following me to the

front door. Before she could escape through it, I lowered my mouth just above hers. She froze in place, waiting for me to move, and her tongue snuck out, licking her bottom lip in anticipation.

I kept my mouth just out of reach, needing her to reach for me. "You're going to have to kiss me, Trouble." My voice was barely above a whisper.

Without hesitation, she tilted her head, rising on her tiptoes, and connected our mouths. A hum rumbled inside me as I pulled her harder to my chest. I tried to keep the kiss slow and lingering, but she raked her hands through my hair, drawing my mouth closer. I stepped forward, pushing her against the open doorjamb, and her body went soft and pliant against mine. Breaking the kiss took all of my willpower, and I left my forehead on hers until we both caught our breath.

"I'll see you in a week, Trouble." My voice was rough, not wanting to let her go. I needed more time with her before I left. I swallowed the thought, and instead, I led her out to her car. I stole one more kiss before I watched her get into her car and drive away.

When I got back inside, I heard a throat clear. "Want to tell me what that was about?" Piper asked from where she and Lucas stood in the kitchen.

"Fuck if I know." I ran my hands through my hair. I was in over my head.

"She give you a 'let's be friends' line, Jaxie?" Piper grinned from ear to ear.

I deadpanned, not reacting to her taunts.

"Don't worry, it happens to the best of them. Not me, but you know... others," Lucas shouted from the other room.

"We're keeping it casual." The words bit at me, and a deep breath escaped on a sigh. I was leaving and didn't fit into her perfect plans. This was enough. Enjoying this *needed* to be enough.

"But is that what you actually want?" Piper's eyes were knowing and probed into what I was holding secret even from myself.

"I'm listening to her. She wants to be friends... well... more than friends." I shrugged. "I'll take what I can for now." When I tried to turn away, she put her hand on my shoulder.

"You see, it's that 'for now' that has me worried." Her eyes were full of concern as she looked to where Sid just drove off.

"Babe, quit picking on him. He never had so much as a crush. This is unfamiliar territory for him." Lucas ducked, dodging my smack.

"I'm just saying I've never seen you this happy. There's something that's changed in you. Right, babe?" Piper stared expectantly at Lucas.

"She's right, man. I'm not sure I've ever seen you this... happy," Lucas said while shrugging.

Am I happy? I thought happiness only came in the form of skating, but Sidney had shown me that the little moments could be just as fun.

"Anyway, boys, I've got to run too. See you tonight." Piper gave Lucas a kiss that had me wishing Sid was still here. As soon as she was through the door, Lucas looked at me. They were heading to her parents' place for spring break.

"Seriously, man, you doing okay?"

Did he think I was going to admit that it felt like a dagger to my chest when she said the words "friends"? She was right, though. There was no point in pretending. Sid had made it clear there was no future for us. I nodded instead.

"K, good, because we've got some planning to do." A huge smile split across his face.

"What?" I wasn't sure I liked the look in his eyes.

"I'm going to propose to Piper when we get back. Already have the ring and everything." He showed me a giant diamond set on a simple band.

"Aren't you young for that?" Although if anyone could make it, it was them.

"No." He shook his head. "I'm dead positive about this."

I wrapped my arm around his shoulders. "Alright then. How are you going to do it?"

"I'm thinking we set up a surprise with all of our friends there to watch, a photographer, the whole thing. Then we could have an engagement party that same night." Any other couple, I would think that was putting a lot on the line, but I was positive Piper would say yes. Lucas clearly knew that too.

"Maybe Sid will get in on it. Help trick Piper so she gets a genuine surprise?"

"Maybe."

SIDNEY

When I got home from work, I hollered out, "Honey, I'm home," in a voice loud enough to echo off the walls. My smile slipped, realizing Mia wasn't home. I dropped my bag with a plop to the ground and flipped the lights on as I walked to the kitchen. My shoulders slumped, and my neck cracked as I rolled it. Stomach rumbling, I checked the fridge, but no matter how many times I opened and closed it, there was still only the sad-looking bag of baby spinach tucked into the back.

I grabbed a box of crackers and a random cheese slice and turned back to my room. Quickly peeling off my uniform that was sticking to my body after a long day, I put on my comfiest pajamas. Armed with a handful of crackers in one hand, I plopped down on my bed.

After fifteen minutes of scrolling Netflix, I closed my laptop, drumming my fingers on top, and a jittery feeling worked its way under my skin. *Dear lord, hold yourself together.*

It had been weeks since I'd been home by myself. Normally, I hung out with my roommates or I was at Jax's place. A huff left me as I reached over the side of my bed and grabbed my bag from the floor. It was a good time to read. I pulled up my Kindle app on my phone and tried to use a book to shut my head off. I had had no problem being alone before. If anything, I had preferred the quiet moments with my books. This constant pull toward Jax, who I'd just seen a few hours ago, highlighted the risk I was putting myself in.

My phone vibrated in my hand, and I smiled at the name. There would be plenty of time to be alone *after*.

Jax: what are you doing tomorrow?
Me: working
Jax: what are you doing right now?
Me: lying in bed

My phone buzzed as his call came through.

"Hello." His rough voice seeped into my gut, down to my core.

"Hmmm" was all that came out when I tried to speak.

"How was your day today, Trouble?" His voice dipped lower as he stretched the syllables in my nickname.

My body heated with his words. This man was going to be the death of me. I pulled at my collar, trying to cool down. "You know perfectly well how my day was," I said, trying and failing to make my voice sound natural. I hated that he had to go home and I couldn't just go to his place tonight.

Jax lightened the mood with his laugh. "I know my day was fantastic. I spent the morning with a girl I'm crazy about." There was a pause as he hesitated a moment. "Sid?" My name sounded like a question.

"Mhmm?"

"What are we doing?" Jax paused, and I was so still I forgot to breathe. "Because this is real for me. I know you said we have a time limit. Are you still firm on that?" His voice was unsure, barely more than a whisper.

My heart clenched in my chest, desperately wanting to give in to this pull of ours and do whatever we needed to do to stay together. The need was so strong I had to clamp my teeth together to stop myself from telling him everything had changed. I wanted to take away all of that worry, but the truth was I couldn't.

There was fun and a connection to be had here, but it was fleeting. Soon, he would be out of here, and where did that leave me? I wasn't giving my heart to someone that already had a first love. Jax's life revolved around hockey. He had a contractual obligation to his team. There was no permanent place for me. Not without giving up on my dreams to follow him.

"I'm firm," I said, clenching my teeth to stop myself from taking it back. My lips wobbled, but I took a deep, steadying breath, preparing for his next words. I listened to his breathing, waiting for him to speak.

"Okay, Sidney." This time, he said my name as if it burned him, and the part of me I'd been hiding from myself, stuffing it deep inside, whimpered, knowing that was the last time he would ask.

Jax cleared his throat before he started on random topics. "Did you know we call tanks 'tanks' because in World War One, the army camouflaged them to look like water and supplied tanks to keep them hidden? Guess the name stuck." The rhythm of his voice made me sleepy, but we kept talking through the night.

It was going to be the longest spring break of my life. I just hoped I was strong enough to handle it.

TWENTY-SIX
SIDNEY

THERE WERE forty-nine hours to go until Jax got back. There was a certain level of patheticness to my hourly countdown, but splitting it up into days didn't feel like enough. Unfortunately, it had the effect of making each hour feel like an eternity. Hell, I'd spent a significant amount of time staring at my watch instead of my textbook. I'd read the same paragraph more than a dozen times, but I couldn't concentrate after the text Jax sent.

King: I miss you.

The simplest message had the air pushed out of my chest as my ribs caved in on my lungs. My eyes burned as I read the three words repeatedly. It was stupid, childish, and ridiculous to miss someone this much after just a few days. But that was how I was made. Deep down, in a place I refused to look, there was a blackness that festered. It liked to whisper in my ear that everyone would leave me, that I wasn't good enough for long-standing love. Hell, I'd felt alone since my mother passed, no matter that she'd had no choice in it. To my younger self, I still felt abandoned.

I'd been fighting against that voice for the last few days, knowing I had absolutely no right to it. Not only was it foolish, but I'd literally been the one to make sure this didn't get any deeper. I continuously reminded myself that I knew exactly how this ended, but in quiet moments, that ugly feeling still crept up, and like Jax could read my mind from hours away, he'd sent that text, reminding me he was still here. That it was all in my head. He was all mine, at least for now. I'd deal with the rest later.

I'd buried myself in the library to occupy my mind. It was a pointless attempt to make time go by faster. Reading had always been a part of me. Textbooks weren't nearly as fun, but with Jax commanding I didn't touch myself, there was no way I could read a smutty book while he was away. Not when he FaceTimed me every night, and just his gravelly voice had me wanting to beg for release. By the way he smirked at me, he knew exactly what he was doing.

Shit, I needed him to get back here, if only to get laid. I closed the book, eyes too crossed to read it anyway, and twisted my hair into a bun, securing it with my pen. I needed something a little less dry, or I'd pass out on my table.

I moved through the stacks and skimmed my fingers over the countless spines. There was a new vibe in here, different from the typical hum of studying students. The lights weren't as bright here, the tall towers casting shadows where I stood. The library had been quiet all week; almost everyone had gone home for the week.

I pulled a book from the shelf, flipping through the boring pages, when my mind went to when Jax and I had been here. How even then, I felt a pull to him, even if I hadn't recognized it.

My thoughts were so consuming I swore I could smell the woodsy scent of him surrounding me. I closed my eyes, taking a deep breath, and startled when Jax's low voice breathed near my ear.

"You didn't answer me, Trouble."

A shudder shot down my spine, and I flipped around, meeting piercing gray eyes. "What are you doing here?"

He crowded me, backing me up until the shelves dug into my spine, and the front of our bodies lined up perfectly. He rubbed his thumb over my lip, freeing it from my teeth before kissing me stupid.

We didn't pull away until my lungs burned with the need for breath.

He kissed along my jaw, nipping at my earlobe. "I had to see you."

Goose bumps covered my skin, and I sucked in a breath. "What about your mom?"

He skimmed his nose down the column of my neck, and his chest rumbled against me. "Who do you think sent me back here? She's looking forward to meeting you at graduation."

My heart rate kicked up as his words took over my brain and panic set in. He wanted me to meet his mom?

He released the pen from my hair and buried his fingers in my hair, tugging my head back. He dropped his forehead to mine. "Get out of your head, Trouble. We're here now, and that's what matters."

A million reasons that was a bad idea came in and out of my brain, but I couldn't voice a single one. I didn't want to.

He kissed the corner of my mouth, then the other. "You promised me now, and I plan on using every second of it."

His words flooded me with a need that I couldn't control. I was done wasting time on doubts. This was our time. I dug my fingers into his hair like I knew he liked, drawing a deep growl from him, and pulled him down into a kiss. One that I filled with every ounce of longing I'd buried inside me. Everything I kept locked away.

He pulled back, and his eyes searched mine until he found what he was looking for, and then he dove back into the kiss. His touch was rougher, more desperate than anything I'd felt.

Jax groaned, raking his fingers up my thighs and under my skirt, and cupped between my thighs. He ripped my panties off, tucking them in his pocket, then slid his fingers through my slick folds, sending a shiver through me.

"Fuck. You are so fucking responsive." He drove his fingers into my core until I was riding them, chasing my release. He bit my jaw, a low growl in his voice. "I can't wait."

I didn't want him to. I worked his belt, then his pants, until I revealed his cock. It was red and angry, straining in my hand as I guided it to my entrance. Jax lifted my right leg around his waist until only the very tips of my toes reached the ground and buried himself into me.

The tendons in his neck strained against the pleasure, and he grunted with each stroke, as if it physically pained him not to go harder.

"Fuck me, Jax."

His thrust turned feral with my permission, slamming me into the shelves, no doubt leaving marks. He worked me, and his hips pounded a hard rhythm. It was ownership at its finest, and he growled out, his orgasm filling me to the brim.

"Fuck, Sidney." His kisses turned soft, tender. "I was supposed to wait. You didn't finish."

I ran my fingers through the damp hair on each side of his temples. "Don't you dare apologize for that. I love you losing control."

He buried his face into the crook of my neck, and I moaned when he licked the sensitive skin. "Don't worry, Trouble. I'm not done with you yet."

He dropped to his knees in front of me and raised my skirt.

"Fuck, you look so good filled with my cum." He licked his mess off my inner thigh. "I can't leave you to walk around like this, or I'll fuck you in front of everyone."

I moaned, my brain flooding with the collision of how dirty but how right this felt. "Holy shit, holy shit, holy shit."

He groaned, hungrily cleaning me with his tongue. "You taste so fucking good filled with my cum."

I whimpered as lust seared through me, and the muscles in my pussy clenched, needing to be filled. He murmured his approval, sliding his fingers inside of me, and praised me over and over again. "That's it, baby. Your pussy is so perfect. It takes me so fucking well. You are so fucking beautiful when you come."

His words pushed me off the edge, and I fell into my orgasm as it crashed around me with such force my knees gave out. He caught me and pulled his fingers from my pussy and sucked them clean in front of me. "So fucking sweet, Trouble."

My mind was too fuzzy to respond. Instead, I laid my head on his shoulder, matching his breaths as I came down from the best orgasm of my life.

Jax stroked my hair and soothed a hand down my back until I could stand on my own.

His eyes met mine. "Your place or mine?"

"Anthony and Mia don't get back until Sunday."

"Fucking perfect." He led me from the stacks and gathered all my things. It felt like everyone's eyes were on me, and for once, I didn't care.

He came up behind me and pressed his rock-hard

cock into my ass. "Let's go before I fuck you on this table."

It was more of a promise than a statement. He was dead serious.

The next two days were filled with quiet moments and cuddles on the couch. He didn't leave my side the entire time, and I soaked up all of his attention.

I leaned my head back on the sofa, humming in the back of my throat as he worked the tendons in my foot with his strong hands. There were empty takeout containers on the coffee table, and the TV was playing something I couldn't be bothered to watch. We'd been playing house, and this was our last night together. I swallowed hard, pushing down the haunted feeling of what was coming.

Jax set my foot down and crawled over me, always attuned to my emotions. He placed gentle kisses along my face, finally landing on my mouth. "When do your roommates get back?"

"Early tomorrow."

He groaned and lifted me from the couch, carrying me to my room. "Then let's not waste tonight."

TWENTY-SEVEN
JAX

THE CLOCK SAID it was two in the morning. I shifted carefully so as not to wake Sid. She'd stayed here, or I'd gone to her place for the last two weeks, not wasting a second we had together, knowing that we were running out of time. I slid my fingers through her hair, letting it fall across my chest, and she nuzzled closer. I gently placed a kiss on the top of her head and breathed in her vanilla citrus scent. It was only late at night that I let the ache of what was coming settle over me. The closer we got, the more I knew I couldn't let her go. That I had to figure this out before it was too late.

Her hand slowly drifted up to my side, curling around my neck, and she tipped her head up, eyes still closed, pulling me forward. My tongue dipped into her mouth in a slow kiss, and I savored every second I got with her.

She pulled back, and my hands trembled,

cupping her face as her gaze searched mine, eyes rimmed with unshed silver. I knew mine stared back, pleading into hers. Her slim fingers traced the lines of my face, the slant of my nose, the curve of my cheekbone. One corner of her mouth lifted in a smile, but the slight wobble gave her away.

You're mine, Sidney, and you're dead wrong if you think I'm going to let you go.

She stared into my eyes, reading everything written there, and she nodded.

One word repeated itself in my head: *Mine.*

She pressed her lips against mine, and I let her lull me with her body. Losing myself in her.

The sun crept into my room when I woke, still tangled with her. Her soft hair was wrapped around us, and my heart ached in my chest. I could never ask Sid to give up her dreams, but I would try my fucking hardest to convince her to take a chance on me. That we were worth everything. Sidney, with her contagious laugh and sassy mouth, had created a gravitational pull that I never wanted to escape. The way she laughed, how she tilted her head when she pieced something together, and now the way she cuddled into my arms. All of it reminded me of home, one that I wanted to keep coming back to. I could feel the void filling up, and I was petrified of the downturn coming toward us. She was worth any compromise or sacrifice. Now I had to prove to her I was worth the same. I had her, she had me, and that was enough. Nothing else mattered. We could make everything work, right? There had to be a way. If she wasn't so freaking stubborn, maybe we could.

"Good morning." Sid's voice was muffled as she turned her face deeper into my chest. She stretched her body across mine, giving me an excellent view. Before I could do anything about it, her phone rang. Sid came to life when she saw the name across her screen. A twinge of jealousy made its way to my gut, wondering who was making her smile that way. I quickly found out I had nothing to worry about when she answered her phone.

"Hey, Dad, how are you?" Her tone lifted with her excitement.

I shifted closer, and she gave me a curious grin, but I was close enough that I could make out his reply.

"Hi, kiddo. How's my favorite kid doing?"

"I'm your only kid."

"I know, but even if you weren't, you'd still be my favorite. *Shhh...* don't tell the others." Sid's laugh filled the room, listening to her dad.

"I'm good," she said. "Same old, same old. Studying, tests, and more studying."

"You always worked too hard," he said.

Some of the joy left her face. Her dad's words were careless. Working hard wasn't something she had to do. Reaching for her goals was a part of who she was. She rolled her shoulders, seeming to shake off his words.

"Where are you now? Feels like it's been forever

since I've seen you." Her voice was light enough, but there was a hint of sadness hidden in her tone.

"I know. That's actually why I'm calling. I'm going to be in town next weekend, and I'm hoping we can meet up for an early supper." Sid's giant smile was contagious as she and her dad set up their date. It was only a few minutes before she was letting him go.

She looked over at me, still smiling, but her eyes widened when she remembered. "Crap, the proposal." Her genuine look of disappointment had me wrapping my arm around her and tucking her into my side.

"Don't worry about it. Enjoy your visit with your dad. I'll even save you some cake." I gave her a playful wink, and I was rewarded when her lip curled up at the side in a sexy grin. We kissed until her stomach grumbled. "Breakfast?"

"Hell, yes."

We spent the morning at a little coffee shop down the street. She sucked the chocolate off the tips of her fingers, finishing her croissant. "What are you looking at?" Sidney's smile was clear through her voice.

"I just thought of what else you could suck on."

Her face turned a bright red, and she clamped her fingers over my mouth. Cute, so fucking cute. "Oh my god, stop. Not even you can make that sound hot."

My smile widened under her hand as I licked her palm. She snatched it back, dancing out of the way, but I snatched it from the air and pulled her onto my lap. "What? You missed a spot," I said, giving her my best innocent smile.

"Anyone ever tell you what a big mouth you have?"

"All the better to eat you with." My cock hardened when her eyes darkened in understanding.

She tilted her head to mine and nipped gently at my bottom lip. "You are in so much trouble, Jax Ryder."

"Is that so?" I gave her a disbelieving look. "What's the punishment? Am I grounded to my room?" Her hands slid into the back of my hair as she settled herself more snugly against my quickly hardening length. I checked the other patrons, but no one looked in our direction. We were tucked into a corner, and it was an older crowd, unlikely to recognize me. She ran her fingers through the side of my hair and leaned down, lips hovering over mine.

"Can I get you anything else?" The server stood beside our table. Her eyes were pinched, and her mouth pursed, staring directly at Sid.

"No, we're fine, thanks. Just the bill." Sid went to stand, but I hauled her back down. "Where do you think you're going?" My voice was light, but my fingers tightened, holding her in place.

"Remember, we aren't making this public."

"You could've fooled me." I nipped her jaw, causing her to grind down on me. I wanted nothing more than to stay here, but, looking at the clock on my phone, she had to go to class, and I was off to practice.

Leaving money on the table to cover both of our tabs, I followed her out the door. We stopped outside the cafe. She tipped her head back to look at me, and I placed a featherlight kiss on the side of her mouth. "I have a surprise for you."

Her head tilted to the side, and her eyes sparkled with mischief, her voice filling with sass. "I'm not sure I want to know what it is."

I had to stop myself from kissing her. "You'll like it, I promise." Playing into her dirty thoughts, I watched as she leaned further into me, drawn by my words. "Be ready Friday night at six." My voice was a demand, not a request.

"I'm not sure I like this new bossy Jax." Her raspy voice and hooded eyes gave away the lie.

She turned and walked a few steps before I called her. "And Sid?"

"Yeah?" She looked back at me.

"Wear something nice."

My breath caught as Sidney walked out of her building, and I let out a low whistle. She was wearing a short black dress that showed off her long legs, and I took three deep breaths, trying to slow the pounding of my heart. Her catlike smile told me she knew exactly what she was doing to me and was wielding it as a punishment for my secrecy. Her eyes roamed over me, taking in my styled hair, black slacks, and tailored shirt. Sid's tongue peeked out, wetting her bottom lip, and lust filled me—it was going to be a long night if I couldn't get a hold of myself, and I doubted she'd approve of me dragging her back upstairs.

Opening the truck door for her reminded me of when we met. I should've known then it was inevitable we would end up here.

"You look beautiful." My voice was lower than I intended, and I closed the gap between us, pressing my mouth to hers. When we finally broke apart, her eyes were full of curiosity, and she pulled away.

I hadn't let on for a second what I had planned for tonight. It had been in the works for weeks, and the anticipation of seeing her face when she realized what we were doing had my heart pumping. After practically begging for clues via text, Sid seemed to have ultimately given up trying to spoil the surprise.

"Hurry and get in. We're on a tight schedule," I said, lifting her into her seat, and grinned at the little squeal she let out.

"What am I going to do with you?" Her voice was gruff with exasperation, but there was a smile on her face.

"Love me forever, keep me for always?" Winking at her surprised expression, I closed the door before she could respond and hurried around the truck.

After a half hour of driving in comfortable silence, I turned into the Ambassador Bridge toll.

Sid looked at me curiously. "We're going into Detroit?"

"Yup, Mia hooked me up with your passport," I said, popping the *p* like she liked to do.

"You're still not going to tell me anything?"

"Nope."

She let out a little huff but returned to looking out the window, searching for clues. I'd booked a spot in a parking lot a few blocks from our destination.

"Don't even think about it," I said when Sid's hand went to open the door. I went around to her side of the truck, opening it for her, and helped her down.

"Jax, what are we doing here?" She shivered. Even in spring, the night air was chilled. I slid my jacket around her arms. I couldn't help the grin that crossed my face when she huffed and followed me.

"We're going somewhere downtown?" Her gaze searched the area for recognition.

"Yes." We were close enough that I was okay to let a few hints slip.

Her guesses were closer. "We're going to a show?"

"Almost." I smiled as she looked incredulously at me for my nonanswers.

As we got closer, more and more people gathered, some of whom were singing in excitement. She turned her head to hear better just as we stepped around the corner. She went still and stared up at the big theater sign. A high-pitched squeal escaped her, and she jumped into my arms. She beamed, eyes bright, and a wide smile took over.

"Congratulations, Sidney, for acing your

midterm." I squeezed her tighter, eyes still roaming over her face. Her smile wobbled before she wrapped her arms around me, tucking her head deep into my chest. She took deep breaths, and I slid her feet back to the ground, wrapping myself around her. Tightness constricted my chest, knowing the emotions she was fighting against. I hoped she lost. I hoped she caved to them and let this happen.

I cupped her face with my hands and gently wiped her tears with my thumb. "This wasn't exactly the reaction I expected." I kept my voice light so she knew I was joking. Her surprised laugh surrounded us.

She looked up at me and placed a soft kiss on my lips. "Thank you. A million times, thank you."

"Anything for you." Playfully clipping her chin with my knuckle, I grabbed her hand and led her inside to watch her favorite play. *Hamilton.*

TWENTY-EIGHT
JAX

MY POUNDING heart echoed in my ears as I sucked down a breath deep into the bottom of my lungs. My legs burned with the effort to propel myself down the rink, but I ignored my body's screams to stop. Instead, I dug into the feeling, knowing that it meant I was pushing myself to my very limit.

The puck felt natural on my stick, like the two were stuck together as I weaved in and out of defensemen. We were tied two-two in the championship game, and like hell I'd let us go into overtime. No, this stopped here, with this goal.

Alex skated up my left side out of view of the players focused on me. I deked right until they moved with me before sending a blind pass to where I knew Alex was just as the defensemen crashed into me, lifting me off my feet. Pain radiated through me, and my lungs refused to take a breath, but I didn't care. All my focus was on Alex's bar down goal.

I heaved my breath and shoved the player off me. He looked utterly defeated, and I patted his head while getting up. "Good game, buddy."

He just growled. Not that I could blame him. They'd been fucking close to winning. Too fucking close, but we'd shut them down like I knew we would.

Our team was huddled around Alex, cheering our victory, but my eyes searched for the pretty brunette I knew would be in the crowd. Somehow, in the last few months, she'd become the only person I wanted to celebrate with.

My breath hitched when I spotted her wide eyes, a smile taking over her face. She bit her lower lip, knowing it drove me crazy. I skated toward her, and her eyes grew wider with each move until only a quarter inch of glass separated us.

"Meet me at the dressing room entrance," I yelled over the roar of the crowd. I didn't want to wait a single second more than I had to.

"What?" She turned her head and moved her ear closer to the glass.

"Meet me at the dressing room entrance." I shouted the words.

She shook her head, and her cheeks turned the beautiful shade of pink I loved so much. She knew that was where girlfriends waited for their men.

I stared her down, hoping she could see just how serious I was. "You better fucking be there, Trouble.

You don't want me tracking you down, and I promise you I will."

A shudder ran through her. Maybe she would like me hunting her. I stored that away for later.

Her hands wrung in front of her, and she nodded. "Hurry."

Fuck. With that word, I raced to the dressing room.

Alex charged into me, nearly knocking me over. "Buddy, that pass was wicked."

"Get off me." I broke from his arms, trying to strangle me like a motherfucking python. "I don't have time for this."

"Your girl meeting you, Jaxy?" Lucas smiled from across the dressing room. This time, instead of denying it, I smiled wide, letting every player in here know she was mine.

Alex patted my back. "You better hurry the fuck up, then. That one's skittish."

Didn't I fucking know it? It felt like any second she could disappear on me, but screw that. I was claiming her today, letting every asshole know who she was with.

Sidney's muffled voice came from the hall. "He asked me to come."

I was on my feet, half-dressed with my hockey pads still on but jerseyless.

Our security guard laughed and pushed her back. "Listen, I've heard that at least a dozen times today. That's what all the bunnies say."

Anger flashed through me, and I pulled the guard

back by his collar. "Call my girl a bunny again and I can promise you will regret it."

Both of his hands flew up in defense. "Sorry. I just—well, you know how it is."

"No, how about you tell me why you stopped my girl from coming in?"

Sidney gasped at my words. There was no way anyone missed them. The place was packed with reporters and fans.

"I—I didn't know. It won't happen again." I must've looked feral because there was genuine fear in his eyes.

"Jax, let him go. I'm fine." I instantly dropped him and moved toward Sid. I was always taller than her, but I was more than a foot taller in my skates.

She chewed on her cheek, her eyes blown wide. She always loved making me jealous. "No one touches you, Trouble."

She smirked in response. "Except you."

"Smart girl." I hauled her off her feet into my chest, eating up her squeal, followed by a giggle. I lifted her high enough so she was a few inches above me, looking down. Our eyes searched each other's while cameras clicked around us. I'd publicly claimed her, but she hadn't claimed me.

Her slow, seductive smile grew, and she leaned down, owning my mouth, showing every single person here that she was mine and I was hers.

At least for now. That thought sank like a stone, and I struggled to take my next breath. Sidney caught it, searching my gaze before capturing my lips again in an all-consuming kiss.

Fuck it. This was worth everything that was coming. She was worth it.

My coach yelled from behind me. "Hurry the hell up, Ryder. You've got press in five."

I reluctantly let her slide to the ground, my grip still tight on her hips. She looked around, her brows pulled together as she took in the dozens of cameras pointed our way.

"Eyes on me, Trouble."

She didn't hesitate, gaze flashing to mine, and I tucked a loose strand of hair behind her ear. "I'll come to your place as soon as I'm done."

It had been three days since we won the Championship, and our lives had been so busy I'd barely seen her. Now, Sid stood in my doorway, looking up at me expectantly. My smile melted from my face as she looked around, brows pinching. *Shit.* My breath caught in my chest, and my throat tightened. I'd been so caught up in everything that I didn't think about how she would react to this. Everything had been nuts since our manager called this afternoon. Apparently, the Boston manager had watched our game three days ago and was so impressed that instead of leaving after graduation, I was heading out two weeks early. It had been a bit of a clusterfuck since that moment. The guys had told a few people, and the news spread fast. Our house had been filled with people for the last few hours. Sid's cheeks were red from the crisp night air, and her head tilted to the side, looking into my eyes. A pit formed in my stomach. I didn't want to tell her this next step. I didn't want to acknowledge the end of our journey, even with the excitement of what was happening to my career.

Sid smiled up at me, looking a bit confused. The house was packed and boisterous with excitement, which was in stark contrast to its normal state. She wrapped her arms around my middle, gently pushing me back so she could get into the house. "What's going on?"

Her smile faded a bit as she saw my serious expression. *Fuck.* I should've told her as soon as I'd heard. If I wanted her to trust I would consider her first, this was a hell of a way to show it. We agreed everything would end once I left, but I was counting on Sid to give a little on this. At a minimum, for her to recognize what we had and be willing to take a chance on us. I didn't need her to follow me to Boston, but I hoped she'd wait for me. I tilted my forehead down, resting it on hers, and ran my thumb over her knuckles. My hand dwarfed hers, skin smooth as my thumb stroked over it. I wanted to pause this moment. Live in it a bit longer.

Pain radiated in my chest, knowing what I had to say, and I did my best to put on a smile. It faltered when I said the next words. "There's some good news I want to tell you about."

She searched my face. "Okay, I actually have some good news too." She drew the words out, hesitation seeping into her voice.

I led her up the stairs to the privacy of my room. She took no time to sit comfortably on my bed, having spent so much time here in recent months. She backed up to lean against the headboard, tucking her knees to her chin. I never wanted to leave this room. I took a breath, trying to act normal, but questions invaded my mind. Would she be happy for me? Had her mind changed at all? Could I possibly let her go?

I met her eyes. "The Bruins called, and they've invited me to early spring camp." I paused before delivering this next blow. "I'll be leaving a week before graduation, but after classes."

Sid's breath hitched, and her face snapped downward, hiding her reaction from me. Her only tell was the barely there tremble as she released her breath.

"Hey." I tipped her chin up so I could look at her. "This was always the plan, right?"

She flinched at my words, and I'd never hoped for someone to tell me I was wrong more than I did at this moment. My breath caught when I saw fire in her eyes, but she looked away and nodded.

Sidney stood, and her body lost its softness that was there a minute ago. "Yeah, of course."

Why couldn't I tell her I wanted the rules to change? That I was a safe bet. The truth was simple: I wasn't. I was everything she worried about. I'd never be around, but I was still standing here selfishly, wishing she would stay with me.

"That's amazing, Jax. You deserve it." Her smile grew, but it didn't reach her eyes. Coming closer, she tucked herself into my chest, and her arms tightened around me. "I had some pretty great news today too. The head of my internship finally called, and they've set up my in-person interview next weekend." She smiled up at me for real this time. "I guess we should celebrate."

I rubbed my thumbs along her cheekbones and leaned down, placing a kiss on her forehead. "Yeah... I guess we should." Except I didn't feel like celebrating. I felt like hiding in here, away from everyone and everything that was going to stand between what we had, wanting to soak up every precious diminishing moment until I left.

When we got downstairs, there were even more people here. I barely recognized any of them. Everyone wanted to be a part of the excitement. An overwhelming need to grab Sid and drag her back upstairs filled me, but before I could, she gave me another small smile, leaving my side, and headed off to see Piper.

Good. Maybe Piper could rub off on her. She was sticking it out with Lucas. She was visiting when she could during the season, and they'd stay together when we were off. She wasn't afraid to commit to him, to accept the challenge of being with a pro athlete.

Piper chose Lucas, willing to make hard sacrifices because she believed he was worth it. I knew Sid was, that we had something special, a once-in-a-lifetime kind of connection. I would spend the next two weeks doing anything I could to convince her to feel the same.

Late at night, I thought about making the sacrifice myself. I could ditch the team and follow her to Ottawa. In those moments, I truly understood why she kept her distance because even in my thoughts, I regretted it. Like she would regret not getting the life she had planned. It didn't stop me from wishing for it, though.

Lucas handed me a beer and wrapped his heavy arm around my shoulders. "Relax a bit. It's the happiest day of your life. Act like it." His voice was loud, but it was missing his usual lightness. His eyes focused on Piper, and worry coated his face. He dragged me into the other room, getting away from the girls for a bit. He was right. It was time to celebrate, not dwell on things we couldn't change.

I was talking to one of Alex's friends when Sid touched my arm. "Hey, it's late. I'm going to head home."

We'd both been busy all night talking to everyone. I'd stolen her away for a hidden kiss earlier, but she'd been preoccupied with chatting. I almost believed she was fine with me leaving sooner, but the way her arms tightened around me and her eyes roamed over me during that kiss said otherwise. We paused for a moment, foreheads pressed together, breathing in each other's air before she pulled back, giving me a weak smile, and walked away.

"What? It's only 10:30 p.m." My brows pulled down. We'd been together every night since I'd come back early from spring break.

Sid's hands ran along her arms, and I tried to meet her gaze, but she looked at the floor. The thought of her not being beside me sent a pain through my chest.

"You're not staying the night?" I stuffed my hands in my pockets, already knowing the answer.

She took a beat but shook her head no. "This party looks like it has a few hours left in it." She adjusted her bag and shrugged. "I'm tired, and I have an early shift tomorrow." Her eyes finally met mine, and there was light in them. "I'm thrilled for you. This is such a huge deal, and I'm proud. Someday soon, I'll be able to say I went to college with that guy!"

Her words stung, and a bitter taste filled my mouth. "If you weren't so stubborn, it wouldn't have to be that way."

It fucking sucks. I knew it would be hard, but it didn't mean we shouldn't try. My jaw clenched, and I stood straighter. The truth she couldn't see was she was the one leaving me.

"No need to make this harder on us. Like *you* said, this was the plan." Responding in a crisp, impersonal voice, she turned and left, with me following a few steps behind her. I stood out on the porch as she drove away, and dread filled me. Everything in me wanted to promise her it would work. That we would find a way and that all of her worries were unfounded, but deep down, I knew I'd break every promise, and she knew it too.

TWENTY-NINE
SIDNEY

"I CAN'T BELIEVE we're graduating in two weeks," Mia mumbled between mouthfuls of pasta. "Did you decide on an apartment?" We were having a long-overdue roomie supper at the Italian restaurant down the street. They made the best rigatoni and a cheese dish with honey that dreams were made of.

I'd been stalking three apartments for the last few weeks, struggling to decide between them. "Going with the smaller but closer-to-work option. I wanted that soaker tub like I need my next breath, but the commute would've been forty minutes." I lifted my hands in a "whatever" gesture.

Mia winked at me. "Think how fit you'll be walking back and forth to work."

"Uh-huh, I wasn't worried about not being fit until this very moment. *Thanks* for that." She gave me a thumbs-up and continued to shovel spaghetti into her mouth.

"It's surreal. It's going to be over. You know?"

A sliver of pain started in my chest. "I'm going to miss you."

Not only was I leaving Windsor, but Mia and I were separating. Me, to start my internship, and her, to go to medical school in Vancouver.

A loud group of girls entered the restaurant and interrupted my thoughts. Looking over my shoulder, I could see they were the girls who sat in front of Jax and me in class. The booth shook as they sat at the table behind ours. Mia was already peeking over, straining to hear what they were saying. They were loud, but I could only hear bits and pieces of their gossip.

Mia lowered her voice. "Something about a girl who's pining over some hot guy at school." She scrunched up her nose, not a fan of tearing someone down.

"Who does she think she is?" I couldn't make out who was talking. They all sounded similar, but I wasn't a fan of this one. "She can't possibly believe he's not going to ditch her at the end of the semester." The girls laughed at her little bitchy joke.

"She can't be that naïve, and those pictures!" The sound of judgment was practically rolling out of another girl's mouth.

"Talk about cheap, climbing all over him in public like that."

A bottomless pit formed in my stomach as what they said sunk in. A rational voice broke through the others. "I mean, obviously, she knows Jax is leaving for Boston. It wasn't a secret."

My breath hitched, and heat flooded my skin as dread slammed into my gut. *Shit.*

Distantly, I heard Mia calling my name. Her face was full of sympathy, which only made this worse. An overwhelming feeling of shame settled over me, and I took three slow breaths to calm my frantic heart.

Mia stood abruptly and walked behind me, looming over their table. Her face pinched, and she raised her chin to glare down at the group. They didn't stand a chance. "How would you like to be talked about like that?"

The girls all looked at her, but she cut them off before they could reply. "You aren't showing any sympathy or consideration for how your careless conversation could hurt others."

The girls glanced in my direction and winced. "You're better than this." The disappointment in Mia's tone had all the girls staring down at the table, only one speaking up.

"I'm sorry."

"You should be." Mia stormed back to our table, quickly paying the bill, and we were out of there. She didn't bring it up, but she glanced toward me every few seconds, eyes roaming over me, checking for signs of a breakdown.

As soon as we got home, we collapsed on the couch and leaned against each other. Mia shuffled endlessly through Netflix, finally choosing a horror movie. Thank god, because I couldn't stand a rom-com right now. She'd been texting back and forth with someone but monitored me as she did. Her brows furrowed in the middle, worry clear on her face. I breathed in deeply and reminded myself I'd known this was coming. I just didn't expect to have it rubbed in my face in such a shit way.

Deep breath one...

Deep breath two...

Deep breath three...

Mia rested her hand on my knee, drawing my attention. "Sidney, those girls were just jealous, but..."

"But what?" My skin itched, and my palms grew warm as the weight of what she was going to say settled over me.

Her eyes were sad, a little too glassy when she replied, "Unless you bail on the Senate, it's not going to work. Have you looked at a NHL Team's schedule?"

My heart squeezed as my ribs caved in with her words. I loved Mia, but I could shake her right now. I pushed out the words even I knew were pointless. "There's weekends."

Mia raised a brow, but softened her tone. "You mean the fifty percent of the weekends where he's not away? So what's the plan, Sidney? You see him a handful of days from October 'til potentially June?"

Everything in me screamed to tell her she was wrong, to explain all the ways Jax and I could figure out living in different cities, hell different countries, but I didn't have those answers, so I settled on.

"I'm going to miss him."

It was the first time I'd admitted it out loud, and an ache throbbed in my chest. Mia looked at me, but I rested my head on her shoulder, watching a girl get hacked to bits on TV. There was nothing to say. I wasn't a defeatist. I'd be fine after graduation. Yes, it would hurt, yes, I'd miss him, but I was moving to Ottawa and starting a new exciting internship. Jax would be preoccupied with his own excitement. I had to believe I'd be okay.

Sensing my unease, Mia asked, "Ice cream?"

I tried my hardest to keep my voice neutral. "I don't think that's going to cut it this time." A heavy weight pushed down on me, and I got up, heading to my room after the movie.

"I hope you know what you're doing, Sidney." Her voice was soft, filled with concern. *Yeah, I hope so too.*

I lay in my bed, and I couldn't stop thinking that I wanted to hit pause to enjoy this time a little longer. I was hurtling toward the end of this chapter of my life, and I wanted a reread. I knew I'd be revisiting my favorite lines and moments for years to come.

Whatever was between Jax and me was deeper, truer. I could see it in his long stares when he thought I wasn't looking, in the way he held me like he refused to let go. I knew because I felt it too. The magnetic pull that brought us together was now ripping us apart.

I'd let myself fantasize, more than once, about giving up everything to follow him. The idea was becoming more than a little tempting, but I knew Jax wouldn't let me do that. Just like I'd never let him give up his dreams. If that wasn't proof of how we felt about each other, I didn't know what was. Knowing that he felt the same didn't make it any easier. It didn't change what was coming, no matter how much I wished it did.

Hearing we had less than two weeks until he left had me shutting down. Going into survival mode, I was building my walls back up and protecting myself from what I'd always known was coming. I knew that there was only one way it would end. I was an idiot for thinking that knowing what was happening would stop it from gutting me.

My feelings had changed weeks ago. He invaded my mind in every quiet moment. The more time went by, the more I believed we belonged together. The universe didn't want us to miss out on this precious thing so few got to experience. I wished it had set us on an intertwined path instead of a diverging one. We were a perfect example of the right person at the wrong time.

My chest filled with ice, and I couldn't help the tears that escaped. This would rip my heart out, and there was nothing I could do about it.

Why did I have to fall for him? Because that was what happened. I skirted right on the line. But he kept showing me all the ways he was different, special, and, honestly, kind of magical. My brain tried to say I had this under control, but the aching crack through my heart, whenever I thought past graduation, had *liar* written all over it.

Me: What are you up to?

I'd been staring at my phone for the last few minutes, waiting for a response. My fingers ran through my hair and pulled at the root. With a groan, I put my phone down on my nightstand. *Get a hold of yourself.*

I tossed my legs over the side of the bed, sitting up, and took a deep breath in, out, in, out. With every breath, the ache hurt more. When I felt like saying screw it and wanting to make all kinds of compromises to be with Jax, I reminded myself that this was how I'd feel most of the time. *Alone.*

There was a hard knock on the front door. Startled, I jumped to my feet, jogged to the door, and peeked through the peephole. I couldn't help the wide smile that stretched my mouth.

"Let me in, Sid. I can hear you there ogling me."

The laugh I let out released all the tension with it. Opening the door, I leaned against the jamb and took him in. He was in his standard gray sweats, of course, and a dark blue Henley. His cap was tipped forward, covering his eyes, but his mouth had my attention. It dropped open, and his tongue licked his top teeth as his mouth formed a sexy smile. He met my eyes, heat gleaming in his.

"Damn, babe, you should greet me like this every time." He reached out and played with the hem of my sleep shorts. I could feel my face redden, realizing I was wearing my skimpiest shorts and a thin T-shirt. Jax nuzzled my neck and ran his nose up the side of my face with his warm breath, leaving a fiery trail behind it. He stepped back and smiled at my disgruntled protest. He held up a bag I'd been too distracted to notice. "I brought dessert."

My mouth wobbled, but I smiled. "You're an absolute saint."

His brows pinched with concern, and his free hand reached up to my jaw. "What happened?"

"Nothing that matters now. Whatcha bring me?" I rubbed my hands together in excitement and pushed away all the achy feelings of earlier. I would have plenty of time for those later.

Jax took out two chocolate explosion cheesecakes and placed them on the coffee table, along with cutlery and napkins. My mouth fell open. "How did you know?" They were my favorite as a kid, but I hadn't had one in years.

"Lucky guess." His smirk was hiding something. *Mia.* She must have been texting him. Sneaky bitch. He'd brought me cheesecake, so I couldn't complain. We sat on the couch, flipping on the TV while we mindlessly ate our dessert. Mouth filling with chocolate goodness, I sighed happily. I was wallowing in my loneliness, harping that being with him meant always being alone, only to have him show up with my favorite dessert, no less. I watched as he stuffed cake in his mouth, eyes on the TV, and an overwhelming warmth filled me. *Hope.*

A few minutes later, he got up, collected our garbage, and headed over to dump it in the trash. He grabbed a blanket on the way back, and a broad smile crossed his face when he looked at me.

"You got something here." His chuckle rumbled through the room, but I stilled as his thumb swiped across my bottom lip, and he sucked it clean.

I grinned. "You can't buy my heart with cheesecake. You need at least a full-course meal for that."

We both smiled as he stroked his thumb over my cheek. "There's the feistiness I know and love."

He placed a quick kiss on the tip of my nose before sitting on the couch, tucking me into his side. I let all the air out of my lungs. *Love.*

Jax threw the blanket over both of us and tucked me closer. The woodsy smell of him felt like an old memory and a warm bed, like coming home. I settled into the normalcy of watching shows with my boyfriend. A regular couple doing ordinary things. No impending wall we were about to slam into, and I let my thoughts drift into daydreams about what it would be like to make this permanent. If I bent on my rules, would he always be like this? I didn't know, but I was starting to think I was willing to find out.

THIRTY
SIDNEY

I FOLDED and unfolded my napkin and trailed my fingers over my thin gold watch, checking it for the tenth time, then rolled my empty wineglass between my palms. I'd finished it in a few sips when I first got here to help with the jitters of seeing my dad. Not that it helped.

He was late. He was always late.

That didn't mean he wasn't coming. *Right*? How late was "didn't show up" late? A sinking feeling started in my stomach and dropped through the floor.

How much longer could I sit here before I became truly pathetic? Pain tightened my chest, and my eyes burned. I would not cry. I should've expected this. I was just so desperate for crumbs that I grasped at the possibility of seeing him despite his words, "I'll fit you in," like I was a business appointment and not his daughter.

I didn't realize how much I'd wanted to see him. To tell him all about my new internship and maybe even about Jax. I knew he'd have issues with it, but maybe after I explained how he was, he'd have some advice. Things were different. Instead, I sat here with a red face, and pitying glances turned my way. The part hitting me the hardest was I knew better. I let my heart soften to the idea of hanging with him, wanting to believe in a different reality.

I was sure my dad would have some reasonable excuse for not showing up. Something I wouldn't be able to refute because it would be utterly rational. "Oh, sorry, kiddo. I couldn't make it because my flight was delayed, and I didn't have enough time between connections." He always had a believable reason. That was, until you realized it was Every. Single. Time.

In reality, it all came down to the fact that I wasn't important compared to his lifestyle. It was damn hard to compete with going on cruises, big celebrity parties, or playing giant arenas. You'd think he would have grown bored with that life enough to find some time to fit me in, but the opposite was true.

My dad spent barely enough time with me when I was a kid, but the longer he was a big-time coach, the more he believed his own excuses. And this right here was why I swore never to date a hockey player. It was a world complete unto itself, and it had a self-perpetuating feedback loop that made the world feel like it truly revolved around them. Asking someone to step out of that loop, to come back to earth and visit for a minute, felt like an imposition.

My hand pressed to my chest and tried to hold my heart together. Jax wasn't like that, though. He was different, *right*?

I couldn't picture him falling into his own feedback loop like my dad did. Jax was constantly thinking about how I felt and made sure I was happy. I was important to him. So why did a part of me feel like, no matter what, one day I'd end up right here again… but with Jax missing on the other side of the table?

Screw this. I refused to let my dad make me feel small. The heat of anger rose up my spine. I covered my bill, and I snatched up my phone, quickly ordering an Uber. It was time to smash some shit.

My heels crunched on the fine gravel as I stomped across the junkyard, making a beeline for the sofa. Everything was still where I wanted it, even though I hadn't been here since the time with Jax. I dug in my clutch for a hair tie, snatching my hair up into a quick ponytail. I tossed my clutch on the sofa and dragged out my favorite bat and the safety glasses.

An hour later, my brow was slick with sweat, and my hands were shaking. I dropped the bat, knowing I'd probably made a callous on my thumb. I looked at my watch again. It was just under an hour until Lucas would get Piper. Flopping onto the sofa, I dug in my clutch for my phone and shot off a quick text.

Me: How's it going? Everything in place?

Jax: What are you doing texting me? How's your dad?

Me: I'm excited for them. It's a big moment and I'm sad I'll miss it.

Jax: Have your dad swing you around when he's on his way back to the airport

Me: Well, that's going to be a problem. My dad never made it.

Jax: WTF?

My phone immediately rang. I hesitated to pick it up when I saw Jax's name scroll across the front. I took a calming breath, and I answered, "Hi."

"Sid, is everything okay? Is your dad okay?" His voice was soft, questioning.

"Yeah, I'm sure he's fine. He does this sometimes." I swallowed down the lump in my throat.

"Does what? Leaves you hanging?"

"Pretty much. You know how it is. Important jobs come first." My voice was barely a whisper.

"Seriously, that's fucked-up. When's the last time you saw him?"

"A year ago." I held the phone away from my face as I took a shuddering breath and clamped my jaw shut, not willing to cry over someone I knew better than to count on. "Jax... I don't want to talk about it."

"I'm so sorry, Sid. I know how much you were looking forward to seeing him." He let out a harsh breath, and I could picture him pacing in a circle.

Just then, Fred drove by in a truck, and a high-pitched beeping sound echoed off the towers of scrapped metal all around when he got to work.

"Trouble?" Jax could obviously hear it through the phone. "Where *are* you?" His voice was pitched low with concern.

With my hand pressed over the mic on my phone, I waited for Fred to shut off the incessant beeping.

"Sid... Sidney?"

"I just... need to blow off some steam," I blurted out. Jax went to say something, but I cut him off. "Enough about me. Tell me about the engagement!" I didn't have to force my voice to lighten as my genuine excitement shined through. "Do you think it's weird if I ask you to FaceTime with me so I can see it too?"

Muffled noise came from the other end. Jax talked to someone but must've covered the phone, just like I did.

"I'm coming to get you." It was a statement, not a question.

"What? Jax, no, you can't. There's not enough time. You can't miss it." I shook my head, even though he couldn't see me.

He paused. "You're right."

Letting out my breath, I thanked god he saw reason. "Have fun. Make sure you take pictures, and don't forget to save me a piece of cake." I forced as much cheer into my voice as I could.

"Whatever you want, Sid." There was noise on the other end of the phone, and I could tell he'd muffled it again. "I've got to run, but I'll see you later."

It used to be that the junkyard could relieve all my worries. It was my haven. My odd source of strength. My immediate confidence booster. The cheapest therapy money could buy. But it hadn't been able to work its magic tonight.

Someone cleared their throat. As if I conjured him from thin air, Jax stood there in a long-sleeved hunter-green Henley and dark-washed jeans. His hair was in its signature ruffled style, and his smile spread as his eyes roamed over me.

I was sure I must look ridiculous in my heels and cocktail dress, standing in the middle of the junkyard with safety glasses on, shit-smashing bat in hand. "How did you find me?" I dropped the bat, turning to face him.

Jax shrugged, lips tipping up in a grin. "The tow truck was a bit of a giveaway."

Instantly, a weight fell from my shoulders, and I ran to him, throwing my arms around him. "You're not supposed to be here! Lucas's proposal is more important than this," I muffled out, my face pressed into his chest, but I had no will to pull away. His strong arms tightened around me, and I met his concerned gaze.

"Lucas's delaying so I could come get you. He won't pop the question until we get there, but you better hurry." There was a smile in his voice, and his tone was warm, comforting.

"Delaying?"

"Yeah, and there's only so many tricks to keep Piper distracted, so let's go. Grab your stuff. And keep the safety glasses," he added with another smirk. "You look hot."

With all my previous worries of the day forgotten, I grinned as Jax pulled me away with him.

We crouched behind the concrete railing and looked down the line of people. Everyone was here: the guys, close friends, what must be Piper's family and friends from back home. Everyone smiled, silently waiting for the signal, telling us Lucas and Piper were in place. There was an electric joy buzzing in my chest, and Jax faced me, gaze peering into my eyes, a grin pulling at his mouth. His giddiness was contagious, and I covered my mouth to stop from laughing.

I barely caught Alex's signal from the corner of my eye, and we jumped out, flipping a giant banner with the words "Will you marry me?" written across it in bright purple letters.

All of us watched with bated breath as Piper's eyes widened. She looked from us back to Lucas, who was already down on one knee. Piper's hand covered her heart, and even from here, I could see her mouth tremble and tears rolling down. She nodded her head vigorously, and a cheer broke out as Lucas pulled her up in his arms, her legs going around his waist.

. . .

The guys had thought of everything. The venue was located only a few blocks away, and my mouth dropped when we stepped in. There was a double-length table filled with Piper's favorite foods. On the other side, there was a dance floor and a DJ setup playing '90s music. Jax and I dropped off our stuff on one of the wooden tables, and he smiled down at me, eyes wide and happy. "You look beautiful."

Heart skipping, I wrapped my arms around his middle. "You don't look half-bad yourself."

He squeezed me to him, kissing the top of my head. I didn't notice the dance floor filling with people until Jax backed up, taking my hand. "Let's dance, Trouble."

I couldn't resist the wicked grin that tilted his lips.

The music had a slow, deep bass undercurrent that screamed of late nights. Jax pulled me close to him, and we danced with my cheek against his chest. I relaxed into his body, letting the warmth seep into my skin, chasing away the pain from tonight. Lifting onto my toes, I whispered, "Thank you."

He kissed my nose, eyes light with joy for his friends. "You have nothing to thank me for."

"Yes I do. Thank you for coming for me. I didn't realize how much I needed you to."

"Sidney..." He ran his thumb along my jaw until I met his gaze, and his voice turned serious. "I will always come get you when you need me. We're a team. I would never leave you hanging."

The air whooshed out of me because I wanted to

believe him. I wanted to give it a chance. I trusted him. It felt like I was hanging over a precipice, unsure what would happen if I fell, but I didn't want to stop moving forward.

"I was thinking we could make a trip to the city the weekend of my internship meeting?" My gaze met his, and I knew he could read my hopeful expression. "We could go check out the apartments I'm looking at? Make a night of it?"

I knew he read between the lines, that this was a chance to see what it would be like if we stayed together. See how we could fit our lives together, even though there were obstacles.

"Eeeee!" A high-pitched squeal had me turning in time to catch Piper as she slammed herself into me. I got caught up in her joy, and soon, I was hugging her back and jumping with her.

Jax stepped back and smiled. "Congratulations. Let me know if he causes you any trouble." He pointed his thumb in Lucas's direction.

She beamed up at Lucas but turned back to me. "I'm happy you came. Lucas told me you almost couldn't make it." Her eyes glowed, joy radiating from her as she hugged me close. "You're practically family now. Wouldn't have been the same without you." She gave me a quick kiss on the cheek before Lucas swept her away to speak with another couple.

I watched them as they moved together in sync. Their situation wasn't much different from ours, and they were taking the jump. Sure, Piper would eventually move to wherever Lucas was playing, but that would be years away. Piper would always be the center of his universe, and if they could have that, maybe I could too.

Jax placed a gentle kiss on my head, pulling me from my thoughts and sending a shiver down my spine. My entire body sank into him. I stayed there with his arms wrapped tightly around me, even as the songs changed. Jax's fingers drifted mindlessly up and down my spine, occasionally stopping to run through my hair, and his breath skimmed my neck, sending electricity down my spine with every exhale. He hummed deep within his chest, rumbling against me every so often, arms solid, content to stay like this. I ran my fingers through the back of his hair. It had grown out a bit since I'd met him, enough that I could swirl it around my finger. He swayed me back and forth in our own rhythm as dancers moved around us. Everything in this moment was perfect.

JAX

Sidney was lying cuddled into my side as I traced designs on her back in long, slow movements. We had been like this for hours, neither of us speaking, both lost in thought.

I couldn't shake the image of her standing in the junkyard in her sleek gray dress, her shoulders tense and her knuckles white with how tight she was gripping the bat. I watched her smash through several vases before interrupting her, and anger at her dad raised in my chest. She hadn't seen him in a fucking year. No wonder she put up boundaries with men.

I gently placed a kiss on her head before I asked, "Is your dad the reason you've been going to the junkyard?" I tucked a stray strand of her hair behind her ears, and her eyes met mine.

"I found it my junior year after he bailed on a weekend with me. I needed some way to blow off steam."

I ran my thumb over her cheek, wiping away a tear trailing over her cheek, and pressed a kiss there. What she was feeling right now was why she didn't want to take the risk. I wanted to promise I'd never miss a date, but I knew that wouldn't be the truth. Life on the road was chaotic, but I had to believe I'd be different.

"What he did tonight." I paused, choosing my words carefully because, no matter how disappointed she was, Sid loved her dad. "You shouldn't have to put up with that. He was an ass for not showing or, at a minimum, not giving you a heads-up."

Shrugging, she settled herself back into me. "I'm used to it."

THIRTY-ONE
SIDNEY

MY NERVES HAD me tossing and turning all night, startling Jax into waking up at an ungodly hour. I was too nervous that something might make us late that we went into the city earlier than necessary.

Nervous energy had me bouncing around in my seat until Jax grabbed my hand.

"Hey." His voice was soft and comforting. "You've got this." He drew lazy circles on my palm, and the gentle strokes soothed my jittery nerves. He didn't let go for the rest of the drive to Ottawa.

We'd spent every available moment together over the last seven days. I wasn't sure how many TV series we'd watched cuddled up as close as possible, only separating to study for finals or to go to class. We soaked up every second we had left, not wanting to waste a single one.

I looked over toward Jax, whose mouth was

tipped up in a smile, his eyes sparkling with pride. I couldn't imagine sharing this moment with anyone else. Jax celebrated my wins with the same energy as if they were his own.

He pulled up to the building to the side of Parliament. To my disappointment, my office wouldn't actually be there.

I leaned over the truck's center console and pressed my lips into his, my fingers digging into his hair as I pulled him hard into me. I tried to express everything I was feeling without words. There was a lightness growing inside my chest, one that glowed a soft amber, that warmed me from within. Hope.

For once, I felt like there was hope, and this time, it was worth a chance. Jax's hands slid up either side of my neck, and his thumbs gently grazed my jaw. I could feel the smile forming on his lips, and mine was quick to follow as a feeling of giddiness filled me. I smiled so wide it hurt my cheeks while his eyes searched mine in silent question before his broad smile matched mine.

"We can do this, Sid."

My shoulders rose with my breath, pushing air into the bottom of my lungs before letting it all go. I pushed down the fear that was a constant presence and all the reasons this should be impossible and said the one thing I'd been dying to say for months. Ever since he'd asked that night on the phone. "I want to try."

"Yeah?" His voice was hesitant, but when I

nodded, he pulled me in for a possessive kiss, one that promised to never let me go.

Tears stung the back of my eyes, but instead of sadness, they came from hope. A hope I hadn't dared to feel in years. "I have no idea how. Honestly, the schedules will be impossible."

He cupped my face with his palms, running his thumbs over both of my cheeks, and promised, "We'll make it work. Just stay with me, and we'll make it work."

I bit my bottom lip, failing to hide my smirk, and he groaned. Jax ran his thumb along my bottom lip, releasing it from my teeth. "If you keep doing that, you're going to be late."

I glanced at the clock, and panic flashed through me. *Shit*. I pulled him in for another kiss, not wanting to leave this conversation like this. "We'll figure it out after my meeting. Together."

"Always."

The building was at least a dozen stories tall, made completely out of steel and glass. I smoothed out a few wisps of hair that had escaped my low bun in my reflection and adjusted my tailored nude blazer. Turning slightly, I made sure I wasn't wrinkled from the drive here. Movement caught my eye through the glass, and my air froze in my lungs. *Shit!* This was probably someone's office window. Heat rushed to my face. I got the hell out of there, heading toward the entrance.

A young man in a security uniform at the reception desk smiled at me, pointing toward where I had been standing outside. He chuckled as my eyes widened. "I can see clear through the glass at the people walking by. Don't worry, it happens all the time."

"Um, thanks." His warm smile helped calm my nerves a little, but it wasn't a great way to start.

He handed me a badge. "Ninth floor. Elevators are on the right."

I tried not to twitch in the elevator as I watched the numbers light up. I was already ninety-nine percent sure I would be the one to get that recommendation from Professor Carter, so this was it. This was the last hurdle. And I couldn't have done it without Jax.

Thinking of him shot warmth through my chest. We were actually going to do it. Don't get me wrong, I was terrified, but he'd shown me time and time again that he was different from my dad. I was finally admitting that to myself. I was still not comfortable that I'd be spending most of the year alone, but he was worth it. We were worth it.

The elevator dinged, and I was met with a sleekly put-together receptionist smiling at me warmly. "Hi, Miss King?"

"Yes, I'm here to see the MP Jones." Swallowing, I could only hope she couldn't make out the little tremble in my voice. My breath caught, taking in the entire wall of windows. The decor was modern and minimal, but the textiles made it look cozy. I took a deep breath in. There was a pleasant smell coming from the fresh flowers on the desk.

A young man, early forties, stepped out of the corner office and leveled me with a smile. "Sidney, right?" His voice was friendly, fitting in with his casual appearance.

"Hi." I went to shake his hand but realized he was holding a coffee. Instead, I gave the world's most awkward wave. This was the member of Parliament I was going to spend my first month shadowing. "It's so nice to meet you, MP Jones."

He laughed it off. "It's Brian. We try not to follow too much formality here." He gestured for me to follow him into his office and sat behind his desk.

His office had wall-to-wall windows overlooking an enormous park. He followed my gaze. "You should check it out. There's a great coffee cart in the middle." His hand jutted out, and I followed his pointed finger to a coffee stand just off the path.

"Thanks. I could always use an excellent coffee." Relaxing a bit, I sat across the desk from him.

He tapped on his computer and pulled up what must be my file. "I'm thrilled you could make it here. Out of all of our applicants, you stood out the most." A spark of excitement ran through me at that. I'd been busting my ass off but was secretly unsure if it would be enough. Taking a deep breath in, I tried not to give away my excitement. "Thank you. I really appreciate the internship."

He clicked through his screen and said, "And it says here, that you were the valedictorian of your high school, looking to be the same for college." *Click, click, click.* "You scored high on your last two interviews." He turned from his screen, looking directly at me. "I'll be frank. You've passed the job criteria. This was more of a personality test to see how you'll fit with us. We believe in achieving excellence, but we also work as a family. We support each other and lift each other up. Does that sound good to you?"

He didn't know how good it sounded.

"Yes, it sounds great." My voice tipped up in a near squeak.

"What makes you want to get into politics?" he asked, turning into interviewer mode but still keeping his voice casual.

"I've known I wanted to be in politics since I was a little girl. It had been my mom's dream before she passed, and I've never let it go since then."

He gave me his sympathies, but I waved him off, long past for the need of them. "I want to make a difference. I want to be a part of the change instead of a spectator."

By the time I stopped rambling, Brian's smile had spread wide. "Just what I was looking to hear. Thank you for coming in. Make sure you grab one of those coffees on your way out."

"That's it?"

"Like I was saying before, we already knew you were capable. This last step was just a check-in to make sure we're on the same page. You are going to fit in great here. Welcome to the team."

My grin was so wide it hurt my cheeks. I freaking did it.

"Samantha will take care of you on your way out. Thanks for coming in. I look forward to working with you."

"No, thank you! Thank you so much!" Desperately trying to rein myself in, I slipped through the door, walking up to Samantha's desk.

"I hear congratulations are in order. Welcome to the team." She flashed a genuine smile my way. "You'll receive an onboarding package via email in the next few days..." She handed me her business card. "If you need any help to situate yourself in the city, call me, and I'll help you out. We have a list of residences that new employees often choose to stay in because they are close by, one of which is the Pavilion up the street." She turned the card over. "If you go to this website, you'll find a registry created by the employees here. Favorite restaurants, best movie theater, hair salon suggestions. Everyone knows it's tough to move somewhere new, so over the years, we've been putting together this database to help ease your way."

My breath caught. Wow. She looked at me with knowing eyes. "Welcome to the family. See you in a few weeks." Her voice was cheery, and it followed me into the elevator.

I was stunned. It was a crazy, incredible feeling to be here. I grabbed my phone, sending a quick text to Jax and one to Mia, who responded with a GIF of an excited monkey. I waited with my phone in my hand for his reply but tucked it into my blazer pocket when the elevator door opened.

I headed to the park to wait for Jax. His manager was in town, working with a player on the Ottawa Senators, and Jax had managed to schedule a quick meeting. His meeting would be short, but neither of us expected just how fast mine would be. I was still overwhelmed with excitement, and I was barely able to restrain myself from dancing on the walk up to the coffee cart.

"Large coffee, please." I handed the attendant my money, going to the table to add my cream and sugar. That first sip had a moan slipping through my lips. MP Jones, aka Brian, wasn't kidding about how amazing this coffee was.

I sat on one of the benches that lined the path and looked at my new office building. It towered over the park, light gleaming off it. I checked the time. It'd been just under an hour since Jax dropped me off. It was fairly early, and the area was teeming with people jumping into cabs, jogging, or biking down the path. The park was full of families taking advantage of the warmth of spring. There was something magical about it. I was practically high on life.

I lost track of time, watching people coming and going. Kids running around, old men playing chess, and couples strolling down the path made me picture Jax being here with me. Speaking of which, where was he? I still hadn't heard from him, and we were pushing on two hours since he'd dropped me off. That put him a half hour late for picking me up.

Where the hell was he? An itch of anxiety crept up my neck. I sent him another quick text, asking him what was up.

After another five minutes of him not getting back to me, I called him. The phone rang out until I got his voicemail. Hanging up, I tried again. Still no answer. He'd never not answered before.

A frown pulled down my lips, and my nerves rolled in my stomach. I sucked a deep breath in, filling my lungs to calm the growing panic.

Deep breath… One.
Deep breath… Two.
Deep breath… Three.

Memories of waking up in the hospital to the news of my mother's death snuck their way through my mind, and dread pulled at my edges. Pushing them away, I waited another fifteen minutes before calling him again. It had now been two and a half hours since he'd dropped me off, an hour later than planned.

This time, I couldn't stop the panic from sinking its teeth into me. He should have been here. At the very least, he should've called back by now. I let out a frustrated growl at the feeling of hopelessness.

Okay, calm down. He was famous. If anything happened, it would be on the news. I quickly scrolled through all the major news sites, but there was nothing mentioning him. I opened up Twitter, searching for his hashtag, and my breath caught in my throat.

Photo after photo of Jax hanging out on a patio

not even ten minutes ago, standing close to none other than Selena Patronne and two people I didn't recognize. Pictures of him smiling, laughing, ones with him taking pictures with fans.

My fingers trembled, and I lost my grip on my phone as a hollow feeling of disappointment sank like a stone in my stomach, replacing the panic that burned through me seconds ago. I blinked rapidly, refusing to cry. It was my fault for believing that he would somehow be different. That I would be more important than whatever was happening in these photos that had him too distracted to even call and give me a heads-up. Looking around the park at all the smiling faces, the playing kids, the happy couples, anger sent ice creeping through my veins. I slowly rebuilt my walls, brick by brick, and waited for him to remember me.

THIRTY-TWO
JAX

I LOOKED OVER AT SID, but she was still turned toward her window. Her entire body was twisted away from me.

I fucked up.

When I checked my phone at my agent's office, I couldn't believe how much time had passed. It felt like a few minutes, not over two hours. When I saw all her texts and missed calls, a sense of foreboding sat like a weight on me. I immediately called her, listened to it ring, trepidation filling me by the time she answered. *"I'm so sorry, Sid. I'm going to be right there." Silence filled the air until finally I heard her take a deep breath.*

"Okay, see you soon."

Sidney's voice sounded wrong, too hard, too brittle. Nothing of the sassy tone she normally gave me. By the time I picked her up, I was a wreck. My hair stood on end from how many times I'd run my hand through it, but she just got into the truck, giving me a small smile. I asked about her interview, and she seemed genuinely excited about how it went. She was so understanding when I said I lost track of time. Too understanding. *Fuck.*

I tried to meet her gaze, but she kept her face turned to the window. She looked tired, and I drove faster to get back to my place. I was going to worship her tonight. Make her feel everything that I couldn't figure out how to say.

When we pulled up to the house, she was the first out of the car, but she waited for me. Her eyes didn't meet mine, and my breath constricted in my chest. She held out her hand, and I followed her to my room. Sid didn't sit on the bed. Instead, she stood in front of me and leaned her head against my chest. She trembled in my arms, and I squeezed them tighter, trying to hold us together. "I'm right here, Sidney. Talk to me."

I slid my hand over her cheek and gently tipped her face up.

"I'm..." Her breath caught. "I can't... I can't keep doing this." She straightened her shoulders, pushing back, and a hard look crossed her face. "This is why we promised to end at the end of the semester."

I stepped back from her. "First, I never promised a goddamn thing—especially not that. Second, we still have time. I'd think if you feel the way you say, you'd want to spend all the time we have left together. That's certainly how I fucking feel."

My chest felt like it was crumbling in on itself. My

voice came out in a plea as I circled her arms lightly with my hands. "Tell me what you need. Tell me what I could do. I'll do it, Sid. I'll fucking do it."

I knew this was real. She was just spooked. Everything about us was overwhelming but worth it.

She inhaled a deep breath, and I could faintly see her quietly counting. One, two, three before she stepped back. My hands hesitated, but they let her go.

She rubbed her palms over her face, pulling the hair out of her bun, and stared at me with tears in her eyes. Her voice was laced with a desperate kind of anger. "I'm such an idiot. I knew this would happen." Her words broke on a sob.

"Sid, I'm sorry. I just lost track of time. It won't happen again."

She laughed, but there was nothing funny about it. "Jax, I knew this would happen, just like I knew it would happen again. I can't do this."

Panic froze the air in my lungs, and I struggled to breathe, my words coming out hoarse. "It won't. I promise it won't. I'm so freaking sorry for forgetting to pick you up, but I promise it won't happen again."

She sniffed, and for the briefest of moments, I thought she was going to say it was fine, that nothing had changed, but what she said next fucking broke me.

Tears rolled down her cheeks, and her lips trembled. "You broke number five. Shattered it into a million little pieces I'll never be able to put back together."

It was like a shotgun to the chest, sending pain radiating from my heart out through my body, and my lungs collapsed as I processed her words. She loved me. She fucking loved me. "I can fix this."

"It's not yours to fix. This isn't something we power through. I thought I could do this. I thought..."

My heart was catching on her words, hoping she would change them. "I thought I could handle this... but I can't."

Every reason I could think of that this was stupid flooded my head. It was one time, I wouldn't forget again, I'd do better. But then she took another slow step back, holding her hand up, and I stopped myself from responding.

"It's not going to be enough, Jax. Your life will be full of amazing things, but it's not the life I want to live."

I shook my head in frustration, needing to make her understand. "I want all of those things too. We can make it work. You said you'd try." My hands tightened at my sides. "Don't you understand? You're already in... you're... inside my skin. Inside my chest. Inside my lungs. Deep within my bones, my heart, my soul. I fucking love you, Sidney."

Anguish flashed across her face. "What if you're meant to leave? What if this isn't a love story but a tragedy?"

"I'm not leaving you. I'm going to Boston, but I'm not going anywhere. You're the one trying to end this."

Her eyes met mine. There were tears pooling, ready to spill, but her shoulders were set in determination. "I'm not going to be able to make the concessions required to make this work. I need certain things in my future, and one of those things is someone to come home to. There are plenty of women who would be okay with you being gone throughout the season, but I would be miserable."

She clenched her hands together to hide them, shaking. "I won't be the reason you feel guilty about doing what you love." Her jaw clenched, and I knew what was coming before she said it. "This is over. We're over. I need this to be a clean break. There's only Professor Carter's final exam left, and we both know we're ready for it. I'm sorry. I need this to stop."

Her words vibrated through my head. This wasn't right. This couldn't be happening. I stepped toward her, then another and another. She didn't move, but she also didn't lean into me.

"I'm ripping my fucking heart out trying to decide between being here with you or with my team." I backed her into the wall. "I can't have both, and the idea of giving one up is fucking devastating." Cupping the sides of her face, I captured her mouth in a hungry kiss. I pulled away, sucking in breaths, and tried to breathe through the pain. "Fuck, Sidney, why? Why can't we just give it a shot? Why did it have to be all or nothing? I can't accept it. My heart won't let me." My fingers trembled on her skin, the world crumbling around me. I didn't look away.

But she did. "It's not your decision, Jax. It's mine. You don't need to choose between the game and me. You just have to let me go." The crack in her voice lanced through my heart.

I slid my hands down her arms and laced our fingers together. I tipped my forehead down to rest on hers and dragged in shaky breaths. Each inhale felt like a dagger sinking into my chest. *She's leaving me.* Desperately, I searched for some other option, some way that we could reverse tonight and pretend that it didn't happen. Somehow I got to keep her in my life. Keep this feeling of finally reaching happiness. Squeezing my eyes shut, I breathed in her citrusy scent for maybe the last time and closed my grip on her fingers, pleading with her. "Come with me."

I could see her heart breaking in her eyes and released her hands to wipe her loose tears with my thumbs, gently cupping her face.

"Please..." My voice cracked.

Sid stiffened, and her shoulders shook, and I kissed down the side of her face, trying to calm her as she took deep, hiccupping breaths. Her heart pounded against me, and she was staring with so much anguish I knew she felt the same. She knew how remarkable what we had was. That separating would be a special kind of torture, but it didn't stop her from straightening in my arms as if steeling herself.

Her fingers glided over my face, thumbs smoothing out my brows, knuckles dragging across my lips. Her gaze took in every detail as I did the same to her. I memorized the patterns of her freckles, the perfect green hue of her eyes, the slight puffiness of her lips. I stared back into her, and I could see what was coming. She wasn't going to let me avoid it this time. There were no more extensions, no more mercy.

"This was a mistake—"

Fuck no. I crashed my mouth into hers, cutting off her words. "Whether it's a lifetime or a moment, not a second of what's between us could ever be a mistake. Love is moment to moment. It's not dependent on how much longer you're together, and I fucking love you, Sidney. It's going to hurt like hell, but it'll have been worth it."

I pressed my lips to hers and tried to get lost in her kiss, washing away everything that was to come —wanting to feel everything that she was—never wanting to stop. I slid her against the wall as she angrily kissed me with sharp nips and bites. Her fingers dug into my hair as she pulled me into her, and she desperately reached for my shirt, pulling it up over my head. Our kisses were frantic, knowing when we stopped, it ended forever. The thought stopped me cold and sent shards of ice through my veins. It would end. It was ending.

I sucked in a shaky breath and stepped back, straightening her shirt. The realization that I couldn't stop her from tearing us apart carved into my chest. She was going to go off and be amazing, and one day, she would meet her perfect guy who wasn't always on the road, and they would have their 2.5 kids and live in their house in the suburbs, and I couldn't take that from her. She deserved to be happy, even when it was crushing me.

Cradling her head in my hands, I wiped her tears with my thumbs and searched her eyes for any other way. She stared at me, looking as desperate as I felt. I needed to let her go. She was begging me to let her be happy. I took a steady breath. "Okay, Sidney. Okay." My voice cracked, but I got the rest out. "If that's what you need, I won't press you, but know I would do anything to change your mind."

Tears streamed down her face as she pulled away from me, turned, and rushed down the stairs, nearly tripping at the bottom. I followed close behind, trying to steady her, but she was already swinging the door wide and racing out. Familiar burning filled the back of my eyes as my vision of her blurred.

She slammed herself into her car just as I heard a sob break from her, and I pulled on my hair to keep from following. This was what she wanted. I was doing what she wanted, but seeing her like this was killing me. She crumpled over the steering wheel, and her shoulders shook. Her pain was an echo of mine.

I couldn't fucking take this. I pulled open her driver's-side door, and her eyes snapped to mine, my agony reflected at me. She hiccupped as another sob racked through her.

"Shhh, it's okay, beautiful. Shh, now. It'll be okay. I promise it'll be okay," I kept whispering, gently placing one arm beneath her legs and one behind her back.

I lifted her out of the car, shut the door, and pressed my back to its side. I slid down until I was sitting on the ground, leaning against it with her cradled in my lap.

"I won't change my mind."

I kissed the top of her head. I wasn't sure who she was trying to convince, me or herself. My fingers gently stroked her back until her breathing calmed. "I know."

It took a long time before I could speak again, voice coming out thick. "What if I quit? If I don't go to Boston."

A shudder rolled through her, as if my words physically pained her. "That's not how love works. We need to let each other go before we take something special and ruin it."

She was right, but she looked so sad, like everything she wanted was conflicting with each other. I sucked in a breath and said the words I didn't want to but I knew she needed to hear. "It's okay to make your own choice."

She leaned into me, her fingers curling into my shirt. "Everyone's going to think I'm an idiot. Hell, I think I'm ridiculous."

"You are not ridiculous." My voice came out harsher than I wanted. I tipped her head back so she could read the truth in my eyes. "You don't want to do long distance. That's an understandable life decision. You have your own dreams and a brilliant career ahead of you." I held her face in my hands and tried to fill my voice with sincerity. "You're made for amazing things. You will conquer the senate. They need to watch out because you are a force of your own. It's not foolish to follow your dreams, and don't let anyone tell you it is."

My fingers stroked through her hair, and I watched it slip through my fingers. "You don't think I'm ridiculous for moving to Boston?"

A laugh escaped out of her. "That's because you're going to be famous!" Anger flashed through her eyes. "Everyone wants to be you. Of course you should go after your dreams. You'd be an idiot to stay."

I shook my head and said, "So I was right because of what? Money? Fame? They don't make my choice any better than yours. We've always known we're on diverging paths—I just didn't want to admit it. I needed to pretend for a bit so I would know what it felt like to truly have you."

I tugged hard on my hair until my scalp shouted in pain. *Fuck, I wish I could stay. I wish I could keep you.*

We sat for another half hour, and I let the feeling of her soak into my memory so I could bring it out and feel it against me when I was desperate. Sidney looked up into my eyes, but I was already staring down at her. She slid out of my arms and pushed herself up to stand.

"To dreams, then." Her mouth wobbled slightly on the words, but she held herself together. All I could do was nod at her in return. I didn't dare try to speak. I moved out of the way of her door and watched long after she drove off.

As I collapsed on my bed, a familiar pain filled me. After Marcus died, I didn't think anyone else could make me feel this way. My phone pinged, but I silenced it. The only person I wanted to talk to had just walked out of my life.

THIRTY-THREE
SIDNEY

I LAY flat on my bed and stared up at the ceiling, replaying tonight in my head. Tears streamed down my face as I struggled to take each breath. It was like a band had tightened around my chest, and each exhale constricted a little more. He'd forgotten me. Just like my dad had said he would. Just like *I knew* he would. I sniffed through my nose and wiped at my tears, but it was pointless. They hadn't stopped in hours.

I thought he was different. I thought we were different, but we weren't. Hell, I already knew love wasn't enough. That the lifestyle was too seductive to compete with. My own dad chose it over me. Pain sliced between my ribs and twisted like a knife until I gasped for air.

I thought he was different.

His arms had trembled as he held me in his lap and looked at me, defeated. My heart had screamed at me to take it all back. Lie and say it was fine so we could be together just to have a few more hours with him.

But it wasn't fine—it was never going to work. We'd both actively avoided talking about the impossibilities of being together. It was one thing to be with a pro hockey player; it was a whole other thing to live in different cities. He would only get a handful of days off during the season. At least if we lived near each other, we could see each other in the morning or at night when they played at home.

If I didn't end it, I would have watched him get further away from me, feeling my heart break hour by hour as we dragged it out until there was nothing left. It was better to end it this way.

Then why does it hurt so fucking bad?

A soft knock on my door had me sitting up and turning toward it. Mia popped her head in.

"I didn't expect you to be home tonight." She took one look at my sodden face and came to sit beside me. "Oh, honey. Are you alright?"

I sucked in a shuddering breath and fought against the wobble in my voice. "No."

Tears rolled down my face, but there was nothing I could do to stop them. I had worked so hard to be strong. But the truth was I was broken, and I wasn't sure I'd ever fit back together.

"I ended it."

Mia stiffened before pulling me into her arms and rubbing my back as I tried to take calming breaths. "Tell me what happened."

She was one of the few people who got why I couldn't just wait for him.

"He lost track of time and hung out with his agent. He was two hours late picking me up."

"Asshole."

I giggled, the sound wet with tears. "No he's not. It just *is*." The words burned down my throat as my tears came harder. I had let myself believe I could handle this, but I was falling apart. "He told me he loves me, and I believe him."

Mia didn't talk, letting me ramble my feelings out to her. "I thought maybe—" I sucked in air. "—maybe we could be different, but it'll be the same."

"I'm not sure I believe that after seeing him with you. He's crazy about you."

My back straightened as I tried to pull myself together, but my mouth wobbled even with my jaw clenched. "I know he wouldn't mean to, but my dad taught me just how impossible it is for players to love someone as much as they love the game. I just let myself forget for a little while."

Pulling my sleeve over my hand, I wiped my eyes with it and met her gaze. "I can't do that to us. You know? I can't accept half of it. We both deserve everything."

I tried to steady my voice. "Instead, I'm choosing me. I have to believe I'm important enough to make compromises for, and that's not possible if I live at the whims of a pro athlete." I sniffed in my next breath. "I wish it wasn't such a big loss. Why couldn't he have stayed the asshole I thought he was? Why did he have to prove me so thoroughly wrong?"

Mia waited until my attention turned back to her. "It's okay to make some concessions for happiness, Sidney. Life is never black and white. You're not letting him go because of your career. You're letting him go because you're afraid."

I wasn't afraid—I was terrified. Not ready to face that thought, I replied, "I can't be the only one sacrificing for this to work. I refuse to feel alone all the time. Someone someday will come along and *be* with me. One day, someone will make their life fit mine and vice versa. I have to believe that." Even as I said it, I knew I would never have something like this again. What Jax and I had was once in a lifetime.

She wrapped me in her arms and flipped on the TV. "Sometimes paths separate, but that doesn't mean you weren't supposed to walk them."

"When did you get so smart?" I said, my voice cracking.

She gave me a wobbly smile that had me looking closer at her. Her eyes were sunken and puffy. She looked like she'd been crying. "You aren't the only one who's made mistakes these past few months. I got too close to the fire and got burned."

"You mean with Alex?" She nodded. "Is that how he got the black eye I saw at the party?"

She laughed at that, and some tension drained from her shoulders. "I may have made the mistake of falling for both Alex and River."

"Oh, shit." It took a second to let that sink in.

"Exactly," she sniffed, but her face didn't falter. "It wasn't fair to come between them. Hell, I didn't *want* to come between them. I just couldn't help how I felt." Her eyes looked at me for understanding.

I lifted my hands up in front of me, making sure she understood. "Don't worry about me judging you. I'm the queen of letting her heart screw things up."

"I had to end it. River blamed Alex. It was a fucking mess."

I held her close for several minutes before pulling myself together and getting up. "One second."

I headed to the kitchen to grab two beers and popped the top off both, handing her one. "Screw 'em. Here's to being successful women. No man can hold us down." The words tasted sour on my tongue, but I pushed them out anyway.

"Fuck 'em!" she shouted and clinked her bottle with mine.

THIRTY-FOUR
ONE WEEK LATER
SIDNEY

JAX SAT on his silver Suitcase and tugged at his hair, completely oblivious to the chaos around him. I was too far away to make out his features, but he was paler than normal and looked like he was wearing two-day-old clothes. My heart ached at the picture he made and I desperately wanted to run to, but my feet remained planted, my body hidden behind the house across the street. My eyes roamed over him, eating up every detail, knowing this would be the last time I saw him, and my chest burned at the thought. I swallowed back a sob and quickly wiped away my tears with the ends of my sleeves.

The yard was pure chaos. His teammates moved in and out of the house, hauling the guys' things into a moving van. All four of them were off to spring camp together.

"What are you doing here, Sid?" Alex's firm voice

came from behind me, and I jumped a good foot in the air, a squeak escaping from my mouth.

"Jesus Christ, Alex. You scared the shit out of me." My hand went to my heart trying to beat its way out of my chest.

He nodded in Jax's direction. "Go talk to him. He'll want to see you. Know that you came."

"I can't." My voice caught on the words. "It'll only make it worse."

I pulled back my shoulders and plastered on a faltering smile. "Anyway, I'm just a fan now. I'll be following along from afar."

Alex shook his head, his hands landing on my shoulders, shaking me. His voice was low and serious. "You could never be *just a fan*. Never. You've got to know that. He would give you anything."

Alex stepped back, a small smile on his face breaking the intensity of the moment. "Now, where's Mia? I'm assuming she came with you" Alex's eyes roamed the alley, searching for where she hid.

Sadness filled my voice, knowing I was breaking a part of him. "She didn't come."

Mia had watched me get ready but refused to go anywhere near them.

Alex's smile faltered, and he shook his head, taking a deep breath in as he stared through me, nodding once, twice, his body rigid, before throwing his coffee against the wall. I jumped back from the spray, and Alex looked at me, shocked, like he'd forgotten I was there.

"Shit, sorry." He looked around one last time,

then wrapped me in a bear hug, lifting me off my feet. "I hope this isn't goodbye but see you later."

He took off toward his house, and I looked for Jax one last time, but he was gone. Tears stung my eyes, and my hands curled at my sides. I said the words one last time. "I love you."

Turning away, I didn't look back at the dream I could've had.

THIRTY-FIVE
TWO WEEKS LATER
JAX

I SHOT the puck and watched it slide between the goalie's legs, and the crowd erupted with the winning goal. Erikson, the starting forward for Boston, tapped the top of my helmet. "Good job, kid."

Pride filled my chest, and I looked around the rink, looking for someone I already knew wouldn't be there. Pain radiated from my heart, and I had to tamp it down. I'd buried everything to do with her since she'd ended it, putting up a wall of ice to stop myself from falling apart.

Everyone was talking a mile a minute in the dressing room. I tried to keep my dark mood to myself, but I could tell that I was sucking the life out of the celebration. I quickly changed and headed back to the place I shared with the guys. It wasn't much different from our old house.

"Hey, man." Lucas beat me home and was

already whispering on his phone. "I love you too. Can't wait to see you next weekend. I booked us a hotel."

A sharp pain went through me as I pictured calling Sid after a game and telling her all about it. Why the hell wouldn't she give it a chance? I deserved a shot at this. We could've made it work.

Lucas hung up the phone and turned toward me. "Listen, man, I know you do your own thing and don't want anyone else's opinion, but this thing between you and Sidney. It was real. You looked at her the way I look at Piper."

"She broke it off." I couldn't help the growl of frustration from entering my voice.

"Yeah, but have you done anything different? You're so caught up in her not wanting to wait around for you, but did you ever consider sacrificing for her?"

"Like quitting the team? Does it really have to be all or nothing?"

"Nah, man, I don't mean quitting the team." He shook his head as if he didn't know what to do with me. "Show her she matters, that it isn't only about your career. That she'll always come first." He ran his hand through his hair in exasperation. "Listen, man, these girls make hella sacrifices. They've got to put their trust in us, even when our jobs are full of temptations. They literally hang their hearts out, and you aren't giving her any reason to believe you won't crush it." He blew out a long breath.

"I told her I love her, and she left me anyway."

"Was that before or after you forgot to pick her up?" His voice was so sharp he practically hissed at me.

"It was a mistake." I left him standing there, still glaring at me.

As I lay in my bed later that night, Lucas's words streamed through my head, and anger rolled over me in waves. Fuck him for saying I hadn't done enough. I'd laid myself bare, told her I loved her. She didn't want it. I closed my eyes but, I couldn't help but pull her picture up as I fell asleep. I typed a text but stopped. Who was I kidding? This was what she wanted. I needed to get over her.

SIDNEY

Banging on my bedroom door had me jumping out of bed. Mia popped her head inside. "Sidney, it's graduation day. Pull yourself together, and let's do this." Her voice was full of forced peppiness, but her eyes were full of concern. It'd been weeks since I'd seen Jax, and that constant ache hadn't lifted.

I barely left my room, and when I had, it'd been to eat ice cream and binge on shitty reality TV. There was a void in my chest, and I'd put it there. Every part of me said that getting involved with Jax was a bad idea, but the force that had brought us together was stronger than I had ever been. It was naïve to think that feelings wouldn't get involved. In my attempt to avoid being brokenhearted, I'd shattered myself. Doubt crept in from the first moment. How could something that I needed hurt so badly?

Ending things had to be the hardest thing I would ever do. One day, I would look back on this and know that it had to happen. Probably while chasing after my kids as my husband made dinner. I wanted a father for my kids who was going to be there for them. Growing up with an absent dad who traveled for a normal job was hard, but hockey players spend six months or more on the road.

I knew all the rational reasons I'd had to end it. I'd played them on repeat since that night weeks ago, when he'd held me until I had calmed after I imploded our relationship.

But when my guard fell, the quiet voice slipped in. Why couldn't we have tried? Why couldn't I have compromised? When I was feeling masochistic, I thought of all the ways that he'd proved he wasn't like my dad. The little things like knowing I'd be tired and showing up with coffee and my favorite breakfast all the way to big things like delaying his best friend's proposal because he believed I belonged there with them. I was a part of their group. He and I were a team.

I pushed my palm hard against the ache in my chest as the pain shredded through my heart. I'd pushed him away. The deeper, darker thing that I was terrified of was if I'd truly ended it to protect my future happiness, or had I done it out of fear of losing whatever this was? Because I lost it anyway, and I kept trying to convince myself I didn't want it back.

I got dressed and came out of my room, where Mia was already waiting for me. Her eyes were soft, and she looked at me like I was a wounded animal. If it wasn't so tragic, it would be funny.

"It's going to be okay. Not every love story is forever." Her voice was calming, but it stung. No matter how many times I told myself that, I came to the same thought. *I wish it was forever*. I wish we'd found a way. I wish we lived in the same freaking country. When I was tired, I let myself picture following him to Boston, and surprising him after one of his games. The way his face would light up, and he'd smile so wide his dimples would show. God, I missed him. The idea of being wrapped in his warmth was like a seduction, one that would cost me the future I'd wanted, the one that had soured with what it cost. No matter how tempting it was, Jax would never want me to do that, leaving me exactly where I was now. Heartbroken.

The ceremony was long, with my dad conveniently forgetting to attend, but an overwhelming feeling of pride still overtook me. *I did it*. I'd started out on this path with a plan, and I'd made it through, and now I was onto phase two. I desperately wanted to call Jax, to hear his voice congratulating me, but the person who understood what I was going through was the person I couldn't reach out to, knowing it would hurt us both. Thinking about where he was right now, I pictured him skating with his team, and a smile tipped my lips. He deserved it. He deserved all of it. He was amazing, and he was going to find some actress or supermodel who was in the business and had a similar schedule, and they were going to have the happiness we couldn't. Jealousy filled me as tears built in my eyes, but I fought against them. I'd done this.

My phone buzzed in my hand.

Jax: Congratulations, Sidney, I'm proud of you.

My heart slammed in my chest that he knew how much I'd want to hear from him today. I felt shattered now that I had. Gently tracing the words over the screen, I typed back.

Me: We did it. We reached for big dreams and somehow, we've made it.

I felt tears drip down my cheek, and rawness scratched at my skin, knowing what I'd given up. Straightening, I wiped my eyes and went to find Mia. Tonight, we would celebrate. Or, at the very least, I'd get drunk enough to forget.

THIRTY-SIX
ONE MONTH AFTER
SIDNEY

I WALKED into my apartment after a few drinks with my new coworkers and sighed at the state of the place. I'd moved here a week ago, and there were still boxes covering the floor, needing to be unpacked.

I hadn't had the energy to put anything away. Don't get me wrong, my team was phenomenal, but when I got home, all I wanted to do was call Jax and tell him about my day. I wanted to tell him about my officemate, who liked to listen to '80s rap, and that I was starting to learn the songs, or describe how awesome my office was, with a small window that looked over the park where I'd found the perfect sweets shop. They made the best chocolate croissants that always made me think of him.

Since I couldn't do any of that, I crashed on the couch and flicked through Netflix while living off takeout. Not my finest moments. When I was feeling desperate, I scrolled through his Instagram feed, looking for glimpses of him. Turned out I had masochistic tendencies because every post hurt.

Mia's voice came through our video call a mile a minute. She was excited because she was already first in her class. *Like I ever doubted her.*

She was happy, and my shoulders relaxed as relief washed through me. She'd never opened up about what had happened between her, Alex, and River, but her smiles hadn't reached her eyes in months. Before I left for my new job, I could hear her crying at night, but she'd always deny it in the morning.

Misery may love company, but I was happy my friend was breaking through it. Which was more than I could say about myself. It had been two months, and the ache wasn't dissipating. I just wanted to call him even more. Late at night, when I couldn't sleep, I let myself think about how things could've turned out differently had I been a little braver.

I pictured myself flying out to surprise him at one of his games. How his broad smile would take over his face and his dimples would be on full display. I let myself imagine the warmth of his arms and tried to remember his woodsy smell.

It was becoming a special form of self-torture.

JAX

River crashed down on our couch beside me. "Just fucking call her, man."

I groaned. "You know I can't do that." Putting my elbows on my knees, I held my head in my hands.

"No, I know you *won't* do that."

It was hypocritical of him to call me out like this—he and Alex were barely talking to each other.

"You're one to talk," I snapped. "Why don't you just call *your* girl?"

He knew exactly who I was talking about. I was so involved with what was happening between Sid and me that I'd completely missed what was happening between Alex, River, and Mia.

He deadpanned, "Because she didn't choose me, *asshole.*" His voice came out hard, and his body stiffened.

I smiled. "Are you sure about that?"

River glared at me. Good. At least he'd stop trying to give me advice.

THIRTY-SEVEN
TWO MONTHS LATER
JAX

"HOW DO you feel about being called this year's most anticipated rookie, Ryder?" the reporter from Sportsnet asked. Jared was clean-cut, with a strong jaw and a lazy grin, no doubt a holdover from his past years of playing pro. I'd watched him on TV since I was a kid and dreamed about this exact fucking moment. Countless other athletes had sat at this same table, answering millions of questions to a room full of eager reporters just waiting for the next sound bite over the years. I'd pictured myself up here more times than I could count.

This should've been a dream come true, but the question grated on my skin, not because it was at least the one hundredth time they'd asked it since they'd started calling me that a week ago. Of fucking course it wasn't—that would be too easy. No, I hated the question because every time I answered was a lie.

I smiled at the reporter, keeping my collected mask in place. "Nothing could make me happier, Jared. Best thing that's ever happened to me."

He gave me a genuine smile and continued the standard questions. This press meeting wasn't really about me. I'd just been thrown up here as filler until our new coach was announced. If you asked me, all this secrecy was bullshit. It was hockey, not a fucking soap opera, but apparently, the league was taking things in a more dramatic fashion because they were announcing the Bruins' new coach on live fucking TV, and I was the lucky bastard being used to fill airtime until he showed up.

I answered on autopilot, no one sensing that the mask I wore of a young, excited hockey player was complete bullshit.

"I know you worked hard for this, Ryder. Sacrificed a lot like all players do. Why don't you tell us a little about that."

Fuck, his words stung. The muscles ticked in my jaw with the effort to keep my carefree facade in place. I was just named the most anticipated player of the season; no rookie wouldn't be high off that. Except Jared was right. I had made a sacrifice to get here, and every day, I wondered if it was worth it because in moments like this, I swore it fucking wasn't.

I swallowed hard and forced myself to answer. "You know, same thing as everyone else. Late nights, early practices. Learned to push through the pain years ago."

The lie tasted like acid and burned down my throat, where it landed heavily in my stomach. I rubbed my palms over my face, hoping I just looked tired after practice and not fucking heartbroken. I needed them to move on with their questions to something more technical related, or I was going to fucking lose it up here.

The same woman who'd announced my entrance walked up to the podium and tapped the mic twice. She wore a black tailored jacket and matching pencil skirt. She was objectively hot. Not that it mattered. Fucking Alex had encouraged me to bury myself in pussy like he'd been doing, but I had no fucking interest. The only person I wanted didn't want me back, and no one mattered but her.

The woman tapped the mic again, and the room went completely silent. She smiled. "I'm excited to announce the new coach has arrived and will be coming out to meet you in the next few moments."

The crowd buzzed with excitement, the reporters too busy talking with each other, speculating who it could be, to pay attention to me. I should care who our coach was—we'd be spending a lot of time together—but truth was I couldn't give a shit, and I wasn't sure when I would again.

The man in question walked through the door behind me, bigger than life. I vaguely recognized him as the coach for the Kraken. He looked like a decent enough guy as he came up to me and grasped my hand, giving it a firm shake. "Good to meet you, kid."

My answer caught in my throat as I met his eyes. They were a familiar hazel brown rimmed with crisp green-apple centers. The world tipped on its axis, everything feeling wrong and out of place as my brain tried to process that he had identical eyes to Sidney.

The woman announced his name, and all the pieces clicked into place. "Let me introduce the Boston Bruins' new coach, Mark King."

Fuck. I tried to push down the rage bubbling inside me as I stared at the asshole who'd practically abandoned the most amazing girl I'd ever met, but my grip tightened on his, not letting his hand go when I really fucking should've.

"You're Sidney's dad?" I practically spat the question, unable to hold back just how pissed I was.

My new coach pulled his hand from mine, breaking our awkward handshake, and stared me down. "So, you're the guy."

"I'm the guy." My blood pulsed in my ears. They looked so fucking similar, him just a hyper-masculine version of her, and my brain finally caught up to the fact Sidney had never told me her dad was a coach.

He must have seen my confusion because he continued, keeping his voice low so as not to tip off the press as to what we were talking about. All they'd see is a regular first meeting between a coach and player. "You know, I'm not surprised she hasn't mentioned me. She's never been a fan of fame or anything that comes with it."

His words confirmed my thoughts. *This fucktwit asshole coach is Sid's dad.*

He didn't notice the tension that filled my shoulders. "She's pissed that I don't see her much, but that's pro hockey life. I don't have to tell you; you know how it is. Who's got time to head back?"

For fuck's sake.

This whole time, I thought Sidney didn't want to stay together once I was on tour because she was afraid of the unknown, but it was clear now that she knew exactly what she was afraid of. Rage roiled in my stomach.

"No, I don't get it. Your daughter is *fucking* spectacular. What is wrong with you?" I hissed the words at him.

Sid's dad—*her dad*—shrugged at me. "You're new to this, kid. Trust me, one day very soon, you'll understand." His hand landed on my arm, and I flinched. "Before you know it, there will be a million people pulling you in a million different ways. Everyone will want a piece of you. Me, the girls, the fans, the press. Young players always think they'll be able to balance a normal life, but it's not possible." He patted my shoulder. "We're better off as lone wolves."

I shook off his hand, and my skin tightened with the effort to keep it together. I didn't want to be a lone wolf. No wonder she hated everything about this life. This was the example her dad had set all these years?

"Sid's fucking amazing," I snapped at him, my

voice carrying through the room. I barely noticed the press staring at us as rage exploded from me until I was screaming at him. "She loves you. You can't even make time to see her? You can't take a fucking weekend out of your schedule?"

His eyebrows rose at my tone. "Kid, you're fucking close to ruining your career. No girl is worth that."

"She's your fucking daughter." My hands tightened into fists. "Not. Worth. It? You have no fucking idea what you've been missing."

"You're making a mistake, Ryder." He didn't look sorry for what he'd done. The asshole looked smug.

I lost control of my anger and shoved him hard until he stumbled back. I took advantage of his off-balanced position and slammed my fist into his face, enjoying the loud crack of bone. "My only mistake was not choosing her."

Noise in the room came crashing back around me as I looked away from her dad. Every reporter in here had their camera pointed at me and was excitedly speaking into their microphone.

I took one last look at Sid's dad, glaring up at me from the floor. "*Asshole.*" I stepped over him, walked out of the room, and called my manager.

He answered immediately. "What the hell, Jax. You know you just ruined your career."

"Get me a meeting with the manager for the Senators," I demanded and hung up the phone. Sidney better be ready because I was coming for her. This time, I wasn't letting go.

SIDNEY

Mia: Facetime 5 minutes.

Me: I'm in the middle of something right now.

Who cared that "something" referred to bingeing back-to-back reality TV shows on my Saturday night. They didn't need to know how pathetic my life had become. The shrill ring of FaceTime interrupted my show as a window popped up on my laptop screen. I was about to close it when Anthony's text came through.

Anthony: Answer the call, Cupcake. You're going to want to see this.

Curiosity officially piqued, I clicked the Accept button and was immediately met with two giddy faces.

"This had better be good."

"You have no fucking idea." Anthony's wide smile took up most of his face as he typed something into the chat. "Sent you the link."

I hesitated a moment too long, and Mia groaned. "Just click it."

The link brought me to a sports news site, and apprehension settled in my gut. I met my best friends' faces. "Guys, I don't want to hear anything about him."

"Oh, honey, this you're going to want to see," Mia insisted, and I clicked Play.

The newscaster was talking in front of a paused video, but I was too focused on Jax's still image to process what he said. Jax looked good, hair in his signature ruffled state, and he was rocking that adorable dimple of his. It was a sweet, torturous type of pain to see him living his new life. For how much it hurt to be separated, I was so fucking proud of him.

I sucked in a breath when the newscaster played the video. The image of Jax standing as a man walked into the press conference room took up the full screen. I sucked in a sharp breath as my *dad* grasped Jax's hand. Holy shit.

I searched the screen for the title, and there in bold letters was "New Coach for the Boston Bruins Meets This Year's Star Rookie." The air in my lungs started to burn, and I was forced to let it out. "What the hell is happening?"

"Just keep watching." Anthony startled me—I'd forgotten they were there.

My dad and Jax stood close together, having a low, private conversation the microphones couldn't pick up. Even without words, I could see Jax's growing agitation. The muscles in his neck ticked, and his hands fisted at his side. Whatever they were talking about, Jax didn't like it.

My dad pulled back and put his hand on Jax's shoulder, continuing to talk. He looked at ease, obviously not seeing the rage written across Jax's face.

"*Sid's fucking amazing.*" Jax's voice carried through the room. Jesus. They were talking about me. It felt like seconds before Jax pushed my dad backward, and I held my breath, watching them. Jax was fighting my dad. Jax was fighting my dad, *for me*!

I gasped when Jax landed a punch and laid my dad out on the floor. *"My only mistake was not choosing her."*

He punched him. He punched my dad. My heart stopped, then doubled in speed as his words sank in. Gratitude and terror pummeled me at what he'd done. He'd just publicly ruined his career. All because he knew how much my dad hurt me. There was no way he'd be allowed to play for the Bruins now. Pain lanced my heart, and my eyes burned with tears. I couldn't let him do this.

"What time did this happen?" I asked my friends, not caring who answered.

"Two hours ago," Mia replied. "Sidney, what's that look on your face? What are you going to do?"

Determination filled my veins. "I'm going to fix this."

I hung up the call with them and immediately dialed my dad. It took several attempts before he answered, and I sucked in a breath when I saw his face. There were some bandages on his nose and a faint purple hue of new bruises already forming under his eyes. By tomorrow, he'd look like a raccoon with two black eyes.

"Sidney, if you're calling to defend your friend, don't bother. I've already cut him from the team."

"Then uncut him."

"What? How do you think this works? Do you think I can just let players go around punching me? You're supposed to be smart."

I swallowed hard, knowing he was right but not

caring. "You owe me. You owe me for every missed birthday or forgotten supper." My voice rose with each word as years' worth of anger flowed from me. "For every time you promised to see me but didn't show up. For every single hour that I waited for you and every tear I cried." I sucked in a breath, making sure to articulate every single word. "You. Owe. Me. Explain to the media it was a misunderstanding or some kind of social stunt and uncut him."

My dad stared at me, stunned for several seconds, before letting his breath out on a sigh. "Okay, Sidney. I'll see what I can do."

"You better, Dad, because I'll never talk to you again unless you fix this."

THIRTY-EIGHT
TWO AND A HALF MONTHS LATER
SIDNEY

"COMING! One sec, I'll be right there." My foot caught on the corner of one of the boxes I still hadn't unpacked as I rushed to answer the door. I let out a high-pitched squeak, jumping on one foot as the sting radiated through my toe. *Shit, shit, shit.*

There was another knock, and I steadied myself before closing the last few feet. I swung it open, expecting to see the Chinese restaurant delivery guy, and the air was sucked from my chest. The face that had been haunting me every time I closed my eyes stared back at me. My trembling fingers reached up to his chest before I could even think about it while his greedy eyes roamed all over me, taking in every detail.

The last time I'd seen him was at his press conference. "You punched my dad."

"Fucking right, I did. Asshole deserved it." I couldn't argue with that. I'd enjoyed seeing Jax hit him more than I should have. Jax grabbed my hand, entwining our fingers, but didn't step into my place. "I know what you said, and I know you don't think I should be here, but I couldn't live with myself unless I got this off of my chest." I watched as his hand raked through his hair and tugged until it stood on end.

"When I met your dad, Sid..." he said, voice stern. "I finally understand, but you're wrong about me. I get you have a history with an asshole hockey player who constantly bailed on you. I get that living with a narcissist would be fucking horrible." Stepping into me, he cupped the side of my neck and stroked his thumb up my jaw, gently coaxing my head back until my gaze met his. "You should know I'm not that guy. I get it's a bone-deep worry for you, but I'm not him."

Warmth built in my chest, radiating through me until my entire body began to hum with a soft buzz, overwhelmed with what he was saying. Jax accepted my silence as permission to keep going. "I get it now. You have it in your head that you're not my priority. You're worried that I'll abandon you like he did. But I'm not worried about that at all because I know damn well that's never going to happen. My career will never be more important than you. Hockey is a part of me, but playing for Boston isn't. It's not asking too much of me to put you first, and I'm all in. I'm all in, Sid."

He took a shuddering breath, not moving his gaze from mine. "It took me a while to figure it out, but there's something you need to hear." He lowered his head closer. "You are worth it." My breath caught, but he didn't stop. "I was in such a dark place when I met you. I was constantly sinking under the weight of trying to live up to what Marcus would've achieved. You convinced me I was enough. You took that weight from me. You saw me when no one else did. I could never put you second."

I sucked in a breath, making a high-pitched sound, part sob, part squeal, and his thumb stroked my cheek again, a smile tipping up his lips. "I'm moving to Ottawa."

"What?" An oily, dirty feeling coated my stomach, washing away my giddiness. I didn't want him to give up his dream for me. I couldn't let him. "But my dad said he'd take you back."

"I turned him down."

"You can't."

"I did." A grin pulled at the corner of his mouth, growing until his dimple appeared. "I'm starting with the Ottawa Senators next week."

His words had me reeling. The last I'd seen him, he'd been punching my dad, and if I knew anything about professional sports, punching your coach wouldn't land you a good trade.

"How," I breathed, worried about his answer, but the smile never left his eyes, and some of my concern washed away.

"Don't tell me you forgot I'm Jaxton Ryder. Best player in our division. Don't tell me you doubted my ability to land a new team."

I rolled my eyes and huffed out a breath, equally exasperated and thrilled to have his teasing tone back in my life. "Serious, Jax. You should've been blacklisted."

His clear gray eyes pierced mine, and his smirk turned playful. "Turns out the Senators' manager has a daughter our age. He heard my interview and agreed your dad got what he deserved. Fuck, I wouldn't be surprised if he went extra hard on him this year."

His words whirled in my head, slowly clicking into place. "You did it for me?"

"Sid, there's nothing I wouldn't do for you." His hands tightened, and he gave me a little shake, his excitement visible in the way his face lit up. "When we have kids, you better fucking believe they will be my top priority. We both have years left to build our careers. But Sidney, when you're ready to start a family, I'll be right there with you. It's not a sacrifice to love you. It's a fucking privilege."

My lungs filled with a shocked breath. *When we have kids.*

He gave me a sheepish smile, realizing what he'd just said. "That's... if you want kids." He stroked his thumb over my cheek in a soothing motion, catching the tears I didn't know were falling.

It took a second to process everything he'd just said. He wasn't leaving me. He was prioritizing me. He was never going to be like my dad. He was moving to Ottawa.

"You want to move here with me?" My voice was

whisper-quiet, and his arms wrapped around my waist.

"Hell yes, I do. I don't know how you ever doubted that," he answered in a clear voice.

"You don't care that you won't be playing for Boston?"

He barked out a laugh. "Not for a fucking second." His hand cupped the back of my neck, tilting my head up. "Will you give us a real chance, Sid? I know you're afraid I'll end up like your dad, but I can promise you I will spend every day proving that wrong. Before you know it, it'll be a distant worry you won't think about, but you have to let me prove it. I won't leave you. I will always put you first. Put our life together first."

"Our life." I mouthed the words.

"I meant all of it when I told you I love you, but I didn't realize that you might not know what love really means. What it can be. It's not just a feeling. It's the importance we put on that person. Love is caring about what the other person needs, and I fucking do. You matter to me."

A hiccup escaped as I cried, and his head lowered, leaning his forehead on mine. "You're worth it. You're worth more. We won't regret this." I watched as his chest expanded with a big breath of air, and he hesitated before asking, "Am I worth it, Sid?"

Jax's face was shuttered, trying not to influence my decision. His worry shifted to hope when my arms circled around him.

"You are," I promised.

A smile stretched across his face, and he picked me up, swinging us in a circle. An overwhelming feeling of home settled over me. This was where I belonged. I couldn't believe I thought I could live without him. When he came to a stop and slid me to the ground, I grabbed his cheeks in my hands and tugged him down until his eyes were level with mine. They burned with tears, but I smiled so wide it hurt my cheeks. "I love you, Jaxton Ryder."

His mouth crashed over mine as his arms wrapped tight around me. "God, I've thought of hearing that again a million times, but nothing's as sweet as you saying it." His fingers smoothed the hair from my face. "Say it again."

"I love you."

JAX

I ran my fingers through Sid's hair, listening to her deep breaths where she was laid out across me. We hadn't left her apartment all weekend, spending every second catching up on the last few months. The time apart had left us both insatiable; I doubted there was an inch of this apartment that I hadn't had her pinned against. Her arms tightened around me, and she mumbled something into my chest.

She better hold on because I was never letting go.

THIRTY-NINE
FOUR YEARS LATER
SIDNEY

JAX'S FACE appeared on my phone screen, his broad smile showing off his dimples. "Hey, babe, you look beautiful."

"You can barely see my face." My voice was full of laughter.

"I don't need to. I know." His grin turned wicked, and I had to fight back my blush.

Running around our house, I asked him about the city he was in as I grabbed my purse and jacket, late to meet Mia. Today, we were celebrating my decision to run in an election. Surprisingly, Jax didn't say much about it, but he did send me a bouquet every day since I'd made the decision. The last four years had had their ups and downs, but he never broke his promise. We made time for each other despite our busy careers, and he was always there for me, even when he was out of town. Sharing moments like this over FaceTime was an adjustment, but it worked, and he was worth it.

A knock sounded on the door. Shit, I was already going to be late. "Coming."

Jax watched me from the screen, but I couldn't make out where he was with the camera so close to his face. "I've got to get this. Hold on."

I pulled the door open and was immediately swung up in strong, muscled arms.

Warmth filled my chest, and tears pooled in my eyes as laughter burst from me. "You're here."

"Always." He kissed me softly before pulling back. "I wouldn't miss this for the fucking world."

Joy flashed through me. "I love you, Jax."

"I fucking love you, and I'll keep proving to you that you'll always be worth it."

EXTENDED EPILOGUE

JAX

"ROOM SERVICE." A loud knock rang through my hotel room.

Fuck. I wrapped a towel around my waist, having barely stepped out of the shower, and entered the large open-concept room. There was a time I'd loved these executive suites with their modern design and extremely comfortable beds. Now, they just reminded me that I wasn't home. Especially today.

It was Sid's and my anniversary, and even though I'd spoken to her late last night, I was still disappointed when she didn't answer her phone this morning. We did our best to be together for the days that mattered, whether that was me staying home or her coming to travel with me.

Our plans for the weekend were to explore Grand Bend for the weekend, spend our nights in a cozy rented cabin and our days on the beach. It sounded fucking perfect to me. That was until I got a letter from our old university congratulating me for being awarded the Excellence Award.

They requested I come down and give a speech to the incoming year's team. My immediate reaction was to excuse myself out of it and volunteer Alex, but Sid had insisted. She'd made an actual spreadsheet filled with multiple reasons why I couldn't cancel that I couldn't remember anymore. Sid decided to use the time to catch up on work so we could rebook the cabin for the following weekend, and now I was here… without her.

At least Lucas was coming in today, also for an award.

A quick rap on the door had me wrapping the towel tighter around my hips and jogging the last few steps to the entry.

"I'm coming. Hold up." I opened the door and was met by a shocked server, staring at me open-mouthed. "You must have the wrong room. I didn't order anything," I said, looking down at the cart covered with breakfast food and topped with balloons.

"You're… you're Jaxton Ryder?" His voice shook, and I did my best to school my expression.

"Yeah, that's me, but I didn't order that." I checked the large clock on the wall, definitely designed more for art than function, and was pretty sure it was nine. Lucas would kill me if I didn't hurry the hell up. Nothing like being late to your own speech.

The server flushed deeper, and his eyes shot to a sheet of paper before returning to me. "A Ms. Sidney King ordered it, sir."

A thrill ran up my spine at the sound of her name. Even miles away, she still had that effect on me. I grabbed the end of the cart closest to me and winked at the server. "I'll take it from here." And I closed the door before he could say anything else.

There were deep green balloons floating above the cart, a large coffee decanter, and a breakfast sandwich wrapped in Ellie's bakery paper. How the hell did Trouble manage that? I took a large bite of the Bacon and Egger, and a low moan formed in my throat. It had been years since she got me addicted to these. I sucked my thumb clean after the last bite and hummed. "So good."

When I lifted the pot to pour myself a cup of black coffee, an envelope fell to the side, revealing itself. *Jax* was written on the front in Sid's curly handwriting. I set my mug down, too excited to see what the minx was up to, and opened it, pulling out a simple white sheet.

I unfolded it and smiled. She'd kissed around the edges, leaving bright red lipstick prints of her pouty mouth. My chest tugged, seeing them, wishing she was here even more.

Happy anniversary, baby. I'm sorry we couldn't be together, but I've arranged some help to make today special even though we're apart. So let's play a game for old times' sake.

Your first clue: Where did we first run into each other on campus?

A smile split my lips, pulling up my mouth until my cheeks hurt. We always liked to play games. Hell, the second time we met, we raced to class. The memory snapped into place, and I knew exactly where to go. I finished getting ready, thankful that men could throw on a suit to be considered professional, and sent Lucas a quick text on my way out.

Me: Meet me at the campus coffee shop.
Lucas: Deal. We've got an hour to be at the rink.

I was surprised to spot Lucas already waiting for me in the cafe. He was drinking from a to-go cup, and there was a second one on the wood table he was leaning against.

"Hey, you spot anything from Sid?" I barely looked at him, too consumed with figuring out why she'd sent me here.

"Morning to you too." Lucas laughed and handed me my cup with Sid's writing on the sleeve.

"You in on this?" I asked, and Lucas grinned.

"Wouldn't miss it for the world." He nodded toward the cup. "But hurry your ass up. We've got shit to do today."

I knew that would be too easy. Don't worry, they get harder.

Jax, no matter how cheesy it sounds, you've truly made me the luckiest girl on the planet. You have an abundance of love you never fail to show me and your friends. Even though I'm not there right now, I want you to know how much I love and appreciate you. How much you mean to me and that life would have been so much duller without you in it. Thank you for never giving up on me. I love you.

Clue two: Where did I take you when you needed to blow off some steam?

She'd signed it with another kiss.

A slow smile warmed my lips when I pinpointed where she was talking about. I took a sip of my coffee, grateful since I'd abandoned the one in my hotel room, and patted Lucas on the back. "We've got to make a stop before heading to the arena."

Lucas raised a brow at me. "We don't have time for that, buddy."

His words were straightforward, but there was a gleam in his eyes I wasn't able to decipher.

I headed toward the door and shot back, "It's only going to take longer if we keep fucking around here. Come on. It's not far."

I pulled up and parked my truck in front of the junkyard Sid had brought me to all those years ago. It looked identical to when I'd been here before, except for the large *"You ditch them. We wreck them."* sign now hung on an angle, barely holding on.

Lucas unbuckled and hopped out of the truck. "Why the hell are we at a junkyard?"

"Not sure, but I'm excited to find out." Delight tingled under my skin at what Sid was up to. We'd been together for years, and we'd never given up on playing games. Although, she's become significantly better at choosing what bets to take on. I walked right up to the counter, ignoring the sneer the attendant gave me. He'd been the one who gawked all over Sid, and the name "Fred" was sewn onto his shirt.

"You know you aren't supposed to be here," he said in a high-pitched voice.

I gave him my most charming smile. "Hey, now. We're old friends. Let me in, buddy."

He huffed out a breath. "You're lucky you're friends with Sidney. She's got you all set up in her spot."

A zing of excitement skated down my spine, and I looked around the dilapidated area for my feisty girlfriend. "Wait, Sid's here?"

"Was here. Ain't no more."

"When?" If he didn't answer soon, I was ready to hop over the counter and shake the answers out. "How long ago?"

Fred just shook his head and buzzed us in. "Better hurry up. Don't have all day."

My brows pinched together. How did he know I was on a deadline?

Lucas shoved me forward. "He's right, Jax. We've got less than twenty to get back."

Dammit. I needed more time.

I practically ran to where her spot was tucked into

the corner. It was exactly as I remembered, a small sofa tucked under and a makeshift awning, and Sid had set up a few vases, a bat, and safety glasses for me. My gaze trailed the space, looking for another note, and closed in on one of the bottles she'd racked. There was a paper tucked inside. Of course she fucking did. When did she even have time? Grabbing it, I tried to shake out her note, but it was stuck in there.

"Looks like you'll have to break it." Lucas caught up and collapsed on the sofa with a grin. "Just hurry the fuck up."

I slid the safety glasses on and lined up to the bottle, fisting the bat between my hands. Memories of her standing behind me, and her soft fingers adjusting my grip, sent heat straight to my cock. *Fuck.* I swung through, shattering the glass, distracting myself from thinking about how her touch felt on mine, back when I didn't have a claim to touch her. When I saw Sid next, I was locking her in our room for a solid fucking week with me after this stunt.

I crouched down and picked up her note, careful not to cut myself on the glass.

"Ticktock. Ticktock," Lucas drawled from the sofa.

"Fuck off, man. Give me a minute."

I could hear Lucas on the phone, telling someone we'd be right there and apologizing for being late, but all my focus switched to the one line written on the page.

Clue three: Where we decided to spend the rest of our lives together.

My brows pulled together. Would that be her old apartment from when I finally showed up there after being traded to the Senators? Or my old place, where she finally agreed to be mine.

"I'm not sure where she's talking about," I murmured, but fuck it, I'd just hit up all the places it could be until I found her next note.

Lucas's large hand gripped my shoulder, tugging me back to look at him. "We're out of time. We'll come back out."

I glared at him, but I knew he was right. No matter how much I enjoyed chasing Sid's clues, we had to make it back to the rink before the ceremony started. We were the guest speakers, so it wasn't like we could skip out.

"Fine. But we continue right after." I raised an eyebrow at a smiling Lucas.

"I promise, buddy." He turned and walked back toward my truck, and I could've sworn he said something about me being an idiot.

We made it to the arena with seconds to spare and rushed our way through the familiar halls to the rink. I stopped abruptly, spotting Alex, River, and Piper, confusion creeping in as a knowing feeling started to take over.

Piper gave me a quick hug, and I looked down at her. "What the hell are you three doing here?"

She let me go, and Alex instantly wrapped me up in a bear hug, drawing a grunt from me. "Couldn't miss your big moment, buddy."

"What?" This wasn't the first time I'd been a speaker at an event, but it was definitely the first time any of them had shown up. Before I could process what was happening, River pushed me forward toward the darkened rink. "Figure it out later. You're late."

Puzzle pieces clicked together in my mind as I took in their smiling faces, and adrenaline pumped through my veins until my heart felt like it was going to pound out of my chest. I took one step, then another, toward the dark rink, my body moving on autopilot as my brain tried to catch up. I attempted to tamp down my excitement, but I couldn't manage it. Every nerve ending in my body screamed at me she'd be in there.

The rink was dark, lit only by a few strategic lights that kept the center in complete blackness. I took a deep breath, letting the anticipation carry me forward.

The second I stepped onto the carpet they'd rolled onto the rink, the lights flipped on, and a crowd of people jumped out and cheered. Distantly, I knew my teammates from school and the Senators were there as I walked further onto the ice, but all my focus was on the beautiful brunette standing in front of me.

She'd stopped coloring the underneath of her hair

white, instead growing her hair out to a beautiful chestnut brown that was currently curling around her cheeks. She wore the navy blue pencil skirt that hugged all her curves she knew I liked and matched it with a plum silk shirt that brought out the green in her eyes. Sidney stared at me, teeth digging into her bottom lip to stop her smile as I walked closer.

A magnet pulled me toward her that nothing in the world could prevent, growing stronger with each second until I practically ran the last few steps. Before I could wrap her into a hug, she held out a hand, keeping a foot of distance between us. She laughed at the displeased look I gave her.

"Trouble, you better hurry up, or I'm taking you in front of everyone."

She huffed out a breath, and a deep pink flush climbed up her neck. "I haven't even asked you yet."

I sucked in a breath, wanting—no, *needing*—to hear it. "So ask."

"But I'm supposed to get down on a knee."

I grabbed her, hauling her into my chest before she could drop, and rested my forehead on hers. "Ask me, Sidney."

Her hazel eyes met mine, the green made more vibrant by the tears pooling in the corners.

"Will you marry me?"

The world dimmed like I was about to pass out before flashing back in vibrant colors. I spun her in my arms and captured her mouth with mine until she made needy, breathy sounds, and the crowd's cheers turned to leers.

I broke apart the kiss and marveled at her. She took deep, heaving breaths that tickled my face, and a slow smile curved her mouth. She looked absolutely devious.

"Is that a yes?"

I kissed her again, unable to stop myself. "It's always been a yes, Trouble."

SIDNEY

I leaned against Jax's hard chest and smiled softly as his arms circled my waist, pulling me closer. We'd been at the rink for hours, hanging out with our friends and family. It had taken me weeks to have this all set up. I'd lucked out with the arena already having a system to put a floor down for parties over the ice, and I was able to rent a few high-top tables that reminded me of the night we met in the bar. Thank god for the boys and Piper, or there would have been no way I could've pulled it off.

A server approached us with a tray of champagne, and I was grateful for the cool liquid. My throat was dry from laughing with our friends as they congratulated us, followed by a few jokes about it taking so long. Once the initial surprise engagement was over, waitstaff brought out food and drinks for the celebration.

It was good to see old friends again, but the warmth of Jax's body against mine had me wishing we were home.

He kissed the top of my head, drawing my attention to him. His dimples were pronounced as he smiled down at me, and I couldn't help but think how lucky I was to have found him. My gaze drifted to his lips, and heat curled low in my stomach before I looked up again. I was met with Jax's dark blazing gaze, and a shiver trickled down my spine at the possession there. I swallowed hard and trailed my fingers down his chest until they hovered just above his waistband.

He made a low sound that vibrated against my side and leaned his head down until his mouth grazed my ear, and his voice came out in a low rumble. "What are you thinking about, Trouble?"

I smirked up at him. "That Sidney Ryder has a nice ring to it."

His groan was so rough it was practically a growl, and I didn't have time to react before he'd hauled me off my feet and tossed me over his shoulder firefighter-style. My cheeks flushed red with embarrassment mixed with a hint of excitement, and I squirmed to get down, only to have him slap my ass to hold me still. If the last several years had shown me anything, it was that I wasn't above enjoying a tiny display of possessiveness.

"Jax," I admonished, not actually wanting him to stop. Was I mortified? Sure. Did I want to see where he was taking this? Definitely.

My eyes caught on a smiling Piper and Lucas, who gave me knowing looks as Jax walked out of the rink. I was never going to live this down. Instead of carrying me outside to our truck like I expected, Jax opened the team's locker room and stalked inside before slowly lowering me to my feet, making sure every inch of him dragged over me.

Before I could say anything, he slid his hand along my cheek and buried it in my hair, his fingers tightening just enough to draw all of my attention. Not that he didn't already have it.

"You have no idea how many times I've fantasized about fucking you in here."

I plastered on a sly grin, but my voice came out raspy. "Oh yeah, always wanted to have sex with me in a smelly room."

Jax met my grin with heated eyes. "Always wanted to claim you as mine."

He pushed me backward until my back connected with one of the cement brick walls that had been painted so many times over the years it had a smooth finish.

Jax dipped his head, running his nose along the sensitive column of my neck, over my jaw until his teeth grazed my ear, sending a shiver down my spine.

"Someone could walk in," I protested.

He sucked on my earlobe before breathing, "That's the point."

My skin flushed with an overwhelming need that settled deep between my thighs, and I was already soaked for him. His strong fingers tugged at my skirt until it was hiked around my waist and I was fully bared to him.

He let out a loan groan and bit the curve of my

neck just above my collarbone at my exposed, panty-less core.

"You knew this would happen?"

"Maybe."

"Fuck, that's hotter than it should be." He dug his fingers into my ass before lifting me in the air, and I wrapped my legs around his waist, sucking in a breath when his hard cock rubbed against my clit. I was going to leave a wet spot, but from the way he looked at me, he didn't care.

I was met with pure lust before closing my eyes and greeting his kiss with my own. He took his time, exploring my mouth with his tongue and nipping at my lower lip until I was whimpering for more.

"Please." I didn't care that I was begging. The only thing that mattered was having him inside me. He flipped me around so that my forearms rested on the wall. I wasn't bent completely over, but my bare ass was completely exposed to him.

His rough fingers dug into the cheeks of my ass, pulling them apart, and he groaned low. "I'm going to fuck you hard and fast, Trouble. You look so hot like this I don't think I could resist, but I'm going to take you long and so fucking slow when we get home, until you can't remember your fucking name and I have you screaming mine."

I trembled in response, and my breath hitched when he pressed his cock against my entrance, swirling it around in my wetness. I hadn't noticed him dropping his pants. He pushed in the tip so that it was barely inside and growled, "Ready?"

I pressed back hard, taking him further inside me. "Yes, Jax."

He filled me in one stroke, the position making him feel larger, until his cock took over my mind, and I was lost to his pounding thrusts. He moved a hand up my thigh as he pounded into me harder and pressed down on my clit before moving his fingers in a circle that always made my toes curl. I was crying his name as my body contracted, and wave after wave of my orgasm crashed over me. He grunted into my neck with a shuddering thrust.

"You are so hot when you come all over my cock." He growled the words as he filled me with his hot cum before pressing me fully into the wall. His arms surrounded me like a cocoon, and he intertwined our fingers. We stayed there as we regulated our breaths, and he murmured his love while placing slow, lazy kisses up my neck. "I love you, Sidney. Now, let's get you home so I can show you again."

I whispered back his love and let him right my clothes, taking care of me like he loved to do.

He kissed me, then whispered against my lips, "I'm going to make you so happy."

I raised on my tiptoes, pressing my lips firmly against his. "You already do."

Soft, wet kisses trailed heat up my chest, pulling me out of my dreams. I hummed as Jax sucked my nipple into his mouth before running his teeth over the sensitive flesh already marked with countless love bites.

He continued upward and buried his face in my neck, breathing deeply, caging me between his forearms, and settled his hips between mine.

The hard length of his cock lay directly over my clit, and I sucked in a breath and asked, "Again."

Jax's low groan vibrated against my chest, and he sucked my earlobe between his teeth before whispering. "I'll never be done with you."

Heat pooled between my thighs, and I rocked my hips against him in approval. "Kiss me."

He didn't waste time capturing my mouth, but instead of our usual famished kisses, his tongue moved over mine in soft, consuming strokes. He took his time with me, worshiping my body until I was lost to him. The air was thick with our love for each other, and I moaned as he sank his cock deep inside me, moving in lazy, languid thrusts. I dug my fingers into his hair, spread my legs wider to take more of him in, and gasped with the pressure of my imminent orgasm. With each stroke, he pulled pleasure from me until I was barreling over the edge of my release.

He groaned, cum filling me with his final thrust, and his comforting weight pressed me into the bed. If I never breathed again, I would die happy.

Jax rolled over, pulling me over his chest, and kissed the top of my head. "Get some rest. This isn't over."

My core clenched, wanting more, even though I'd just had a mind-bending orgasm. He really was going to be the death of me. I yawned, my eyes growing heavy, and mumbled my words as I fell asleep. "I love you."

I woke up wrapped up in Jax's warmth, and I snuggled deeper into his arms. A strip of sunlight streamed through the hotel window and lit the side of his face, casting him in a golden glow. A giddy feeling fluttered in my chest. *We're engaged.* I was going to keep this incredible man forever. I dropped my nose to his skin and sucked in a deep breath, and his woodsy scent filled my lungs.

I didn't know what time it was but wouldn't be surprised if it was after eleven. Jax made good on his promise, keeping me up all night, letting me nap in between taking me again. I had no idea that many orgasms were possible, and I was starting to wonder if he was dipping into pleasure Dom territory.

I shifted, and Jax groaned, holding me still, and his voice was gravelly with sleep. "Don't even think about getting out of this bed."

I smiled at his sleepy tone. "We have to get up. Checkout is in like a half hour."

"Book the room another night," he grunted.

"Listen, I'm not Mrs. Ryder yet. I don't have famous privileges."

He had me pinned to the bed so fast it stole my breath, and he dropped his chest to mine, letting me feel the weight of him. He searched my gaze before he smiled wide in that mischievous way of his.

I raised a brow, cautious of that look. "Whatever you're thinking—"

He cut me off. "Marry me."

My words came out on a laugh. "I beat you to that one. Remember I asked you yesterday?"

He lowered his head and ran his nose along mine. "Today. Marry me today."

My skin tingled with excited anticipation, but I was shaking my head no. "There's no way we'll get an officiant, let alone a license."

He kissed me softly, stealing all of my thoughts before saying, "We'll get River to officiate like he did for Lucas and Piper's wedding, and don't worry about the license." He gave me a cocky smile. "I'm famous, remember?"

I searched his expression, expecting to see a hint of a joke, but he was dead serious. I'd never cared about a large wedding, wasn't one to dream about my dress as a little girl. The only thing that mattered to me was him. "Okay."

"Okay?" His gray eyes held mine, and his voice was unsure, like he needed assurance.

I smiled up at him. "Yeah, let's do it, but you're going to have to get off of me because I've got to get ready."

He flew off me at near-inhuman speed, already pulling up his pants before I sat up. He yanked on his shirt, and his fingers flew across the keys on his phone, already getting everything in motion. He was halfway to the door, then spun around, rushing back to me for a deep kiss. "I'll text you the plans. See you in a few hours, Trouble."

I could barely breathe after the intensity of the kiss, so I just nodded and collapsed back on the bed as he rushed out the door.

It took several calming breaths before I could grab my phone and FaceTime Mia and Anthony. I didn't give them a chance to say hello. "Mia, I need you to get down here right away and bring the silver floor-length slip dress you bought in senior year."

"Hello to you too. Aren't you in Windsor? That's like two hours away." Mia laughed, but Anthony studied me.

"I guess you better hurry because I'm getting married, and you're my maid of honor."

"Shut the fuck up," Anthony said at the same time Mia squealed so loud I had to pull the phone away.

She sucked in a deep breath before speaking. "So I take it the proposal went well."

I nodded, and my skin flushed with the memories of last night. I cleared my throat. "You could say that."

"Congratulations, Cupcake. I'm sorry I won't be there." Anthony had moved to France, following Curtis, and I couldn't be happier for them.

"Considering the fact that we decided to elope this morning, I think I can forgive you."

Mia laughed. "Well, I'll be there in two. Have your soon-to-be husband use his clout to get you a hair appointment."

Husband swirled in my head and warmed me from within. In a few short hours, I would be Mrs. Ryder.

JAX

River stood in front of me, with Alex and Lucas lined up to my left as we looked across the hotel ballroom toward the large set of double doors. We'd lucked out, and they'd had an arch setup with flowers from a wedding the previous night, and it only took a few season tickets to get an express marriage license.

I took a deep breath. I wasn't nervous. Instead, there was an excited hum running through my veins. This was better than being drafted or the feeling of my first NHL goal. This was everything I'd ever wanted.

I stood with rapt attention as Piper walked in first, wearing a simple dress she must have had with her, followed by Mia. She smiled at me so wide her cheeks must've hurt. We didn't see her much, but I was grateful for the support she gave Sid. She was always there for her when it counted, and it didn't surprise me at all that she'd dropped everything to be here.

Lucas played a wedding song on his phone, and my heart started to pound as adrenaline coursed through my veins. I held my breath until Sidney stepped through the doors, and it all rushed out of me.

She was stunning, wearing a light silver gown that hugged all of her curves and hung to the floor. She'd swept her hair up in some kind of curly updo that I couldn't wait to dig my fingers through. She walked slowly, her eyes never leaving mine, and stopped directly in front of me.

"You clean up good," she said, trailing her fingers over the lapels of my suit, and gave me a shy smile.

I ran my fingers down her exposed neck and played with the spaghetti strap of her dress, riveted by the goose bumps that followed my touch. "You're beautiful, Sidney."

River cut in. "We are gathered here today..."

I completely zoned out, too focused on Sidney, until I heard a soft laugh ripple through my friends. I shifted my gaze toward River, who was already smirking at me. "Do you have prepared vows?"

Sidney had a soft blush across her cheeks as she took a small piece of paper from Mia. I gave her an encouraging smile as she read. Her voice started soft but grew with confidence with each word.

"With all my heart, I, Sidney King, take you, Jaxton Ryder, to be my husband.

I promise to cherish and love you,
Your partner in parenthood,
Your ally in conflict,
Your greatest fan,
I will be your sidekick adventure,
Your comfort in sorrow,
Your accomplice in mischief,
Your strength when you need.

I want to play this game with you all the days of my life."

I leaned in and captured her mouth in a deep but quick kiss. "Sorry, I had to do that."

Our friends laughed again, and I shifted back only far enough that I could hold her hands. I wanted her to see the sincerity in my gaze. I started my vows. I hadn't written anything down; I knew exactly what I was going to say. I may have thought of this moment a time or twenty before. A smile took over Sid's face as I spoke.

"I, Jaxton Ryder, promise to you, Sidney King, before our friends,

to honor and love you,

to nurture your dreams,

I pledge to always be there for you.

When you fall, I will catch you.

When you cry, I will comfort you.

When you laugh, I will share your joy.

No matter what lies ahead of us,

I promise we will always be forever."

River's voice cut through the room, sending a whoosh of happiness through me. "With the power vested in me, I now declare you man and wife. You may kiss your bride."

I lifted her from the ground and claimed her lips with mine, spinning us in a circle. Our friends cheered around us, and a laugh bubbled from my chest. This might not have been planned, but it was perfect. I kissed her once more, then dropped my forehead to hers, my words shaking with how much they meant to me.

"I love you, *Wife*."

Join [Jessa's readers' FB group](). **ARC SIGN UP EXCLUSIVE**. You'll get updates on my current projects and all kinds of fun extras.
If you liked this book please leave a review on Goodreads and Amazon. I'm dying to hear what you think!

The Gentlemen Series
READ NOW

She's a kick@ss thief and the heads of her rival gang, Beck, Nico, and Rush need her help.

Whychoose, Multi-POV, Badass Heroine, Tons of funny banter, All over 20 years old, Forced Proximity

By Jessa Wilder & Kate King

The Blissful Omegaverse Series
READ NOW

In a world where Omegas are cherished, Alphas are revered, and Betas are forgotten I wouldn't have changed a thing.

Growing up in foster care, my friends and I took care of each other. Ares, Killian, Rafe, and Nox, were my everything: my first loves, my only family, my pack. Until the same night they told me we'd be together forever, I presented as an Omega, and everything changed. By Jessa Wilder & Kate King

KEEP IN TOUCH

Follow Jessa on:
Tik Tok:
Jesswilderauthor

Instagram:
Jessicawilderauthor

Website:
jessawilder.com

THANK YOU

Thank you so much for reading Rule Number Five. If you liked it and are looking for a way to help this author out please review it!

Your time and support means so much to me.

Thank you to Emily, who's always there to listen to me freak the hell out and to all of my beta readers. Without you, none of this would be possible.

A huge thank you to Kate King. The lessons we learned over the past 2 years of writing together made this possible today. We went from baby author's to USA bestsellers and for that I will be forever grateful and I'm excited to get back to some of those projects.

Printed in Great Britain
by Amazon